More Praise for

WE ARE
THE
LIGHT

"*We Are the Light* is the book America needs right now. A novel that embraces our national heartbreak and division with love and compassion. Matthew Quick is the patron saint of the damaged and outcast and no one writes with more heart and empathy. You'll love this book."

—**Nickolas Butler, bestselling author of**
Shotgun Lovesongs* and *Godspeed

"*We Are the Light* is a beautifully written and emotion-packed novel with a huge heart. Matthew Quick takes us on a searing and unforgettable journey through grief and empathy and how even the most broken of us can be repaired."

—**Harlan Coben, #1 *New York Times***
bestselling author of *Win*

"Matthew Quick has always been a brilliant chronicler of the ways in which we get broken, and the spectacular ways our lives can fall apart, and yet his greatest gift is the way he tries to find, within every story, an opportunity to put some of those pieces back together. In *We Are the Light*, where unexpected connections offer a way forward, Quick writes with such honesty and openhearted understanding of the pain and joy of being alive."

—**Kevin Wilson, *New York Times***
bestselling author of *Nothing to See Here*

"Filled with everyday guardian angels, this bittersweet, redemptive meditation on rebuilding after the unthinkable reminds readers that beauty can be found even among shattered pieces. *We Are the Light* is a perfect read for anyone in need of an insightful, optimistic view of humanity's capacity for compassion and growth."

—*Shelf Awareness*

"Matthew Quick is one of the few fiction writers who, inspired by Jungian insights, makes a solid contribution to the impact of analysis. Like all significant works of art that reflect truths we might have known, had we not lost our way, *We Are the Light* is subtle and intimate, compellingly strange and hauntingly familiar, an initiation into the depths of suffering and love. It will not only break your heart—it will break it free."

—**Joseph R. Lee, Jungian analyst and cohost of *This Jungian Life* podcast**

"A story of unexpected twists and turns on the road to recovery after a shattering tragedy. . . . When it comes to facing tragedy and trauma, Quick's novel shows us that it definitely takes a village to heal and move on."

—*Kirkus Reviews*

"An illuminating epistolary novel . . . A crackling narrative builds to an excruciatingly honest disclosure. The author's fans will love this."

—*Publishers Weekly*

WE ARE THE LIGHT

—⬦⬦⬦—

MATTHEW QUICK

AVID READER PRESS

NEW YORK   LONDON   TORONTO   SYDNEY   NEW DELHI

AVID READER PRESS
An Imprint of Simon & Schuster, Inc.
1230 Avenue of the Americas
New York, NY 10020

First Avid Reader Press trade paperback edition November 2023

AVID READER PRESS and colophon are trademarks of Simon & Schuster, Inc.

For information about special discounts for bulk purchases, please contact Simon & Schuster Special Sales at 1-866-506-1949 or business@simonandschuster.com.

The Simon & Schuster Speakers Bureau can bring authors to your live event. For more information or to book an event, contact the Simon & Schuster Speakers Bureau at 1-866-248-3049 or visit our website at www.simonspeakers.com.

Interior design by Carly Loman

Manufactured in the United States of America

10   9   8   7   6   5   4   3   2   1

Library of Congress Cataloging-in-Publication Data has been applied for.

ISBN 978-1-6680-0542-2
ISBN 978-1-6680-0543-9 (pbk)
ISBN 978-1-6680-0544-6 (ebook)

For the wise and generous Jungian
who finally got me to click my heels together three times.
Thank you.

VOCATUS ATQUE NON VOCATUS DEUS ADERIT

"Invoked or not invoked, the god is present."

—WRITTEN ON CARL JUNG'S HEADSTONE

I.

Dear Karl,

First, I want to apologize for coming to your consulting room even after receiving the letter saying you were no longer practicing and, therefore, could no longer be my—or anyone else's—analyst.

I realize that your consulting room is connected to your home and since you've stopped practicing it's probably become *part* of your house now, making it off-limits to me. I was on autopilot. Every Friday night at seven p.m. for almost fourteen months. That's a hard habit to break. And psyche kept saying, "Go. Karl needs you," which was initially confusing because I'm the analysand and you are the analyst, so I'm supposed to need you and not the other way around. But you always told me to listen to psyche and that the goal of analysis was to individuate and know the Self well enough to align with it. Well, my psyche really wants a relationship with you. It keeps saying you need my help. Also, Darcy told me to keep going to analysis. And I just generally wanted to go, as well. I've really missed our weekly "analytic container," our two hours. Friday nights.

It was hard to manage everything without our sessions, especially at first. Many people offered to find me a new you, but I kept telling everyone I'd wait for Karl. I have to admit, I didn't initially think I'd be waiting so long. Please don't feel bad. The last thing I want to do is guilt-trip you, especially given all we've been through, collectively and individually. I just want you to understand. And you always say that I should tell you everything and never hold back.

I, too, haven't been able to return to work since the tragedy. I tried a few times, but never made it out of my car. I just sat there in the faculty parking lot watching the students streaming into the building. Some would look over at me with concerned expressions and I couldn't tell whether I wanted them to help me or if I wanted to be invisible. It was the strangest sensation. Do you ever feel that way? I'd grip the steering wheel so hard my knuckles would turn white.

Isaiah—my boss and friend and principal of Majestic High, in case you forgot—eventually would come out and sit down in my passenger seat. He'd put his hand on my shoulder and tell me that I'd helped a lot of kids already and now it was time to help myself. He comes to my house all the time too. Because he's very religious, he'll say, "Lucas, you're one of the best men I've ever met and I'm absolutely sure Jesus has a plan for you." Sometimes he and his wife, Bess, cook me dinner in my own kitchen, which is nice. They bring all the food and everything. Bess always says, "Lucas, you have to eat. You're wasting away to nothing," and it's true. Isaiah's a great friend. A good man. Bess is a fantastic woman. But Darce—you'll remember that's what I sometimes call Darcy, dropping the last syllable—says I can't tell anyone about her transformation, and so it's hard, because I can only nod and press my lips together whenever Isaiah and Bess say God has a plan for me, which makes them think I'm agreeing, rather than holding in a tremendous secret.

I went to their church a few Sunday mornings, back in January, for what Isaiah calls "worship." I was the only white person there, which was interesting. I like the gospel singing. The first time I went, the purple-and-gold-robed pastor called me up to the altar and put his hand on my head and loudly prayed for me. Then he asked everyone in the congregation to come up and lay their hands on me while they also prayed. I've never in my life had so many hands on me. It was a kind gesture that I appreciated, but the funny thing was that I couldn't stop shaking, even when the touching and praying ceased and the singing started again, which was uplifting. I thought I was having a seizure.

I kept going to Sunday service, but after a few weeks no one prayed for me anymore and I kind of felt like I was invading something—like maybe I was an interloper. When I told him how I felt, Isaiah said, "Ain't no unwelcomed guests in God's house," which was nice, but Darcy said I shouldn't wear out my welcome and so I stopped going to church, even though I liked and maybe even needed it. Perhaps I'll go back at the end of the year for the Christmas season if Isaiah keeps asking me. Darcy said maybe that would be okay.

Last December, I attended seventeen of the eighteen funerals. Well, at least part of each. The funeral homes tried to make it so that no two services overlapped, because that's the way we bereaved wanted it. But a few funerals ended up partially conflicting, mostly because everyone wanted their burials to happen before Christmas. I would have made at least an appearance at all eighteen, but the police wouldn't let me into Jacob Hansen's service. And I have to say your Leandra's—which I attended in its entirety—was perhaps the best. I liked the way you personalized everything and resisted a more traditional format. I didn't even know your wife played the cello until you showed that video of her in your living room the day before the tragedy. It made me realize how one-sided analysis can be, since you knew almost everything about my Darcy, and yet, I didn't know your Leandra's profession. I'm not sure I even knew her name before the tragedy, which is hard to believe, especially since we'd see you two at the Majestic Theater and we'd always exchange waves and smiles from a respectable non-boundary-crossing distance.

I also admire how you led the funeral yourself without the help of a minister or rabbi or priest. I'm not sure I would have been able to do that, even though Darcy's funeral was just staged for appearances and her casket was obviously empty.

If you were worried about missing Darcy's funeral, please don't be. Like I said above, it wasn't real. And I'm not sure anyone but me even noticed your absence at all the others.

Anyway, in the video you screened at your wife's funeral—as you will certainly remember—Leandra was practicing for a solo she was to perform at a Christmas-themed show and the song she was playing really made me believe that I had to tell you about my numinous experience. It seemed like a sign. Proof that you and I were in this together and that I wasn't going insane.

You'll remember that the song was "Angels We Have Heard on High."

I was surprised at how such a small woman could handle such a big instrument. And I marveled at the ethereal sounds your wife massaged out with her wonderful bow work. It was miraculous watching Leandra playing at her own funeral and I almost ran up to the pulpit right then and there. It was like God had come down from heaven and commanded me to tell you the good news about the tragedy, which was strange because I'm not religious. I'm not entirely certain that I even believe in God.

I didn't run up to the pulpit, of course, but sat on my hands. And then Leandra's version of "Angels We Have Heard on High" played over and over again in my brain, producing a sense of ecstasy. My body was right there in the pew, but my soul—or psyche—was somewhere high above, marveling at the early morning sunlight streaming through the stained-glass depictions of saints.

I don't remember anything else until I was standing at the back of the crowd that had gathered by Leandra's open grave. Darcy's best friend, Jill, was holding my hand. I was wearing dark sunglasses when my soul slipped back into my body. And you were crying violently with a hand on your wife's white casket. It was like your black suit was heavy armor, because you were hunched over in a way that aged you, making you look more like ninety-eight than seventy-eight. You couldn't catch your breath, so it became impossible for you to speak, let alone conclude the funeral. No one knew what to do because there was no priest or minister or rabbi to take the lead. And you wouldn't let anyone else help you. You kept waving—and even literally pushing—people away. Then you started saying, "The service is over. Go home. Please just leave me alone." Everyone was feeling cautious and unsure until Robin Withers—the town's head librarian, whose husband, Steve, was also killed, in case you don't know her—put a hand on the casket, crossed herself, kissed you on the cheek, and then gracefully departed. That seemed to calm you down. So everyone followed Robin's good lead, including Jill and me, who were the last two people to exit.

But when I made it to Jill's truck, I looked back and you were still crying all alone, only there were two men nearby smoking cigarettes next to a backhoe. They had on shark-colored jumpsuits, black gloves, and beanie hats. And their dead eyes were watching you.

Jill tried to stop me, but I broke free of her arms and strode over to you. You were crying so hard I thought maybe you were dying, but I told you about Darcy having wings now and my seeing your Leandra and all of the others rise from the lifeless pools of blood, back at the Majestic Theater. And I described for you their collective graceful ascent toward the heavens. Their white feathers sparkling like opals. The steady pulse of flapping. The dignity and glory and compensation. I don't know how much you heard through your sobbing. I'm happy to give you a more detailed report whenever we resume our Friday-night sessions, which is what this letter is in service of. I'm very much open to being questioned.

I miss sitting on the worn leather seat and staring at your large black glasses. I miss the little forest of totem pole cacti by the windows and the "phallic energy" those strange green plants would supply us. I miss seeing the deep wrinkles in your face, which always reassured me, because they appeared hard-won—like they had been etched by the accumulation of great wisdom. But mostly I miss the healing energy that always flowed so naturally between us.

Bobby the cop says I'm not allowed to knock on your door anymore, which I have stopped doing, if you haven't noticed. But psyche says I must keep trying to reconnect with you in one way or another. Psyche says it's vital. That your very life might depend on it. Darcy suggested writing letters, as a safe compromise, saying, "What harm can a letter do? No one was ever hurt by words on a piece of paper. If it's too much for Karl, he can simply refold the paper, slip it back into the envelope, and read it later." She also said I was a pretty clever correspondent. We used to send letters when we were in college, since we attended different universities back in the early nineties. And I have always loved writing, so I thought, why not?

I don't know if you remember, but early on—when you first started analyzing me—you . . . well, you looked deep into my eyes for what felt like fifteen minutes and then you said, "I love you, Lucas." It really made me uncomfortable at the time. I even went home and googled *What to do when your therapist says I love you*. That was back before I understood the difference between an analyst and a therapist. Pretty much everything I found on the internet said I should immediately stop seeing you, because your saying "I love you" was unethical and boundary-crossing. And I almost did stop coming to analysis, mostly because I was afraid. Other than Darcy, no one had ever said "I love you" to me before. Not with sincerity. But then, as we spent two hours together every Friday night, I started to get better and I began to understand what you meant when you said your soul could love my soul because it's everyone's soul's purpose to love, just like it's the job of our lungs and nose to breathe; and our mouths to chew and taste; and our feet to walk. As we banked more and more Friday nights together, I started to believe that you actually did love me—not in a sexual way or even a friend way. You loved me the way the best of a human being naturally loves the best of any and every other human being once you remove all the toxic interference.

That's why I feel it's important for me to say, "I love you too, Karl," especially since I never managed to say that to you before now. I wanted to so many times, because you helped me clean up so many of my complexes. Darcy kept daring me to tell you I love you, but I obviously couldn't before now.

I love you, Karl.

And I want to help you.

You can't hide in your home for the rest of your life.

You are not a shut-in; you just can't be.

Psyche keeps saying I need to break through your neurotic bubble of isolationism.

You need to help me, obviously, but you will also resume helping many other people once you have properly mourned Leandra's murder and healed your heart. I'm absolutely certain.

Is there anything I can do to speed up the process?

What do you need?

I'm willing to do just about anything.

Your most loyal analysand,

Lucas

2.

Dear Karl,

I didn't expect you to write back after only one letter, so rest assured, my determination has not been daunted by your lack of a reply. Quite the opposite, actually.

I didn't, however, know the appropriate amount of time to wait before I wrote the second letter. Was one week too long or too short? Based on all the work we've done together, I'm guessing you might say something like, "Well, perhaps you shouldn't make up arbitrary rules. Perhaps you should trust psyche to guide you. What does psyche want? Get very quiet. Close your eyes. Breathe. Drop down. And then listen."

Just a few hours after I slid the first letter through the outgoing mail slot at the Majestic Post Office, I did exactly what I thought you'd recommend. Meditating on a public bench under the Japanese maple tree near the Wawa. And psyche clearly said to write you again right away, immediately—that very night! The impulse was commanding. But I figured I had better give you at least a fair shot at responding, just so our correspondence wouldn't turn into an ugly Lucas-only monologue.

Darcy agreed, saying, "You don't want to come on too strong when wooing widowers," which she meant as a joke. She used to kid me about going to see "my boyfriend" on Friday nights and would jokingly tell Jill I was cheating on my wife with you. I didn't ever tell you about that teasing before because of what you said about keeping our analysis sacred, meaning not telling anyone about it. You used to say it was like cooking rice with steam. If you take the lid off the pot, all the steam evaporates and then the alchemical process can no longer take place. But I had to tell Darce about my analysis because she balances the checkbook and Jill was her best friend, meaning that she told Jill everything, back when Darce was still human. I don't think Jill told anyone about the therapeutic relationship you and I had and hopefully still have. I asked her recently and she said she had sensed it was private and therefore kept the information to herself. Jill's all right like that, which is why I don't understand Darce's need to keep Jill in the dark now, regarding Darcy's wings and her choosing to remain behind here on earth. I consult with Darce every single night, but I'm not allowed to tell Jill about that, which I think is just plain cruel.

But that's who I'd like to talk about tonight—Jill. Because something bad happened and I'm not really sure what to do about it. This was primarily the reason why, even after Bobby the cop's sternest of warnings, I started obsessively coming to your consulting room again, hoping you'd be willing to grant me an emergency session. I was pretty much able to handle the Majestic Theater tragedy—horrific as it was—on my own, but this thing with Jill has really eaten away at my conscience, especially since it's the one secret I've kept from Darce. Since she's no longer human, I sort of think she might already know what happened, but it's hard to tell. Even if she forgives—or miraculously already has forgiven—me, I still don't think I'm going to be able to forgive myself.

I wanted to tell you all of this face-to-face, which is why I didn't include it in the last letter, but I just can't hold it in anymore.

I can't remember how much I've said about Jill in our sessions—honestly, I'm having trouble remembering all kinds of things these days—so I'll just start from the beginning and assume you've never heard about Jill before.

Darcy absorbs the energy of others nicely and quietly, while Jill radiates energy. Darcy often de-escalates. Jill almost always escalates. Sometimes escalation is good and sometimes de-escalation is better, which made them quite the team.

To put everything in context, you have to understand that no one has done more for me in the past so many months than Jill.

Have you ever been to the Cup Of Spoons coffee shop? Across the street from the historic and now infamous Majestic Theater? Even though I've never personally seen you at the Cup Of Spoons, you definitely have eaten there, right? Everyone in town loves that place. Well, Jill owns it. She's the blonde in the kitchen, the one who comes around and asks how your day is and knows your name and smiles at you in a way that seems to do more than the caffeine ever could. She was one of the few people in this world who could make Darce laugh until she cried. Darce once literally peed her pants when she and Jill were laughing one night after a few too many bottles of wine. Jill was doing impressions of me when that happened, spoofing on how careful I always am about everything.

Anyway, after the tragedy, while all of you were being treated at the hospital, I was being interviewed at the police station. I, of course, waived all my rights because I hadn't done anything wrong. Darce said it was fine to do this. And so I let a nice woman photograph the blood on my hands and take samples from under my nails and then—in a room with a video camera recording me—I told a few detectives and police officers exactly what had happened in the Majestic Theater. Naturally, I left out the part about Darce and Leandra and the fifteen others turning into angels, but I was one hundred percent truthful about everything else.

It took me a good hour or so to remember the following, but then it hit me. One of the police officers used to be a teenager I worked with a few decades ago. He was looking at me differently. The others appeared almost afraid of the words coming out of my mouth, but Bobby's eyes were welcoming and reassuring. Several times during the interview, he said, "Mr. Goodgame helped me when I was in high school. I probably wouldn't have graduated if it wasn't for him." I don't know why he kept saying things like that, but it really helped me get through the interrogation. And when I concluded my testimony, Bobby declared me a hero, which seemed to annoy the other police officers in the room, probably because they wanted to remain objective and not rush to any conclusions, which is always the best way. Still, I appreciated Bobby's taking my side and his understanding the more-than-obvious facts that explained why I had blood on my hands.

When I was finished being video recorded, I was surprised to find Jill yelling in the front part of the police station, saying that I shouldn't have been interviewed without legal counsel, which was when I told her it was okay because I hadn't done anything wrong—and I really hadn't.

"We're going to get you out of here right now," Jill said, which was strange because it was only her there, so I didn't really understand why she was using the plural pronoun.

Outside in her parked truck with the heat blowing on full blast, she let the engine idle for a long time before she looked over at me and said, "Is Darce really gone?"

Because Darcy had sworn me to silence, back in the Majestic Theater, I didn't know how to answer that question, so I just stared at my hands, which Jill incorrectly took to mean that my wife had indeed been killed and therefore no longer existed, which I have already told you is not correct. This is when Jill began sobbing uncontrollably. Her chest heaved so hard I thought she might choke to death, so I grabbed her and—in an effort to get her to stop coughing—pulled her close into my body, which worked, although it took her more than thirty minutes to calm down. At some point, I began to stroke her hair, which smelled like honeysuckle, and tell her she was okay, that everything was all right, and it really was, even though I couldn't exactly tell her why.

Jill stayed the night at our home and then sort of unofficially moved in with me. She closed the Cup Of Spoons for the month of December so she could accompany me to the seventeen sometimes-overlapping funerals and she ran interference for me whenever anyone wanted to ask questions I didn't want to answer. Reporters quickly learned to fear her. And Jill was also very good at keeping my mother at arm's length during Darcy's funeral, which—and you'll be happy to hear this—also helped to keep my mother complex at bay. Whenever my mother tried to corner me at the reception, Jill would interrupt and say, "Excuse me, Mrs. Goodgame, but I need to steal Lucas for a moment." Whenever Mom would say, "But I'm his mother!" Jill would pretend like she didn't hear Mom and then pull me away by the hand. When my mother first flew up from Florida, it was Jill who told Mom that she had to stay in a hotel and not in my house, which I didn't even realize was a possibility.

I don't know whether I would have made it through all those funerals if I didn't have Jill. And she was very supportive when I couldn't find my way back into the high school. She always echoed everyone else, saying I had already helped so many teenagers and now it was time to help myself, which was kind and made me feel a little better about my malaise.

The problem happened when Jill tried to outthink my grieving.

It was maybe four or so months after the tragedy, right before you had Bobby the cop gently tell me I'd be arrested if I didn't cease knocking on your consulting-room door and peeking through your windows every Friday night. Jill and I were sitting at Darcy's and my kitchen table, eating tuna-fish sandwiches that Jill had brought home from the Cup Of Spoons, when she said, "I think you and I should go away for a few days. Specifically, the first week in May." When I asked why, she reminded me that it was Darcy's and my wedding anniversary—our twenty-fifth—on

May 3. Jill knew because she was Darcy's maid of honor. Her offer put me in a bind. I wanted to spend my twenty-fifth wedding anniversary with Darcy, but Jill thought Darcy was dead, which was why Jill was always hanging around our house now. Jill wanted to take me somewhere Darcy and I had never been so that the pain of missing my wife might not be as bad, which was sweet of Jill. I said I would think about it, but when I met up with Darcy later that night in my bedroom with the door locked, Darce said, "You're going!"

"But I want to spend our twenty-fifth anniversary with you, not your best friend," I protested, which was when Darcy put her foot down and said Jill wasn't yet ready to know the truth about my wife being an angel and, therefore, there was no excuse that would get me safely around going away with Jill for my anniversary. I sort of saw the sense in what Darcy was saying and—as she promised to fly to wherever Jill and I would be staying—I didn't see the harm in traveling, especially since Jill and I would be in separate rooms, so there would be more than enough time for Darcy and me to be intimate on our anniversary.

Jill booked us two rooms in a seaside hotel in coastal Maryland. We drove to the little island and I could see a small, squat, trapezoid-shaped lighthouse from my bedroom window, which I thought Darce would like when she arrived later that night, as she loved lighthouses.

Jill and I hopped on rented bikes and rode around with helmets on, sipping water out of the hydration pouches we wore on our backs. Then we lay on the beach and went swimming in the cold ocean whenever we got too hot. When the sun set, we showered up and had a seafood dinner at the hotel restaurant.

As we leisurely made our way through three bottles of wine, Jill talked nonstop about Darcy, telling stories I had heard a million times before. Like the one about how they used to sneak out of their bedroom windows in the middle of the night when they were kids and then meet in this field where the Walgreens now is. And they would bathe naked in the ghostly moonlight. And listen to crickets. And sweat in the summer heat. She told me about how Darcy and her ditched their senior prom dates for two other guys they met on the Wildwood boardwalk during prom weekend. They ended up driving to New York City with these guys, who turned out to be junior Wall Street traders fresh out of college. The four of them ate a picnic breakfast in Central Park.

Darce and I were only friends in high school. I didn't even go to our prom. She and I didn't fall in love until I started writing her letters when we were both away from Majestic for the first time. Darce and Jill were an odd couple—especially when we all were kids. Darcy was short and small with chin-length black hair. My wife was always cute and approachable. Jill was as tall as most boys. Her straight blond hair cascaded down to her butt. She floated through the high school hallways like a goddess. I would have never dreamed of speaking to her back then. As adults, Jill was the one who was always nervously telling jokes and Darcy was the one who was always quick to laugh, throwing her head back and roaring with her mouth wide open. My wife was easy to please and Jill was a pleaser. Jill's looks often made other girls self-conscious but my wife was always very comfortable in her own skin. Jill was impulsive. Darcy was thoughtful. All of the Jill and Darcy puzzle pieces just naturally snapped together. For every tab, knob, and loop one had, the other had a corresponding blank, hole, or socket. They were a perfect fit.

But—back in the Maryland seafood restaurant—Jill was talking about how Darcy was there for her when Jill divorced Derek, who used to hit Jill hard enough to leave bruises in places that were easily covered by clothing. Derek, who I never liked, was able to avoid legal trouble because his brother was a high-powered lawyer and Jill only started talking about the abuse after all the bruises had healed, so there was no documentation. Instead of cracking open the crabs in front of her and enjoying her meal,

Jill went on and on about how she might have killed herself if it hadn't been for Darcy's help, and then she started really slurring words, which was when I realized she had drunk almost all of the wine by herself. So I helped her get into her bed upstairs, put some bottles of water on her bedside table, and then slipped away to wait for Darcy in my own room.

The lighthouse was spinning its great beam of light around and every so many seconds my window became illuminated. There were light-blocking shades, but I didn't want to keep the beam out. I pictured Darcy using it to find me. I also pictured the gigantic smile on her face when she saw we were staying near a real working lighthouse, the rhythm of which she could appreciate all night long. There were mosquitoes and biting flies, but I opened the screen anyway and waited for Darcy.

I must have fallen asleep because a knock at the door woke me up. I was still half dreaming when I made my way over to see who was there. I figured they had the wrong room, because Jill was passed out and Darcy would surely use the window. But when I opened the door, I was over-taken by a rush of passion, which could only have come from a loving wife on a twenty-fifth wedding anniversary. Hands groped my back as a mouth greedily sucked my own. It felt like she was trying to extract my soul. Before I knew it, I was on my back. And aroused. And then I was inside her. And her hair was brushing against my cheeks. When I began smelling honeysuckle, I started screaming, "Get off me! Get off me! Please! Stop!"

And then Jill had my face in her hands and she was whispering, saying everything was okay and that she was sorry and that we were just drunk and that it didn't mean anything, but I couldn't stop shaking. It felt like I was about to have a seizure. And then it felt like there was someone inside me trying to carve his way out with knives that were too blunt to cut so they just scraped and scraped but never broke through to the exterior of me. And so I lay on my back, moaning, which upset Jill, I know, because she started crying. Then she said—over and over, almost chanting—that she was a horrible person who didn't deserve love, which immediately shifted something deep inside me. Without thinking, I grabbed Jill and held her. I told her that the best part of my soul loved the best part of her soul. And even though she didn't respond, I kept telling her the best part of my soul loved the best part of her soul until she fell asleep in my bed.

Then I watched the great lighthouse beam go round and round until the sun came up. Darce never arrived, of course, because she didn't want Jill to see her wings. The shock of seeing her best friend as an angel might have killed Jill dead. A small part of me resented Jill for keeping Darcy away on our anniversary, but the resentful part of me vanished by morning, at which point we ate our continental breakfast in the hotel lobby before deciding to leave a day early and making the long, mostly silent drive home.

When Jill pulled into my driveway, she shifted into park, turned off the engine, and stared at the lower half of the steering wheel for a long time before she said, "Did I ruin everything?"

I, of course, told her she hadn't and that we should chalk it up to the wine and that we didn't ever need to talk about what had happened in Maryland again. She thanked me and made a half-hearted joke about being an alcoholic, but I didn't laugh. Instead, I looked into her eyes and said, "You are worthy of love." I was surprised to see that I had taken her chin in my hand and she was looking up at me with wet eyes, but she eventually swallowed and nodded a few times, which was when I let go of her.

Inside my house, we ordered a pizza and watched a forgettable movie from opposite ends of the couch, where she fell asleep and spent the night.

When I met up with Darcy in our bedroom, I told her everything that had happened except for my being inside Jill for that brief moment. And Darcy told me that I had done what was necessary and that she was proud of me, which made me feel awful for obvious reasons. But then she said that Jill and I needed each other and she was happy that we were taking care of one another. I sort of fell forward at this point and Darce wrapped me in her wings and held me until I felt so hot I thought I might spontaneously combust into flames.

When the sun rose, I woke up naked on the bedroom floor. I immediately replayed everything that had happened. I began to feel nauseous when I got to the part where I had lied to Darce. I wondered whether she had seen me with Jill. Since becoming an angel, Darcy seems to know everything about my new life without my having to tell her, which has taken some getting used to, to say the least. But she said nothing about what happened between Jill and me in the hotel room and I haven't said anything either. For the first time since we started officially dating back in ninety-two, I began to feel a little distant from my wife, which made me worry that my marriage might be in trouble.

I thought it would help to speak with Jill, but she wasn't in the guest room or on the couch. She was already back at the Cup Of Spoons serving breakfast to the good citizens of Majestic, PA.

The next thing I knew, I was speed walking, and then I was outside your home, on the sidewalk, looking to see if I could catch a glimpse of you, but your shades were drawn like always. I didn't want to risk getting arrested, so I kept walking. For some reason I walked past Jacob Hansen's home maybe eighteen or so times, daring myself to look over and see if Jacob's younger brother, Eli, or their mother might be in the front yard watering the flowers or something. I fantasized about one of them waving at me in a friendly, forgiving way. But no matter how many times I walked past, I couldn't make myself look. Not even once.

Like always, whenever I passed my fellow Majestic townsmen and townswomen, they nodded or tipped their hats like I was a saint or a superhero or some such nonsense, which is really starting to bother me. Whatever miracle happened in the Majestic Theater, I wasn't responsible for it, no matter what the rumors around town might say. But I got to wondering whether those rumors had made me irresistible to Jill, who—even in her late forties—is still more beautiful than any movie star you can imagine. It's like the hometown-hero narrative that the local and then national media pushed has bewitched everyone except me, which has been more than a little disorienting, to put it mildly.

Did you have many reporters bothering you back in December? Jill used to throw snowballs at them when they were camped outside my home for those first few weeks. When it got really cold, she started filling up balloons with water and firing those too. Bobby the cop told her she had to stop doing that. She used to get so angry. I'd just sneak out the back door and hop fences whenever I wanted to get away and take my walks. Sometimes they found me and followed me around town. I'd just ignore them. I actually could block all of that out pretty well by hiding deep inside myself. But after Christmas, most of the media people went away to chase fresher stories.

Darce says my hometown-hero persona is good cover, meaning the misinformation that's been circulating since the tragedy allows my wife to hang around Majestic and visit me every night. She says if people knew the truth, angel-hunting season would begin and then that would be it for our relationship, which I guess I can understand. I don't want my wife to be hunted.

I asked Darce whether we should be worried about you keeping my confidence, especially since I'm now writing these tell-all letters, but Darcy says I'm protected by that piece of paper we both signed at the beginning of my treatment, the one that says we agree to keep our analytic container sacred, meaning what we discuss must be kept a secret from everyone outside of our container. Even though you tried to end my treatment prematurely, psyche tells me I can still trust you to keep all of this confidential.

What do you think about my Maryland story?

Does it make you secretly hate me a little?

Have I disappointed you?

You can be honest.

I can take it.

Seriously.

Your most loyal analysand,

Lucas

3.

Dear Karl,

Since you still haven't written back, I'm thinking maybe I've told you too much too fast, and yet there's so much I still haven't said. I've been quite selective. But I forget that you are also still in mourning and have clearly—via the letter you sent terminating my analysis, as well as your silence—expressed your need for physical, mental, and emotional space. I worry that I'm overwhelming you, especially since I am no longer paying for your time.

I do have money.

The life insurance company accepted Darcy's death certificate, which Jill sent them, and so they paid out on the small policy. And Isaiah arranged for me to be on paid leave, so I still have health insurance and a biweekly paycheck, which Jill keeps track of for me. I find it hard to believe it's a matter of money, but I'd be willing to accept an increase regarding your hourly fee. You'll eventually need an income again, right? I am happy to give you what money I have. Just name a price and I'll have Jill write a check. Even if it's just letters and no face-to-face meetings. A phone call down the line, to break the ice. And then who knows?

Darcy says I should keep sending these letters regardless of whether you write back. She says it's the writing that helps me most and that no one is forcing you to read them. That my envelopes might sit on your kitchen table for weeks or months until one day psyche will command you to open and read. Then perhaps you'll be moved to restart my analysis. And we won't have to make up for all the lost time because we'll have a handy detailed record of everything that's been happening to me right here in black and white.

I have mixed shaky feelings lately.

Again, I don't want to shame you, but the lack of a reply—especially after all the hard emotional work I've already stuffed into envelopes—has touched my father complex a bit and has me worried about my abandonment issues creeping back into my primary operating system. I've been trying to bring that to consciousness and be aware of it, like you always say.

It's like when Freud rejected Jung and then Jung had that breakdown where he slept with a loaded pistol next to his bed just in case he needed to exit the planet.

You'd want to be Jung and not Freud, I realize, so maybe that's a bad analogy.

But regardless of all that, this is the last time I'm going to begin a letter with a hedge or an apology. It should be clear by now that I feel conflicted about writing you, even though I also feel one hundred percent compelled at the same time. "Karl needs you!" psyche continues to scream every day. "Don't give up on him!" And so I will soldier on and try to win the battle for Karl. The best part of my soul loves the best part of your soul. I want you to know that statement is accurate and feel its truth as self-evident. "Like the sun rises and sets daily," you used to say.

I remember you told me about Jung visiting a tribe of indigenous people and how they told him that they helped their father, the sun, cross the sky. They viewed it as their life purpose—helping their sun god make his journey each and every day. That's how Jung learned humans actually affect and maybe even cocreate God. And that's why we need to avoid serving our neuroses, because it separates us from the Self and therefore limits our ability to help God manifest in the here and now.

Maybe with these letters—even if you are only reading and I'm doing all the writing, for now—you and I can help our own metaphorical sun god cross his metaphorical sky.

Darcy says that my writing you is in service of separating my true inherent self from my neuroses, which can only improve everything both in consciousness as well as in the unconscious.

I remember when you used to tell me that my unconscious was always talking with your unconscious, both of which were in conversation with the collective unconscious and that all of this dialoguing was necessary and important and maybe even divine.

I realize that I don't have to remind you of all of this, since you have been studying Jungian thought for your entire adult life and I've only been submersed in it for less than two years. But you told me to listen to my soul, saying, "Psyche always knows!" while shaking a finger over your head. I can still see the hopeful twinkle in your sky-blue eyes. It continues to give me strength.

Maybe you're wondering if I've been keeping up with my dream journal, writing down all that my unconscious is trying to communicate nightly. Unfortunately, I don't sleep much these days because I like to spend my nights with Darcy. Perhaps you will consider these nightly visitations to be encounters with the numinous and therefore worthy of documentation and analysis, so I look forward to discussing my supernatural marital experiences with you, just as soon as you reengage. I don't expect you to doubt the truth of my claims, but I have nonetheless been collecting angel feathers as proof. Each morning when I wake from the trance of being with winged Darcy I find small white feathers in my bed. They're tiny. Maybe only an inch in length. Much smaller than what I observe when I gaze at Darcy's magnificent wings—feathers that measure seven to fourteen inches long—so I'm thinking that what I'm finding must be undercoat feathers, which, for obvious reasons, are much smaller than the top-coat feathers of angel wings. What do you think? I've filled an entire gallon ziplock bag. It's ready and waiting to be examined.

But the real news I have to share today—and, yes, I realize I've buried the lead—is that I have a mysterious visitor in my backyard, whom we first discovered on Monday night.

I was in the living room reading *Castration and Male Rage: The Phallic Wound* by Eugene Monick, having finally completed his *Phallos: Sacred Image of the Masculine*, which was the last book you recommended back when we were talking in late November about the dark feminine rising in our culture and the need for pure phallic energy to clean up toxic masculinity. Anyway, Jill was emptying the dishwasher when she yelled in from the kitchen, "Lucas, someone's put up a tent in your backyard!"

I set down *Castration and Male Rage* on the coffee table and quickly made my way into the kitchen. It was twilight and the trees that lined the western portion of our property were blocking out what little light there was left in the day. A small two-person tent glowed orange as a jack-o'-lantern at the edge of the yard. Jill asked if I was expecting a camper, but, of course, I wasn't. Then she asked what we should do. I had no idea, so we ended up observing the tent for more than half an hour. I guess we were hoping whoever was inside would need to pee or something and step out so that we could identify him or her, but nothing happened whatsoever. The tent just continued to glow from within as we stood in the kitchen—with the lights out—peering through the window over the sink.

"Should we call the police?" Jill asked, but I thought that might be a bit rash, given that no crime had been committed, to which Jill said, "Trespassing is a crime."

"But it's a victimless crime," I answered. "I'll just go and see who it is and then we'll decide what to do."

"Well, you're not going alone," Jill said, and then grabbed a broom from the closet, which I immediately understood was meant to be used as a weapon if necessary. That made me smile, because who would be afraid of a broom unless it was attached to a wicked witch? And one look at Jill's face would let anyone know that she's not evil.

We slipped out the back door and made our way across the lawn. I took the lead and Jill followed close behind, clutching the broom handle like a sword, so that the straw end was pointed at her stomach.

"Hello," I called out when we got closer, but there was no answer. It was no longer twilight and I felt dumb for not bringing a flashlight, but I wasn't about to turn around, and anyway, the glow from inside the tent made it just possible to see. "We mean you no harm. I own the house here. And this is my friend Jill. We were just wondering if we might be able to have a chat."

When there was no response, Jill leaned into me so that our biceps were pushed together. It was warmish out and I could feel light perspiration on her skin. When she looked at me, I shrugged, because I had no idea what to do.

That's when Jill started poking the tent with the end of the broomstick and saying, "Hey, you in there. This is private property. Come on out."

"We just want to talk," I added, trying to soften Jill's words, but still there was no response.

"Okay, we're calling the police," Jill said, and then pulled out her cell phone. When she began tapping in numbers, I put a hand on top of the screen and held up my index finger.

"I'm going to open the tent," I said.

"Lucas," Jill said, meaning, *No, don't*, but I ignored her.

"If you don't say anything by the count of three," I said to whoever was inside, "I'm going to slowly unzip your tent and see what's going on in there, okay?"

Jill shook her head no, but I said, "One," and raised both of my hands up at Jill, meaning, *relax*. She sighed heavily and gripped the broomstick a little harder. "Two," I said. "I'm coming in after I say 'three.'" As I let some time pass, I wondered if Darcy had anything to do with this orange tent magically appearing in my backyard. It somehow felt like she might be involved. "Okay, three. I'm coming in."

I got down on my knees and slowly pulled up the tent zipper. When I stuck my head inside, Eli Hansen looked up at me with eyes that seemed to say, *Please, please, please*. He had lost a lot of weight, which made his nose and ears and teeth look too big and everything else look too small. His pale skin suggested he hadn't seen a lot of sun lately. And his unwashed shaggy brown hair was like a frozen explosion, with clumps shooting out in every direction. Before I pulled my head out and zippered the tent flaps back together, I saw a stack of books, a reusable grocery bag of what I imagined was food, a large jug of water, some clothes, and a sleeping bag.

Jill grabbed my arm, which is when I realized I was sort of frozen there on my knees, so I stood up and made my way back to the house with her trailing close behind. Halfway across the lawn, I turned around and yelled, "Eli, you can stay as long as you like."

In the living room, I told Jill all about how I had been counseling Eli at the high school before the tragedy happened and that I had also, after the tragedy, sort of done to him what you, Karl, had done to me—meaning I just accidentally disappeared from Eli's life, leaving him to deal with his problems by himself. Only he—being just a teenager—obviously didn't have an angel wife to comfort him through the nights. He had instead simply lost a brother to the Majestic Theater tragedy. And even though Eli wasn't in the theater when it happened, he might have had it worse than us because everyone in the town thinks his brother is a monster, while the rest of the deceased Majestic Theater victims have been deified and their left-behind survivors continue to be treated like saints.

"What exactly was wrong with Eli?" Jill asked. "What were you helping him with?"

I told her nothing was "wrong" with him. Eli had just needed to vent about many things.

Eli had come to my office at the beginning of the school year—back in September—because he was feeling lonely. He at first presented as awkward and shy, but warmed right up once I got to know him better. But he didn't really like anything except watching classic monster movies with his older brother, whom he wouldn't say much about, no matter how many times I asked about Jacob. Almost immediately, I started to get the sense that Eli was sitting on a great big secret that would need to be teased out of him over time, which is exactly what I had started to do. But then the tragedy happened and our work together was cut short.

"But maybe I should have worked quicker?" I asked Jill. "What do you think? Is that why Eli's in our backyard right now? What does this mean? What should we do? How do I fix this?"

I admit I was rambling and pacing and probably acting a little out of character, which is most likely why Jill called Isaiah, who arrived with Bess.

I was surprised when Jill got into the car with Bess and they drove away, leaving me alone with my best man friend, who put his hand on my shoulder like he always does and said, "That boy out there is hurting real bad," before explaining that Eli—who was at one point academically ranked among the top-ten students of his class—hadn't been doing any of his assignments since the tragedy and had recently stopped attending school altogether, which made me feel guilty about abandoning him and all of the students who relied on me the way I relied on you, Karl. The irony is not lost on me.

"I can go out there and talk to him," Isaiah said. "We could tell him that he has to go back to school and graduate. We can say he has a bright future ahead of him and all of that. But something tells me he didn't set up that tent because he wanted to be lectured."

"So what do you think he wants?" I asked.

"What do *you* think?" Isaiah replied. "What's your gut say?"

I closed my eyes like we'd do on Friday nights in your consulting room. I quieted my thoughts, dropped down deep inside, and asked psyche what it wanted to do about Eli. When I opened my eyes, Isaiah said he was glad to see me praying and—when I didn't correct him—added that he was going to make a man of faith out of me yet. Then he said if there was anyone who could help Eli it was me. "Even considering all that's happened," he added. Isaiah's words made me feel a little sick to my stomach here. "That boy's in your backyard for a reason," he added. "How you going to answer God's call, Lucas? How are you going to serve the Almighty? You have spiritual gifts. I've seen them. You simply cannot hide that kind of light."

Isaiah grabbed my head and pulled me so close that my forehead was pushing into his collarbone. He held me in his strong arms as he began to ask his God to help me with the task that had been set in front of me. Even in his prayer he said I was a good man who had helped many teenagers and compared me to Samson when he was chained up by the Philistines after they had cut his hair and blinded him. Then he said, "Lord, give my friend and colleague Lucas here the strength to knock down the pillars he's been asked to push against and to restore order and harmony in an effort to save that boy out there. You know I pray for all of them daily, Father, but that one out there needs extra. And Lucas here is just the man to give what he needs, as we both know. In the name of the Father, the Son, and the Holy Ghost, Amen."

When Isaiah released me, he squeezed my shoulder harder than he ever had before—so hard that I winced—and then he pulled me in for another big man hug. Next he slapped each one of my cheeks twice before he filled me in on what was going on at the high school and the fact that his daughter, Aliza, had just announced that she was expecting a baby. Except he laughed because Aliza said she *and her husband* were pregnant, which prompted Isaiah to say he and I were getting to be old men and soon we wouldn't understand anything the younger people said to us.

When Aliza was a senior at Majestic High, many years ago, she started coming to my office a lot because she was having what she called a crisis of faith, meaning she wasn't sure she believed in the religion that she had inherited from Bess and Isaiah. She felt conflicted about this to the point that she wasn't eating. I mostly listened to her, but I remember saying that it was her job as a young woman to decide what was best for her as she made her way out into the world. I remember how tortured she looked, because her parents wanted her to keep singing in the choir and teaching Sunday school to little kids, but the energy to do those things wasn't in her heart. And I remember wondering how Bess and Isaiah could be such caring people and still produce a daughter who was scared to tell her parents what she really felt. It made me sad but I never talked to Isaiah about it. I kept Aliza's secrets.

After her high school graduation ceremony, she found me on the foot-ball field and kissed me on the cheek and hugged me and held on for what felt like an inappropriately long time while she whispered, "Thank you," into my ear. Later that summer, she flew across the country to UCLA. And I hardly ever see her these days, as she's made California her home and seldom visits Pennsylvania.

Sitting post-prayer with my friend in my living room, I was happy for Isaiah and pregnant Aliza and Robert, her husband—and I said so—but deep inside I was mostly worried about Eli being in my backyard.

What did he want?

What did he need?

Why was he choosing me?

And what if he had come to punish me because he thought I had done something wrong? It would be easy to see how his young mind might have gotten the story mixed up after sorting through the various reported details from the Majestic Theater that night and the erroneous news stories and misinformation that's still on the internet, not to mention how the rumors have been tainted by the disorienting effects of post-traumatic stress.

I was surprised when Isaiah showed me his overnight bag and told me that Jill was going to stay with Bess until the morning—so they could "talk like women do"—and Isaiah was going to sleep on my couch just in case anything got weird with Eli.

"Cain and Abel," Isaiah said. "You've dealt with the first and the hardest case. Now we have to deal with the young shepherd who is little more than a lamb himself. That boy doesn't have a mean bone in his body, but if recent events have taught us anything, it's that you never can tell. So let's think this through and go slow."

I think he meant that tragedy does funny things to the brain, which I don't have to tell you. I'm sure Jung would agree too.

That night, when I locked the bedroom door and met with winged Darcy, she pointed out through the window to the glowing orange tent and said, "That boy is the way forward."

I asked what she meant.

"That boy is the way forward," she repeated.

"It would be hypocritical of me to keep writing Karl and not engage with Eli, right?" I said. "This is some kind of spiritual test, right?"

"That boy is the way forward."

Winged Darcy wouldn't say anything else.

In the morning, Isaiah got up and went to the high school, but the boy did nothing, even when Jill returned at dinnertime and poked his tent some more with the broomstick.

Eli's been out there in the tent for four days now. No one has seen him exit or enter, and I've been watching pretty closely. The whole thing seems strange and—sorry to get crude here for a second—I do wonder how he is relieving himself.

Now that I've written you this letter—using our therapeutic connection to fill my tank again, so to speak—I'm going to attempt to speak with Eli just as soon as I return from the post office.

Do you see me when I walk by your home and wave? Sometimes I imagine you peeking through the blinds and smiling back at me. I pass by several times a day, hoping the stars will align, as the old poets say.

I really miss you.

Your most loyal analysand,
Lucas

4.

Dear Karl,

Do you know Sandra Coyle?

She's a lawyer.

She's on the school board.

Frosted shoulder-length hair?

Heavy tortoiseshell glasses?

Expensive pantsuits?

Her husband, Greg—the golf pro at the Pines Country Club—was killed in the Majestic Theater and immediately transformed into an angel. I saw Greg fly up toward heaven just like the sixteen others, including Darcy and Leandra.

Did you know that Sandra was the first one to speak with the press about what happened at the Majestic Theater? Only she used plural pronouns, saying things like, "*We* won't let this tragedy go answered. *We* will fight. *We* will petition politicians. *We* will make order out of this chaos," before she consulted the rest of us.

On the internet, there's a clip of her filmed on the night of the shooting. She's staring into the camera with her makeup smeared and her hair disheveled and blood splattered across her neck and she's pointing a long finger at the lens as she says, "*Shame* on the politicians who make it possible for a teenager to purchase guns and ammunition. *Shame* on the gun sellers who took money from a nineteen-year-old and clearly insane boy. *Shame* on the parents who raised this killer."

Watching the clip made my stomach feel queasy, because I'm not sure you can allocate the shame so neatly and easily. Maybe shame on the town of Majestic for producing Jacob Hansen, who was twenty-one on the night of the tragedy and not nineteen. Was not Sandra herself a member of our community? Maybe shame on the Majestic school system, which I was a part of. I'd spent the majority of my adult life doing everything humanly possible to prevent this sort of tragedy from manifesting. I don't think I could have tried harder, even though I never worked directly with Jacob. And there were many other people—like Isaiah, for example—who had dedicated their entire careers to producing compassionate young people. Isaiah is in no way deserving of shame.

Sandra didn't know that her husband had turned into a graceful, calm, and peace-radiating angel with beautiful wings, so I initially forgave her for being so indiscriminately upset and lashing out so haphazardly.

But in the immediate aftermath of the tragedy there was also no way she could have known the facts about how Jacob's guns were acquired or why he decided to shoot his neighbors while they watched a classic Christmas movie in a historic theater. So Sandra's righteous rage made me feel more than a little uncomfortable.

Don't get me wrong. I understand her pain. And I certainly understand the very human need for retribution. But the steadiness and certainty of her hatred—especially after seeing her husband killed right in front of her eyes—felt disconcerting to me, although I didn't say anything about that at first, except to Darcy, of course, who said, "Sandra wasn't gifted with a vision. You have the advantage. You mustn't forget that."

And I understand that winged Greg couldn't resist the ecstatic pull of the light and therefore decided to fly eternally toward it, leaving Sandra all alone to make sense of what had happened. Only Darcy was able to temporarily resist the great light's pull. She's told me that she won't be able to resist forever and that I need to prepare for her eventual departure. That's what we work on every night together in our locked bedroom—our inevitable separation. But I realize that I am privileged. And maybe I'd have just as much hate in my heart—maybe even more than Sandra—if Darce didn't grant me the ability to see angels and then remain behind while I acclimated to her new reality.

"Spiritual handholding," Darcy calls it.

Shortly after the tragedy, Robin Withers—our town's head librarian, whom I mentioned before—organized a support group of sorts for the survivors. I can't imagine you weren't contacted and given an invitation to join, but as you have never attended any of the meetings and still aren't responding to my letters, there is no way for me to know for sure. I asked Robin whether you had been invited and she assured me that you had been, but perhaps she lied to me. I don't know why she would do that, but anything is possible in this crazy new world, especially since grief makes people do all sorts of funny things.

At first, the meetings were therapeutic. Grief counselors volunteered to speak with us collectively and individually. I spoke privately with a nice man named Travis, but I felt a little awkward about it, even though he was kind. Halfway through our session, I started to feel like I was cheating on you—so I stood up, told him I had a Jungian analyst to confide in, and then excused myself. He followed me out into the YMCA gym. They had set up makeshift rooms using portable screens and curtains.

And Travis kept saying it was important for me to work through everything properly, as I was facing what he called a "monumental psychological task"—one that he confidently said he could help me navigate.

I could tell that Travis was sincere, but he wasn't going to put a Jungian lens on things—like we do—and so I felt he would only be messing up what we had already started. I thought about the sanctity of our therapeutic container, keeping the steam in to cook the rice, and making sure the alchemical process remained uninterrupted. I smiled and thought, *Karl would be proud.*

I did, however, attend the lectures and "circle shares" and sat through all the crying and tried to allow the best of my soul to love the best of everyone else's soul. And sometimes I held the hands of the other victims or let them soak my shirt with tears. And it felt purposeful, being there at these meetings where we all communed and tried to make sense of what had happened.

Every night, I asked Darcy if I could tell the group about my numinous experience, arguing that it would be cathartic for everyone to understand that their loved ones did not suffer and were not afraid, but were instantly transformed into higher beings who were far more beautiful and enlightened than humans could ever be. I had felt the awesome benefits of that knowledge and it seemed like I was cruelly hoarding a panacea. Darce argued against my disseminating that information, proposing that my Jungian analysis with you had prepared me to be the perfect vessel for the sacred, meaning I was able to contain the divine knowledge without psychologically cracking or mentally dissociating or suffering a disintegration of the soul.

"Telling the unprepared and the uninitiated could literally render them insane," Darcy argued. "It's only for those who have eyes to see and ears to hear. The mystery is not for everyone. This is the esoteric."

But what if it is also universally medicinal? Balm for the soul? I kept thinking. I don't believe I'd be able to do anything at all—not even get out of bed in the morning—if I hadn't seen the dead rise up and transform, if I wasn't having nightly conversations with an angel who wraps her wings around me and makes me feel whole again. The feathers my wife leaves behind as proof have saved me over and over.

"There will be a task," Darcy says, "and you will know it when you see it."

So I kept my mouth shut about angels and all the rest, but I tried to help the others in the ways I mentioned above.

All of The Survivors—which is what we had begun to call ourselves—got together on December 26, for a second Christmas of sorts, only we didn't open presents or eat a ham-and-pineapple dinner or sing carols or even exchange cookies. We just sat with each other in the library. And almost everyone cried into each other's bodies as we talked about how impossible it had been the day before to simply be around those who weren't inside the Majestic during the tragedy, because they didn't understand. And they really didn't—not even Jill.

You probably saw that Mark and Tony—the couple who restored and owns the historic Majestic Theater—hired someone to drape a huge black silk sash over the cathedral-like face of the movie house, in memorial of all who were killed. They also declared that the theater would be closed indefinitely out of respect for the bereaved, which most would consider to be a nice gesture. But neither of them had been there the night of the shooting, so they really don't get that a black silk sash doesn't do much to heal anyone. Also, going to the movies had always been Darce's and my equivalent of going to church. "It's where you go to restore your faith in humanity! It's where you go to believe! To laugh and cry and smile like a kid again," Darce used to say, and I agree. We went at least once a week. So Mark and Tony shutting down the movies felt like an extra punishment in some ways. And the community's additional loss depressed me greatly.

I couldn't make myself cry with the others, because I had winged Darcy comforting me every night.

Sandra didn't cry a single tear at the meetings, nor did she hug or hold anyone. Instead, she fumed. I'm not suggesting that she wasn't sad about losing her husband, Greg, especially since they have two elementary-school-aged children, who thankfully weren't in the theater when the shooting happened, but were home with a babysitter. Even though Sandra never approached me, I would notice her pulling members aside and sort of lecturing them in the corner of whatever room we were in. Her face was always tomato red, but not from crying. Sandra was an exploding volcano. And she was always wagging her index finger in people's noses. Sometimes little beads of spit would fly out of her mouth, almost as if they were trying to escape the heat of some terrible furnace.

Three or so months after the tragedy, maybe at the end of March, Sandra began to actively repurpose The Survivors' Group, turning our attention away from healing and toward activism—specifically gun control. I have nothing against politics. I own no guns. If I never see another gun of any kind, even a toy gun, I will be grateful. So I'm not against what Sandra is trying to do. But the goal of our meetings quickly morphed from comforting each other to something that felt more like score settling.

At one point, I got brave enough to stand up and make a brief speech in defense of finishing the first task before we began the second, saying that surely we'd be better equipped mentally and spiritually after we finished mourning, at which point maybe we could vote on the next steps to take. I could see that I had spoken sense because almost all of my fellow members were nodding and holding eye contact with me.

But Sandra flew into a rage and began pacing around the room yelling things like, "How will you feel about your little mourning period if another young man kills another group of innocent people before we get around to doing something about it? Will we write the victims' families, saying we had to heal ourselves before we did anything to fight back, but we're terribly sorry for your loss? Does that sound responsible to any of you?"

With her hands on her hips, Sandra scanned the room, daring anyone to make eye contact with her. No one could. Not even me, and I'm backed by a legitimate angel.

Then Sandra said, "I'm surprised, Lucas," which made my blood run cold, because—from the icy tone of her voice—I knew she was about to deliver her finishing blow, which she did, saying, "I'd think you of all people would be in favor of taking swift and merciless action."

I couldn't breathe. It was like Sandra had reached out some invisible hand and crushed my windpipe. I was five years old again and my mother was standing over me, yelling, "Shame on you!" I knew right then and there, I would never again attend another Survivors' meeting. And I didn't. That was the last one for me. Everyone visited my home and begged me to return to the group. Everyone except Sandra, which is how I know it was her intention to psychologically assassinate me. Or maybe Jungians such as yourself would say she wanted to psychologically *castrate* me.

At first, Jill and Isaiah and Bess all asked me many times why I wouldn't return to The Survivors, but I couldn't tell them. Darcy said it was best to bide my time and gather strength before I made a play, which she said I most definitely would, if only to save the others from the darkness that had taken up residence in Sandra Coyle. But when the political signs started going up in the front yards of Majestic residents and Sandra began making appearances on the local news channels and radio talk shows and even podcasts around the world, my friends got the picture pretty quickly.

Whenever I see the other Survivors around town now, they always say they miss the early days of the group and ask if I would like to meet for tea or a walk or a talk on a couch. I always take them up on the offer and almost every time I end up hugging the other Survivor and my shirt becomes soaked with tears. "I wish there was something we could do, other than be angry," they all say to me, and I've been thinking long and hard on what the solution could be.

Darcy kept saying the answer would find me when I was ready and that it was a blessing not to know the exact battle plan before I was spiritually and psychologically prepared to implement it. I can see the logic in that thinking. I have to admit, it's often quite helpful to have an angel around.

Sandra seems to grow more and more powerful by the week. She recently forced her way onto the high school auditorium stage, and from what Isaiah told me, the presentation she delivered to the student body was not exactly in line with my best friend's educational philosophy. Isaiah said, "That woman is suffering unmercifully, but she *unmercifully* wants everyone else to suffer even more than her." We'll just leave it at that because I don't want to speak unnecessarily ill about a fellow Survivor.

I'm not angry with Sandra. But I can't help concluding that she pushed me out of the way in order to do whatever it is that she's now doing. Maybe she will get some reasonable gun laws passed that will prevent future tragedies, who knows? Maybe the ends will justify the means. It's certainly possible. But I can't shake the feeling that I've let down the others by submitting to Sandra Coyle.

I really didn't know what to do about all of the above until Eli Hansen set up his tent in my backyard.

Did you think I forgot about the cliffhanger I signed off with in the last letter?

Write me back and I'll tell you all about Eli.

This is a story you definitely want to hear.

Trust me.

Please write back; it would help me tremendously.

To be honest—and despite the good face I'm putting on to keep these letters relatively upbeat—I'm just barely hanging on here.

I could really use a session.

Your most loyal analysand,

Lucas

5.

Dear Karl,

Well, you didn't write back. I thought maybe the Eli teaser might tempt you. Perhaps I didn't wait long enough. Actually, there was no way you could have responded by the U.S. postal system this quickly, but I had hoped maybe you'd hand deliver, call, or email. Because a lot has happened, and quickly, I decided to write again today. A million words want to jump onto the page. So let's get started, shall we?

After I dropped off the last letter about Eli setting up his tent—well, wait a second, that one was *two letters ago*, I think. Regardless, after I slid that through the mail slot in your front door, I became determined to speak with Eli. (I know I wrote I'd use the post office, but I want you to read these letters ASAP and I made sure no one saw me violating the stay-away order that Bobby the cop laid down.) It was the fourth day that Eli had spent in the orange tent and I was beginning to worry that he might never leave.

As I strode home, politely greeting everyone I passed just like I always do, I mentally played out the conversation I would have with the young man. I didn't want to seem didactic. I hoped that I could get him talking and that I would simply listen, which is what I do best by nature. After thinking through all of my options, I decided that I might ask to enter the tent and then—provided I was given permission—sit cross-legged on the floor and just stare softly into Eli's eyes, like you used to do, whenever you would send your psychic self into me or try to find me "on the astral plane." I decided that this was perhaps the most effective way to let Eli know the best of my soul loved the best of his soul, and that I was glad he had set up his tent in my backyard. I welcomed him. I was here with him. I was willing to bring my full self to this moment—all of me. And I was also more than willing to continue the work we had started earlier in the year.

But as I walked down Main Street and the Majestic Theater's great black silk sash came into view, I began to feel quite hungry and before I knew it I was sitting in the Cup Of Spoons with a BLT sandwich and a large glass of ice tea. It was funny, because after one bite of Jill's signature midday dish, which is an absolute favorite of mine, I began to feel queasy and couldn't lift another piece of food to my mouth if you paid me a billion dollars. Jill came out from the kitchen and asked what was wrong with the meal, so I came clean and told her I was worried about speaking with Eli.

Jill said, "Maybe just wait until I'm finished up here. We're closing at seven tonight."

And so—since it was already almost five p.m.—I agreed to take a long walk and then meet Jill back at the Cup when she got off.

It was a warmish spring night and there were a lot of people on Main Street, so I immediately turned onto lesser-traveled roads to avoid living in the usual inaccurate Lucas Goodgame hagiography. I walked past your house eighteen more times, but I couldn't force myself to turn my head and see if you might be in your yard or looking out a window—or maybe even reading my latest letter. A few times I thought I heard you calling my name, but when I stopped and closed my eyes and listened harder, I realized that your voice was only coming from inside my head, so I eventually kept walking.

I also walked by Eli's home exactly eighteen times, hoping that I might see his mother and then glean some useful information that would help solve the mystery of why her second-born son was camping in my backyard. But I also couldn't make myself look over to confirm whether or not Mrs. Hansen was out and about. For some reason, I felt compelled to literally run whenever her home came into view and I ended up sprinting so fast back and forth in front of the Hansen residence that I broke into a sweat and was soon lathered up with perspiration.

Right after the eighteenth pass, Bobby the cop pulled up in his squad car and asked if everything was okay, which, of course, it was.

"Why are you sprinting past the Hansen house, Mr. Goodgame?" he said, but in a cheerful way.

"Just working on my cardio," I replied, and then he suggested maybe working on my cardio far away from Mrs. Hansen.

"It's just not a good look, you know?" Bobby added, which made me feel sick to my stomach again.

"I'm just running," I reemphasized.

"I know," he said. "But why not jump in the cruiser and I'll give you a lift to the Cup Of Spoons?"

"How did you know I was going there?"

"Wild guess."

I told him I was too sweaty and smelly, but he said he didn't care about that and insisted I get into the cruiser, at which point I asked if he were arresting me. To which he replied, "Why would you think that?" in a way that made me feel a whole lot better. So I decided to get into the cruiser after all. And before I knew it, I was back at the Cup Of Spoons and Jill was handing Bobby a BLT sandwich, "On the house," because he had found and brought me back to her. Which is when I realized that someone had called Jill and told her I was running past either your house or Mrs. Hansen's.

Was it you?

I won't be mad if it was. But why didn't you just come out and talk to me yourself if you had some sort of concern?

I, of course, asked Jill who had tipped her off. She insisted that she had no idea what I was talking about, but her left eyebrow kind of arched like it always does when she's lying. As we drove home in her truck, I decided to let that mystery go, because I still had to deal with Eli, which would require all of my mental reserves.

Because I hadn't been feeling well enough to eat earlier, Jill brought home her famous three-bean soup and a hunk of crusty French bread for my dinner, which I tried to get down but couldn't. Jill said that I was nervous about confronting Eli and "for good reason," which made me feel even worse. Then she said, "My God, Lucas, you're turning green," which is when I threw up in the sink, after which Jill got me into bed and gave me some medicine that made me fall asleep almost instantaneously.

An awful noise woke me up in the middle of the night.

I sat up in my bed and looked around, but I was still half asleep. It took a few minutes for my eyes to adjust and my brain to come back online, but when it did, I stood and walked over to the window, which Jill must have opened for me, because neither she nor I like to sleep in air-conditioning. (It gives us sore throats.) I could see the tent glowing like a jack-o'-lantern again. It looked extra bright because there was no moonlight whatsoever. I heard this bloodcurdling moaning that reminded me of what I heard after the shooting was over, back at the Majestic Theater. It almost sounded like a psychic operation without anesthesia. Like someone was trying to extract Eli's soul out there in the tent.

The next thing I remember is walking down the stairs in my home with Jill following close behind, saying, "We need to call the police. That boy needs help."

I couldn't, of course, tell her what winged Darce had said about Eli being the way forward, so instead I kept saying, "No police."

"Your neighbors are going to call the police if they haven't already," Jill answered, but I just ignored her. When I reached the back door, she turned me around so that I was facing her and then said, "I don't think you're ready for this."

I could tell she was afraid, but I wasn't quite sure of what. I wanted to get to the bottom of Jill's fear, but I thought it best to triage, and Eli's moaning was concerning enough to pull rank, so I exited and made my way toward the orange glow.

Eli must have heard my back door open, because he immediately tried to quiet his suffering, but managed only to turn down the volume, as I could still hear him whimpering softly. I wondered if he had buried his face in his sleeping bag, but when I unzipped his tent and stuck my head inside, I saw that Eli had his face in his hands, which were literally dripping with tears. When I touched his shoulder—just like Isaiah had done for me many times—Eli flinched, so I pulled my hand back, and then I remembered my plan.

I entered the tent, pulling the zipper closed behind me, and then sat cross-legged across from him and softened my gaze before I tried to find him on the astral plane. After five or so minutes, he dropped his hands and began to stare back at me. I could feel his breathing slowing and I could sense that he was relaxing a bit.

Finally he said "I didn't know what else to do. I didn't have anywhere else to go."

"It's okay," I said, and then continued attempting to do what you had done for me many times in your consulting room, when you psychically entered me, when the best part of your soul wrapped itself around the best part of my soul.

"What are you doing?" he asked, but in a calm way, so I told him that I was trying to calm him down and that it was working, so maybe he should just go along with it, which he thankfully did.

We sat in silence for a long time, quietly looking at each other. I could feel Jill outside worrying and wondering what was happening inside the tent, but, somehow, she knew better than to break our man spell with words or by entering, which I appreciated greatly. And I could also hear the steady beating of Darcy's wings high above; I could feel her looking down on me with angelic approval, since angels can easily see through thin tent fabric. I wondered if Jill might decide to tilt her head back and search for the origin of that beating-wings sound, but she never let out a cry of joy or astonishment, so I don't believe she ever looked up, which was both a pity and a relief.

As I sat in the tent with young Eli, I could feel his pain and frustration and loneliness leaving his body. I could literally feel his muscles relaxing and his psyche regaining a stronghold.

And then I was laying him down on my living room couch and covering him with a sheet and telling him he was okay and that he had come to the right place and that I was going to help him get better no matter how long it took. I could feel Jill watching with approval from the dark corner of the room and I began to wonder where the necessary strength had come from, because I could feel the power of what the best of my soul was doing for Eli, which was awesome in the true sense of the word—filling me with a sense of awe.

Just before the boy drifted off to sleep, with eyes closed, he whispered, "Mr. Goodgame, I don't hold you responsible."

Before I had a chance to reply, he had lost consciousness.

Jill followed me up the stairs and then whispered, "Are you okay?"

"I just need to be alone," I said in the kindest way possible, and then slipped into my bedroom, locking the door behind me.

Darce had already flown in through the window and was smiling proudly at me.

"The boy is the way forward," she said once more, but with renewed vigor.

I was too exhausted to reply. Instead, I collapsed into her celestial body, at which point she wrapped me in her warm, massive wings and I passed out.

When I woke up the next morning, I was in my bed and Darcy was gone, but I collected fourteen small feathers from the bedding, proving that I had not imagined the previous night's numinous encounter.

Jill was, of course, already downtown—just like every other morning— serving breakfast to the good citizens of Majestic, PA.

I found Eli asleep on the couch, so I put on coffee and made scrambled eggs and toast. As if by magic, he shuffled into the kitchen just as I was putting his hot plate of food down on the table. Turns out he takes his coffee black, like me. We ate, listening to the sound of forks and knives tapping and scraping the plates and the loud gulps of men swallowing, after which Eli loaded the dishwasher and I scrubbed the egg pan.

When we finished, Eli said, "I'm not going back to school and I can't go home."

"Okay," I said.

"What exactly do you mean by 'okay'?"

"*Okay*," I said once more, trying to sound as understanding and innocuous as possible, which seemed to shift the mood.

I think he was expecting a lecture or a set of instructions or something, because he leaned his right ear a little closer to his right shoulder and raised his eyebrows, as if to convey uncertainty.

"People say you've gone crazy," he said after a beat. "Like legitimately insane."

I hadn't heard that before, but I wasn't surprised. I decided to keep listening, rather than reply. I did my best to remain curious, because you always said that's the best thing to be in every situation.

"Are you?" Eli said when it was clear I wasn't going to respond without further prompting. *"Bonkers?"*

"Do I seem mad to you?" I asked, and then held eye contact until he looked away, taking another page out of your Jungian analysis playbook.

Finally, he angrily said, "It's everyone else who seems crazy," which is when his eyes began to well up again, until a big fat tear slid down his cheek, which he immediately wiped away with the back of his wrist.

"Sometimes walking helps me," I said. "Do you want to take a walk with me?"

He nodded and then we walked all day long. I bet we walked at least eighteen miles, hardly saying a word to each other. But having the boy next to me on the journey seemed to help a great deal. And as the day went on, I began to feel certain that he also found my being next to him just as helpful, if not more so. And so we kept walking, getting stronger together. Our trust in the Eli-Lucas link increased as we continued to use it.

Jill brought us home lasagna slices for dinner, which—after all that walking—we ate greedily together in my dining room.

"What did you two do today?" she asked at one point.

And Eli simply said, "We went for a very long walk."

"Did you enjoy it?" Jill asked, and Eli and I both nodded in unison.

On a whim, I suggested the three of us walk up to Main Street after dinner and get ice cream, which Darcy always loved to do in the spring, when nights were pleasant as the one we were gifted that day. Eli and Jill were keen, so we walked to We All Scream For Ice Cream, which I'm sure you must know, because it's a Majestic town favorite. Although, come to think of it, I've never seen you there before. I had only ever seen you—outside of your consulting room—at the Majestic Theater, because we both loved the movies so much. Remember how, on the night of the tragedy, right by the historic black-and-white pictures from the forties and fifties in the lobby, Darce and I even exchanged pleasantries with you and your wife, Leandra, which was unusual, because you always said we needed to keep our analytical container sacred, meaning no contact whatsoever outside of analysis. *You must remember*. It was the first and only time we ever spoke outside of analysis. You and I exchanged smiles and audible hellos. Darce said, "Merry Christmas," to Leandra, who said, "Happy Holidays," back to her. It was the first and only time our wives ever spoke. I can't decide if that chance meeting feels quite ominous or quite auspicious to me now. You could frame it either way. But it definitely feels significant, right?

Regardless of whether you eat ice cream or not, whether you know the oral delights of We All Scream For Ice Cream—where Darcy and I actually once worked together for a summer—the first sign of trouble on the night Jill, Eli, and I went for cones happened when a few people saw us walking down Main Street and then immediately crossed to the other side of the road, which made every bone in my body vibrate the wrong way. Then Wendy Lewis—who now owns We All Scream For Ice Cream—wasn't as friendly as she usually is to this former ice cream scooper and loyal customer. She gave me a big smile when I walked through the door, but her face darkened when she saw Eli. Jill tried to make it all right by asking Wendy if anything was wrong, but Majestic's self-proclaimed Queen of Ice Cream would only say, "Everything is fine," but without making eye contact.

Then, as we sat outside licking our cones in the warm blooming night air of spring, whenever people passed, I noticed that they weren't looking at me the way they usually do—as if I were a hero. It was like I'd stepped out of the Lucas Goodgame hagiography, but somehow accidentally this time. Instead, they were looking at Eli as if he were a horrid, disease-spreading, murderous monster. Then these people would give me a questioning glance that seemed to say, *What are you doing* with him? A few customers approached the ice cream store as if they wanted to make a purchase, but when they saw us there, they turned around and walked away. It was as if Eli, Jill, and I had all forgotten to wear clothes and our private parts were grotesquely on display.

Eli pretended not to notice and at one point I thought maybe I was imagining things in my troubled head, but then a group of teenagers whose names I know but won't repeat began staring at Eli in a bad way that was impossible to deny. After a minute or so, Jill got upset and yelled, "Take a picture, why don't you? It lasts longer!" When one of the teenagers raised her phone to literally take a picture of us, Jill threw what remained of her ice cream cone at the picture taker, who ducked with impressive athleticism. Ice cream exploded onto the windshield of a parked sports car, which made all of the teenagers pull out their phones and begin to record both the mess and us, adding commentary that was condemning and cruel. Eli jumped up, threw his cone in the trash can, and stormed off. And so Jill and I followed.

Once we were off Main Street, Eli began saying things like, "I didn't do anything! It's not my fault! It's not fair! I thought that if I were with you, that maybe they'd let up, but it didn't work! And no one wants to listen! My life is over. *Over!*"

Jill and I kept saying we absolutely were listening and wanted to understand, which was when I could tell that Jill had taken a liking to Eli, who was relatively easy to root for, truth be told. He's a good kid with the right sort of heart, which would enable him to endure the present horrors, if only the right people would hold him in the manner he needed to be held.

"The boy is the way forward," I heard winged Darcy saying in my head.

But—even after the kind, understanding, and sympathetic words Jill and I had shared with Eli—when the three of us arrived at my home, Eli strode across the back lawn like a thundercloud and disappeared into his tent without saying another word.

"Let him calm down," Jill said, which seemed reasonable, so I sat in a lawn chair behind the house and watched the tent glow orange—and I remained ready and waiting to intervene should Eli start to moan again.

I will be a sentry of emotions for Eli, I thought, and then sat up a little taller. Straightening my spine. Permitting the phallic energy to erect within my whole body and drive the mission, allowing myself to burn, and to remain in that state of incinerating intensity while directing the entirety of my phallic energy at the mission or target. Doing what you had taught me during our sessions.

And that's when I understood exactly what needed to be done.

I resolved right then and there to be for Eli what you, Karl, had been—and I hope will be again—for me. Suddenly, I understood that I had to earn the benefits of our analytic container, and that maybe you were even testing me—seeing if I was worthy of more of your instruction, teaching, and care, especially after what you saw that night at the Majestic Theater. The shock and disapproval on your face rendered me psychologically impotent for a time. But I have come to see it as a necessary part of my masculine development. And I'm going to prove I'm a worthy analysand, Karl, and not a lost cause. I aim to be the best Jungian analysand you've ever had and reclaim my position on your "roster of men." I'm going to do it by creating my own "roster of men" to encourage and nurture in an effort to bring out their absolute best. I'm, of course, starting with the boy, just like Darcy suggested. I decided to deploy all you had already taught me. So I have one name on my official roster of men—Eli—although I am thinking of adding Isaiah, because I love him like a brother. But one man at a time, maybe, at least at first.

The next day—after that night in the lawn chair, watching over Eli—is when everything really started to fall into place, regarding the way forward, but I think I'll save that part for the next letter. I've already written a lot today and I have actually become quite busy lately, almost like an orchestra conductor, only I'm not making music, but something even more unexpected.

Does that sound unhinged?

Ha!

I've never felt more hinged in my life.

I'm seeing the field clearly, maybe for the first time. My certainty is unprecedented. My sureness transcends the physical realm.

Psyche is singing.

And you want to hear this song.

When I catch you up, I am sure you are going to be extremely proud of me. I'm performing an initiation of sorts. I'm going to help Eli cross over the threshold. The entire town is going to help make him into a man, just like in olden times, back when we had rituals for healing wounded boys on the threshold of adulthood.

Maybe you'll even wish to get involved with Eli's new project, who knows?

Both Eli and I would very much like that. We hope to include everyone who was in the Majestic Theater when the tragedy happened, even Sandra Coyle, if she can behave herself. You can't just pick and choose when it comes to healing. We must heal all who wish to be whole, and we must do so completely, thoroughly, and with the entirety of our souls.

Your most loyal analysand,

Lucas

6.

Dear Karl,

I ended the last letter with an upset Eli brooding in his tent and me sitting up erect on a lawn chair, like a sentry of emotions—I know because I keep copies of everything I send you and reread every single word before I settle back in to write the next installment. But I teased what was to come in hopes that you'd write back, which you haven't.

That's okay. I'm not angry with you. Quite the contrary. No matter what, I will never ever be upset with you.

But back to where we left off in the story.

I sat up all night long in my backyard and whenever I looked toward the heavens, I saw Darcy flying, carving a figure-eight infinity sign into the night sky, as if she was saying she'd be with me forever. Her wings were illuminated by starlight, which created an otherworldly effect that was so beautiful, human words cannot describe it. You simply have to feel it in the present moment to understand it. The sight was so transcendent that I didn't even mind when she spent the whole night soaring and never once descended to speak with me.

She'll get close enough for touching only in the safety of our bedroom with the door locked. I don't know why.

But as I had Eli to watch over, there was no way I was going to abandon the mission on night one, so I had to settle for the occasional glance, lifting my face up to the heavens every so many minutes, and feeling deeply held by the consistency of Darcy's flying. It was almost as if she was demonstrating her approval of—or was actively blessing—my new venture, which gave me a tremendous confidence.

When the sun rose, Darcy faded into the soft morning light, slowly disappearing, although I wondered whether she was still there, only the sunlight had made her invisible somehow. I have never seen winged Darcy during the day, so it's a working hypothesis for now.

I've googled on the internet but have found there isn't much reliable information regarding angels. The first thing that comes up is the professional Major League Baseball team, which tells you a lot, right there. When I went deeper into the search results, much of what I discovered conflicted. One article says this and then another says that. I read so much incompatible material, I decided to discard it all and take up the task of learning about angels myself, relying only on what I can observe, stockpiling empirical evidence, which I have and will continue to share here.

"Did you get any sleep at all?" Jill asked, when—just before leaving for breakfast duty at the Cup Of Spoons—she stopped by my lawn chair.

The sun was already up, so I said, "Aren't you late?"

Apparently, she was able to reach her kitchen assistant in the middle of the night because he was up playing video games. Randy had agreed to open so that she could get an extra hour's sleep, which was when I realized she must have been watching me watch Eli until the early morning. I never turned around and looked back at the house, so maybe she was in the window the whole time. I didn't know. Then Jill bent down and kissed my right cheek, before saying, "You be careful, okay?"

I wanted to know why she said that, and ask, *What was the danger?* but part of me was also afraid to know the answer, so I let her walk away.

I sat there for another half hour or so before I yelled, *"Eli?"*

I yelled his name twice more and the deafening silence made my heart beat a little faster.

But then, finally, he said, "I'm coming," right before emerging from the orange tent with his hair all mussed and a tired, sad look in his eyes.

I led him into the kitchen, where I cooked us breakfast, and then we ate in silence, once again listening to the sounds of our utensils banging against our plates. Then—just after slurping down the last sip of my coffee—I said, "What if we continued the work we were doing at the high school together, only this time we'll be free of the rules I had to follow when you were a student and I was a faculty member?"

"What do you mean?" he asked from behind the coffee mug he was cradling with both hands, and I noted the skepticism.

So I quickly pivoted to talking about my experience with Jungian analysis and began telling him all about you, which I realize violated the covenant we had made and risked letting all the steam out of the pot before the metaphorical rice finished cooking. But desperate times call for desperate measures, as they say. And I do believe I did a good job selling Jungian analysis. I told him about the embarrassing anxiety attack I had in my office during a counseling session with one of his classmates—how the EMTs were called to the high school and I was wheeled out clutching my chest because I thought I was having a heart attack.

"So you didn't have a heart attack?" he said, because—as I told you when I first started analysis—I had let everyone in the high school believe I had. Then I told Eli how you helped me understand my father and mother complexes as you slowly built a temporary scaffolding around my psyche so that we could fix the broken parts. The whole time I was speaking, he returned my eye contact and nodded in all the appropriate places.

"We'd be starting at ground zero here. But I do believe that I can help you heal and then you must get your life together and launch yourself into the world as a man," I said to Eli.

He asked what I meant, and so I told him about phallic energy and the need for a goal or target and the necessary drive to insert yourself confidently into the world, saying I would initiate him into the world of men, like men had done for boys throughout the ages, before modern times.

"How exactly are you currently inserting yourself into the world, Mr. Goodgame?" he asked, but without sounding sarcastic. He was genuinely interested.

So I told him that my goal was to redeem and ultimately save him, by any means necessary. Eli's resurrection was my singular mission and I was willing to do anything in service of making him whole again, which kind of stunned the boy, I know, because he frowned at his lap.

When he didn't say anything for a minute or so, I said, "What is it?" which is when he said he didn't believe I had done anything wrong, regarding his brother, and therefore I wasn't required to make him my "pet project."

"And yet, you set up a tent in my backyard," I said, surprising myself, because my words sounded more weighted with authority than I had previously thought possible.

He searched my eyes for a long time, just like I used to search yours, looking for whatever I could latch on to, whatever would make me believe I could trust you.

"Fate has brought us together, Eli," I said with even more authority. It felt like I had left my body and some higher force had temporarily taken control.

Then I had a good idea. I pulled out my phone and called Isaiah. As it rang, I pushed the button that allowed everyone in the room to hear the conversation. When my best man friend answered, I said, "Good morning, Isaiah."

"Lucas! You caught Bess and me walking from the car into the Lord's house, where we will be praying very hard for you this beautiful blessed morning."

"Thank you," I said. "I've got you on speakerphone. Eli is with me."

"I'm going to pray for you too, Eli. And I'm glad to be here on the phone with you and my favorite counselor of teenagers. What can I do for you two gentlemen?"

That's when I quickly explained my plan to get Eli a high school diploma. I asked Isaiah to give me carte blanche regarding a senior project that would earn Eli the necessary credits to graduate. I made it clear that I didn't know what it would be or how long it would take. And then I relayed Eli's desire not to return to school, saying he never wanted to set foot in the building again, but perhaps Eli might be interested in completing his high school degree under my supervision.

When I finished, Isaiah said, "Eli, you're in good hands. I'll take care of everything on my end. If Lucas Goodgame says you've done enough to graduate, you will graduate. No questions asked. I would, however, like to be kept abreast of your project, and if I can help in any way whatsoever, do not hesitate to call me. You hear, Eli?"

The boy looked at me with amazement, so I nodded at the phone on the table, meaning, *Please respond*, at which point Eli said, "Yes, sir."

"That goes for you too, Lucas," Isaiah said.

To which I also replied, "Yes, sir."

"Well, Sunday worship is about to begin. I'll put in a good word for your project with the Big Man," Isaiah said, and then ended the call.

Eli searched my eyes and then said, "You're going to be *my teacher*?"

I thought, *I'm going to be your Karl*, but I didn't say that. Instead I told him to help me make lunch, and then we were filling ziplock bags with peanut-butter-and-jelly sandwiches and nuts and dried fruit, which we shoved into a backpack along with bottles of water. Before I knew what had possessed me, we were in my car driving out of Majestic. And soon enough, we were at the bottom of Raptor Mountain. We hiked up the rocky trail toward the lookout, where we sat on a boulder and watched birds of prey soar through the sky, surfing the invisible air currents.

"Why did you bring me up here?" Eli asked.

I told him how Darcy and I used to come to Raptor Mountain almost weekly, saying, "This was one of her favorite places in the world. Every time we visited—and we climbed this huge pile of rocks hundreds and hundreds of times—she'd talk about how she had always wanted to fly. With burning envy, she'd watch the birds through a pair of binoculars, all while saying things like, 'I'd cut off an arm if I could only soar like that for a single hour. Look how majestic they seem. How they just *are* up there in the sky without any of our complicated emotions. Life is simple for raptors.'"

"Mr. Goodgame, I'm really sorry about your wife," Eli said, which was when I realized that maybe he felt uncomfortable talking about Darce, considering what his older brother had done, so I decided to change the subject.

"What do you want to do for your senior project?" I asked.

"What even *is* a senior project?" he said, because that wasn't a regular thing that Majestic High students did anymore. So I explained that once upon a time, each senior took the fourth marking period to research a topic of their choosing and then they were required to give a presentation. The rules were intentionally lax to encourage academic freedom and creativity.

"Why did the school stop doing them?" he asked, but I didn't have a good answer, so I just shrugged. At which point Eli said, "So this is just something you and I are going to do together? No one else will be involved?"

"It can be whatever you want it to be," I said, shielding my eyes from the midday sun as I gazed upward at an eagle circling high above. Then I wondered if winged Darcy ever came here and if she now flew with the hawks and eagles and vultures, and if so, had she, in some way, finally—and maybe even ironically—gotten exactly what she had wished for so many times when we were sitting on these very rocks?

Eli and I leisurely ate the food we had brought, as we continued to watch the birds of prey command the air like avian sorcerers.

And then on the hike down, I asked if his mother knew where he was, which produced a long string of expletives. Apparently, he didn't care what his mother knew or didn't know and he held her personally responsible for the tragedy at the Majestic Theater.

"When we were little, she used to lock Jacob in a dark closet for hours. She beat him with a wire hanger," Eli said in a way that let me know his mother had, of course, done similar things to him, and probably worse.

I didn't verbalize that particular observation. Instead, I asked if his mother would come looking for him, to which Eli proudly replied that he was eighteen and therefore a man, so it was an irrelevant question.

Karl, I remembered your telling me—during one of our first sessions— that I was almost fifty years old and yet I was still not a man, which made me feel sorry for Eli, who was trying to will himself into manhood without doing any of the necessary tasks. And here I was trying to help him when I hadn't even been able to finish my Jungian analysis with you and therefore was in some sort of transitional state between puer Peter Pan and true manhood. But the circumstance was what it was, and so I took a deep breath and settled into the role with which I had been tasked.

We were both tired on the ride home. At one point, I looked over and Eli's head was resting on his left shoulder and his eyes were closed, so I tried to remain very quiet and concentrated on staying awake so we wouldn't crash.

The boy slept the whole way.

I was surprised to hear him speak when we were pulling into my driveway. "Maybe this is crazy," he said, "but would it be possible to make a feature-length movie for my senior project?"

When I shifted into park, turned off the car, and looked over at him, he returned my gaze with a palpable vulnerability. I understood that it had taken a lot of courage for him to voice what psyche was asking of him and so I said, "I think that's a fantastic idea!" Then before I truly understood what I was saying, I added, "And maybe—for the presentation part—we can even screen it in the Majestic Theater."

He stared back at me, trying to blink away his concern, until I finally realized what I had just suggested.

We sat there in the car staring at each other, neither of us willing to say what we were both thinking, which was that some sort of higher force was dropping bread crumbs and that maybe this moment was the first crumb we had actually picked up, right before agreeing to follow the trail.

I was just about to voice the thought when Eli opened the passenger-side door, got out, and then strode across the back lawn and directly into his tent, zippering the flap shut behind him.

When Jill came home later that evening with hamburgers from The Cup, I told her to let Eli be but refused to tell her what we had been up to during the day, saying it was "man stuff," to which she replied, "Are the two of you going to start living in a cave and hunting with spears as well?" but in a friendly, jokey manner, which made me laugh and say, "Maybe."

Isaiah dropped by later that night. After I filled him in on day one of Eli's senior project, Isaiah said he wanted to pray with me. We put our hands on each other's shoulders and bowed our heads so that our hairlines touched and closed our eyes. Then—in a booming voice—he said, "Dear Heavenly Father, please bless whatever crazy venture my friend Lucas has begun, and please be with Eli as he starts to heal and work his way through his pain and, ultimately, find the path that You have already mapped out for him. *Amen.*"

I echoed his "Amen" and then Isaiah hugged me hard, patting me on the back and saying, "It's really good to see you working with young people again."

When I locked my bedroom door that night, winged Darcy was waiting for me, so I asked her if she soars with the birds of Raptor Mountain now that she has the ability to fly, but she only engulfed me in her wings and held me tightly in a way that let me know she was proud of me. The last thing I remember hearing before I lost consciousness was her saying, "The boy is the way forward," like she had many times before. And I felt the truth of that statement vibrating harmoniously through every bone in my body.

The next morning, I was able to add four angel feathers to my collection, pulling them by the quills from the comforter, and each one felt like a confirmation of everything I had learned to believe in since we last spoke.

I think you once said Jung would call it a "compensation," but I might be remembering that incorrectly. It's been a long time since you and I have talked Jungian philosophy.

I'll write again soon, but for now, I must sign off.

Your most loyal analysand,
Lucas

7.

Dear Karl,

Did you know that you can buy real feathers on the internet?

This was a surprise to me, although it probably shouldn't have been. Eli and I decided on natural pheasant feathers, because they create an almost tiger-striped appearance when you line them up uniformly. It's almost on-the-nose ironic, because Eli wants to make a monster film, where he plays the misunderstood but ultimately humane monster, à la Frankenstein's. Except—instead of an abnormal brain—our monster will have a healthy brain and won't kill any little girls or any people at all. (Eli could rattle off many other comps in addition to Frankenstein, but monster movies are not exactly my forte, to say the least.) Eli and I debated for a long time about what the monster should look like, taking into consideration our limited budget and the fact that we have no special effects team or makeup artists. (Eli is bringing a little over four hundred dollars to the project, which we initially thought would be mostly funded with the life insurance money Jill was able to secure after Darcy's pretend funeral.)

Eli kept saying things like, "How can we—given our limited budget and time restraints—convey a feeling of otherness that will simultaneously repel and intrigue a general audience?"

It turns out he's even more passionate about classic monster films than I had previously realized, but in an intellectual way. He sees them as metaphors, of course. Like I mentioned earlier, he and his brother, Jacob, used to binge classic monster movies every weekend, before Jacob "went south," as Eli puts it. They at one point had quite the DVD collection, but their mother inexplicably sold it at a pawn shop a few months before the tragedy, saying she needed the money to buy food and pay the mortgage, even though she apparently has a pretty good job working in the city as some sort of director or manager for a popular TV news program, which I'm sure you would recognize if I were to say its name, but I won't because I don't want to politicize these letters. You always said that politics was the road to splitting and binary thinking, which I learned firsthand when Sandra Coyle shamed me out of The Survivors' Group.

Don't worry, I have been conscious of Eli's unconscious fantasy: me taking up the role of big brother—playing Jacob, if you will. To combat that, I have kept the role of the father or initiator firmly at the forefront of my mind and have resisted the impulse to backslide into some sort of puer Peter Pan boy adventure. I'm all business here. I've put aside all of my own needs to be fully one hundred percent in service of bringing out Eli's potential—helping him to individuate, as Jung says.

I did, however, talk Eli into covering the monster with feathers, arguing that feathers on the shape of a man who has no wings is quite the metaphor. "Kind of like a clipped Icarus," I said, which made him laugh, and then reply, "Okay, *Daedalus*," which I took as progress, since that's Icarus's dad, which—like any myth-studying Jungian—you already know. Also, a feathered man was something we could create ourselves. Eli eventually accepted the genius of my idea and soon we were ordering the supplies.

As I mentioned before, we were able to buy twenty feathers for $13.32—including shipping and taxes—via the internet. We guessed we'd maybe need one thousand feathers, so fifty orders of twenty feathers. When we ordered that amount, the bill came to exactly $666. This pleased Eli greatly, as he initially thought our movie would also be a psychological horror film, although cleverly disguised so that it will present as something much less sinister. Apparently, according to Eli, 666 is the best number when it comes to horror tropes. I thought you'd appreciate that little bit of synchronicity.

Because we would need to ask for volunteers to populate and help bring our film into existence, I've been encouraging Eli to write something a little less sinister and even perhaps upbeat, arguing that maybe the good citizens of Majestic, PA, could use a pick-me-up, considering all that had transpired. He was, of course, resistant to that idea at first, but after we downloaded Final Draft—a script-writing software—onto my computer and began to flesh out an actual story, I was able to begin pressing on the more tender parts of Eli's heart and I do believe that we are now headed in the right direction.

It was Eli's idea to use a wetsuit—with gloves and booties—as the base layer of the monster costume, so we purchased that off the internet as well. Arguing that it would be "killer," he also talked me into ordering a springbok pelt for the monster's "back piece." It arrived in the mail with an actual bullet hole in it, which left no doubt about how the fur had been acquired. For obvious reasons, I found this detail quite disturbing, but Eli quickly countered, saying the bullet hole would only add to the metaphorical realness of the monster, whose psychology was inspired by Majestic's post-tragedy collective unconscious, and therefore the monster must be a visual representation first before it would sink down to "the deeper level of metaphor."

It's been heartening to watch the boy come alive as he strides toward the target he's set up for himself. The synapses of his brain have been firing away. And the early days flew by like seconds as we took turns typing up our ideas. The same sense of timelessness continued when we sewed the pheasant wing feathers into the wetsuit, wrapping the quills with thread, and then pushing the needle through the tough, thick neoprene with our even tougher silver thimbles, both of us alternating between the jobs of feather-liner-upper and tailor. All of this we mostly did in the living and dining rooms.

Jill kept us fed well, but otherwise gave us a wide berth, often saying, "I can literally taste the testosterone in this room," before going out back to lay in Darcy's hammock and watch movies on her phone. Well, I guess she was also always trying to get Eli to sleep indoors, but he ended up in his tent most nights anyway.

There are times when I feel as though Jill might be a little jealous of—and maybe even threatened by—the attention I am now giving Eli. I sometimes catch her standing in the doorway watching us at work and the look on her face—just before she realizes she's being observed and, therefore, consciously forces a smile—well, I'd classify it as reluctant resentment. It's almost as if she now too sees a little bit of monster in Eli—maybe the type of consuming monster who steals your housemate away from you. So I have been trying to reassure Jill, asking her opinion on various plot points and costume design choices, but she always rebuffs me, saying, "I'll leave you men to play *monsters*," overemphasizing the last word, which makes me sad, because the judgment in her voice feels oppressive. I sometimes wonder if she doesn't understand the necessity of what Eli and I are doing because she wasn't in the Majestic Theater when the shooting happened. But then I think, neither was Eli, and I'll be stumped again.

I've consulted Darcy multiple times about all of the above, but she'll only say the same six words to me these days: "The boy is the way forward." It would just about kill Jill if she knew that her best friend was refusing to even discuss her concerns, because—back before my wife sprouted wings—Jill and Darce discussed every single feeling and thought either of them had. No matter how serious or trivial. Now Darcy doesn't seem concerned with Jill's well-being in the least, which even I feel is a bit harsh, given all Jill has done to take care of me.

Sometimes I even say to Darcy, "Jill went to all of the funerals with me. She took care of the insurance paperwork. She pays the bills and keeps my checkbook balanced. She even does my laundry."

But no matter how many times I list all that Jill has done for me since my wife became an angel, Darce says nothing to acknowledge her best friend's efforts. She only repeats the same six words: "The boy is the way forward." Which is driving me a little nuts.

Eli and I purchased a stock boogeyman mask and then sewed the remaining feathers into the green rubber with the bone-white quills pointing upward, so that the monster would be wearing a nest-like crown.

When Eli put the costume on for the first time, he looked in the mirror and proclaimed himself "Prince of Monsters!" which made me laugh, but also feel a little dark deep down inside. I'm ashamed to admit this, but something within started screaming, *No! You, Lucas, are the true Prince of Monsters!* It did not feel like the best part of my soul saying that, and so I tried to push it back down, swallowing it, hoping that my psychic stomach and liver and intestines would break the idea down and then dispose of it completely.

It was at this point that I restated my desire to include all the people who were there when Jacob shot up the Majestic Theater, to which Eli said, "There's absolutely no way they'll agree to work with me."

"We'll never know unless we ask," I countered, but he flopped down on the couch in his monster suit, and by the sag in his shoulders, I knew I had deflated him a bit. I had to suppress the urge to scold him for bending the feathers sewn to the back of his legs, but figured the monster would have to sit down eventually or else the film wouldn't be realistic. So I swallowed the desire to keep the monster costume in prime condition and mustered up as much enthusiasm as I could before saying, "Listen.

We're going to need people to act in our movie. We're going to need a crew and film equipment and someone who knows how to use a camera properly. I'm pretty sure I can talk Jill into providing the catering for free. I can guarantee Isaiah and Bess will help. And a few teachers at the high school owe me a favor or two. But we're going to have to make further alliances, for sure. There's no way around it. And who could possibly better understand the themes and subtext of our film than the people who witnessed the origin story of the monster firsthand?"

"So you're saying you want to make this meta?" Eli asked. "Like *self-aware.*"

I wasn't exactly sure what "meta" meant at the time, but as the word took the sag out of his shoulders, I pointed a finger at the monster's face and said, "Exactly!"

"Huh," Eli said, before adding, "wow! Yeah, I can see how that could heighten pretty much *everything.*"

"What if," I said, treading carefully, trying not to lose momentum, "I contacted my old Survivors' Group buddies and I set up a pitch meeting to test the waters before we go completely public with a casting call that will, of course, prioritize those who were either in the Majestic Theater the night of the tragedy or are in one way or another connected to the deceased or their survivors."

"Would I have to be there?" Eli asked.

I told him that of course he would, as he was going to be the lead actor and the director and the writer and probably a dozen or so other things, so therefore the cornerstone of the whole enterprise. Not to mention, this was also his senior project, what he needed to complete in order to graduate high school. "And I'm not about to let you coast," I said, for emphasis.

He mulled that over for a bit before standing up and then pacing the room, saying he needed to break the costume in because the base-layer wetsuit was really tight on his body and was made to be submerged in water and yet he'd be wearing it dry. He also mumbled something about creating heat vents because he was "sweating oceans." Then he stopped pacing, looked at me, and—with great enthusiasm—asked, "What if I came to the pitch meeting in character?" When I raised my eyebrows, he added, "And you only referred to me as the monster or the Prince of Monsters, which—come to think of it—could be our movie title. *Wow!* What do you think?"

Admittedly, I had decided to agree with whatever made Eli stand up erect, whatever produced the most phallic energy, thinking maybe his psyche knew best what was necessary for his redemption, but I also thought his wearing the costume was an excellent idea, especially given how much work we had put into designing and making it.

How could the other Survivors possibly doubt our commitment after seeing the actual monster costume? I thought and then smiled, mentally resting into the sweat equity we'd already banked.

"What about the *Majestic* Prince of Monsters?" I countered, thinking maybe I just needed to get him into the library meeting room and the unveiling of Eli's real identity would take care of itself. Then I thought, *Maybe he'll be so proud of the response we get, he'll just triumphantly take the mask off himself and everyone will cheer like a scene right out of the movies.*

He pointed an index finger back at me and—in regard to my addition to our title—said, "*Yes!* I like it. The *Majestic* Prince of Monsters."

Then I pulled my phone out of my pocket and began making calls, starting with Robin Withers, who—after hearing my pitch about art helping us to heal—immediately granted us use of the Majestic Public Library's meeting room the following Tuesday night at seven o'clock, saying, "We've all been talking about the need for something other than Sandra's campaign, which is fine and important and absolutely necessary, but—well—everyone's missed you, Lucas. And it's wonderful to know you'll be rejoining us and the world at large," which made me feel even more confident, even though I hadn't yet mentioned the words "monster," "movie," or "Eli."

"Why aren't you telling them exactly what we're up to?" Eli asked when I was in between calls. He had taken off the monster costume at this point and I noted how sweaty and red he looked.

"Let them see our genius in action," I said, patting him on the back, and when I winked, he immediately winked back, which made it feel like we were fully aligned and therefore unbeatable.

After asking various people to pass on the message—through one or two degrees of separation—I was able to contact pretty much everyone who had witnessed a loved one murdered in the Majestic Theater on the night of the shooting. Additionally, I invited Mark and Tony—the owners of our historic movie house and Majestic's best-known film aficionados— as well as Isaiah and Bess, who I'd asked to come along for moral support.

All agreed to be there except Sandra Coyle, whose assistant—a young woman named Willow—said her boss had a conflict that most likely could not be pushed. So I said, "Please tell Sandra that Lucas Goodgame specifically extended a personal invitation and specifically requested that she attend because there are no hard feelings and I'd like to unite all who survived the Majestic Theater tragedy."

The assistant read back the full message, just to make sure she had gotten every word correct, which she absolutely did, and then I breathed a sigh of relief, because there was no way Sandra Coyle could say I had snubbed her or tried to cut her out of our film. And she was absolutely the type of person who would say such a thing, just to poison the whole ordeal. I know because she is very much like my mother and maybe even Eli's mother, although I have never met Mrs. Hansen face-to-face.

Although for the next week Jill was enthusiastic around Eli, she desperately tried—during every private Eli-free moment we shared—to convince me to cancel the meeting at the library.

"But everyone from my original Survivors' Group except Sandra Coyle has already agreed to attend," I'd protest.

"Yes," Jill would reply, "because you didn't say you wanted them to star in a monster movie about the shooting that killed all of their loved ones."

"It's a metaphor that's designed to heal!" I'd roar.

"Grieving people don't care about metaphors!" Jill would retort, matching my volume.

"Have you not seen the monster suit?" I'd say, and then stare at her like I was resting my case, because the winning quality of the costume was entirely self-evident.

"You really have gone mad, Lucas," she'd say, and then storm out of the room.

We had the same argument over and over again, and I thought we were deadlocked until Tuesday afternoon—just hours before our big meeting—when Jill came home early from the Cup Of Spoons with Isaiah. Eli was out in his orange tent resting up for the big night when my two best friends walked into my living room and asked me to sit down.

"Why didn't you say anything about the monster movie aspect of tonight's meeting?" Isaiah said in a way that let me know Jill had definitely betrayed my confidence, yet hadn't quite managed to pitch our film properly, which was understandable as she wasn't really privy to all of Eli's and my in-depth and ever-evolving creative discussions.

I tried to explain that it was a metaphor, but Isaiah wasn't interested in the artistic merits of what we were trying to accomplish, which was unfortunate, being that he is a well-respected educator and role model.

Then Jill and Isaiah took turns trying to convince me to postpone the meeting and maybe write up a proposal that they could vet for me and Eli before we shared anything with the other Survivors, saying that maybe we weren't thinking clearly, but had gotten lost in a tangent, which was fine for Eli's senior project, but maybe not the best when it came to handling the hearts and minds of Survivors who were still grieving and suffering from post-traumatic stress disorder. I was kind of surprised that my two best friends couldn't see the genius of what Eli and I had mapped out, but then I remembered that almost all creative geniuses were misunderstood at first, so maybe this was just a universal part of the artist's journey—our first psychological hurdle.

If I couldn't win them over with the artistic merits of our film project, I thought, well, then maybe I could sell them on the healing aspects. So I described how Eli had come alive as we worked on the script and I told them that I had never seen a young person so committed and enthusiastic.

I reminded them that the kid had literally dropped out of school. But he'd been working on his senior project ten to twelve hours a day and with a smile on his face and a spring in his step. Yeah, maybe his brother did a monstrous thing, but Jacob was still a human being. And Eli loved Jacob. He really loved him. And we adults have a responsibility to make sure the sickness that took Jacob doesn't spread, because it can really easily and I should know. Then I couldn't stop repeating the same question, without giving anyone enough time to reply—*Do you understand what I'm saying?* I began talking faster and faster, as if speed would force them to finally comprehend me. I told them it really wasn't that hard to get what I was saying. But the looks on their faces suggested otherwise. The more I spoke, the more they seemed afraid of me, until I began to worry I was turning into a monster right in front of the people I loved most in the world.

When I realized I was screaming at a deafening volume, I shut my mouth and closed my eyes and then the room was silent for a long time.

"What's going on in here?" Eli said.

I opened my eyes and there he was standing at the edge of my living room, searching Isaiah and Jill for answers with a tentative boyish look in his eyes that seemed to be prematurely saying, *I'm sorry.*

No one answered Eli's question.

He tried to make it okay by saying, "Mr. Henderson, you're coming tonight, right? And you too, Jill, *right?*"

There was so much earnest enthusiasm in his voice, so much hope, that I thought I might have to strangle both Jill and Isaiah dead with my bare hands if they gave the wrong answer. Happily, they both said, "Yep," and then stared at their feet.

"Perfect," Eli said. "I'm going to graduate high school for sure, but we're aiming to do much more than that. We're going to heal the town. We're going to do something positive. Mr. Goodgame's been superb. I'm learning so much. More than I deserve probably, so thank you, Mr. Henderson, for this opportunity. You won't regret it. I'm going to make the school look good, don't worry."

Isaiah had a hard time meeting Eli's eyes, but he eventually did, which was when the boy said, "Mr. Goodgame and I have a lot of prep work to do, so you won't mind if I steal him away, will you?"

Eli caught my eye and then nodded his head in the direction of the back door. It took me a second, but then I caught his drift and followed him out to the tent, where we hid—listening to "chill-out" music on Eli's phone—until it was time for the meeting.

It's funny, I didn't ask him directly whether he had heard the screaming I was doing or if he knew what prompted my freak-out, but I could tell he had heard and he definitely one hundred percent knew. And lying there in the tent, Eli didn't tell me that my yelling at Isaiah and Jill was okay and that he had my back and we were in this together, but I also absolutely knew that one hundred percent too.

"Mom once held Jacob's head underwater in the bathtub for a long time because he had *quote* gotten too dirty *unquote* while we were playing outside," Eli said in a way that let me know his mother had, of course, done something similar to him, and probably worse. I tried to think of a comforting response, but ended up staying silent, which I think Eli appreciated.

Maybe an hour or so into our tent chill-out session—still lying with my hands clasped behind my head, just looking at the afternoon sun trapped in the orange fabric above—I said, "We're going to make a monster movie to end all monster movies," mostly because that was what Eli wanted to accomplish.

"Don't forget about healing people too," Eli said, because that was what I had been emphasizing for the past few weeks, trying to elevate the boy's ambitions while modeling healthy masculinity.

When he held his fist up in the air, I pounded it, and the success of our project felt absolutely inevitable there in the suburban quiet of an average June afternoon in Majestic, PA.

Your most loyal analysand,
Lucas

8.

Dear Karl,

Before I tell you about the pitch meeting at the Majestic Public Library, I want to let you know that I have been keeping my mother at bay—religiously sticking to the rules you set up for me—refusing to allow Mom's parasitic thoughts to enter through my ears and infect my "personal life software." And I do believe that this has been beneficial not only for me but for everyone else in my life too, especially Eli and Jill.

I've even recently reread the Grimm fairy tale "Iron John" in an effort to remember all that we discussed when I first started my analysis with you. Stealing the key from under Mother's pillow and then running away with the hairy rusty-skinned man into the woods. The hero disobeying and having his finger and long hair turned to gold as an unable-to-be-hidden consequence. And then being sent away to experience poverty and struggle, but with the promise that Iron John would come to help if the hero says the strange god-monster man's name three times.

Karl, Karl, Karl.

Six times a day, I say your name thrice, and yet you never arrive to gift me a horse and armor and warrior brothers.

But then again, I have been thinking a lot about how Eli just sort of appeared and I wonder if you had anything to do with that.

Is the boy the metaphorical equivalent of a horse and armor?

And are the other Majestic Theater Survivors my sibling warriors? Don't worry.

I haven't gone completely insane.

I realize that you didn't literally make all that has happened happen, but I am starting to see that maybe you prepared me for everything that is currently transpiring, giving me a lens to see and a cipher to translate the chaos into meaning and maybe even purpose.

My mother has been calling my cell phone obsessively, leaving voice messages that are demanding and anxiety-provoking and crazy-making. She routinely fills my in-box so that it is impossible for Isaiah or Jill to record words—and so my friends are constantly reminding me to delete Mother's long rambles.

It certainly helps that she's far away in Florida. And I have paid attention to her phrasing, just like you taught me to do, noting whenever she says things like, "I'm your mother so I have a right to know what's going on," and "Your refusal to speak with me is ruining my retirement," and "I'm losing sleep because you won't call me back," which isn't true, because I call her back every Sunday at seven p.m. and give her thirty minutes, which she mostly uses to download all of her anxiety into me, speaking a million words a minute in a desperate effort to get it all out. She doesn't ever ask me questions about how I feel, which is strange because in all of her voicemails, she claims that she desperately wants to know "what's going on in her son's brain."

"Is Jill living with you now? Has she moved in?" Mom will ask instead, and—before I can get a word out in response—then add, "You have to be careful with beautiful women, Lucas. I'd never trust anyone who moved in so quickly—literally just hours after Darcy was killed. The sheets of your bed hadn't even cooled!"

I try to tell Mom that Jill stays in the guest room and that we are not romantically involved, but the words get stuck in my throat on account of what happened in the Maryland hotel by the lighthouse, and a deep sense of shame washes over me. It feels like I'm being slowly dipped in a vat of boiling water.

When Mom starts telling me the many things her current boyfriend, Harvey, is doing wrong regarding their relationship, suddenly I'm a little boy again and I'm in bed with Mother and she's telling me about her work problems or how my dad is an inferior man or how her own father—my Pop Pop—never loved her as much as he loved my since-deceased aunt Regina. I know that Mom wants something very specific from me, but no matter how hard I try, I can't figure out what that is. And a pressure begins to build in what you call the root chakra—at the base of my spine—until a tingling explodes and makes my skin buzz in a way that feels like ten million insects are crawling all over me. This only intensifies whenever I think back to my childhood. Back then Mother was always asking me to lay my little head on her chest. She would stroke my hair as she sang Joni Mitchell's "River," even though it was hardly ever Christmas season when she sang that song, because—back when I was a boy—she sang it almost every night year-round. And maybe that's why—to this day—I don't let anyone touch my hair, not even Darcy. And hearing Joni Mitchell songs gives me anxiety attacks.

As I listen to Mom these days from seven to seven thirty on Sunday nights, I try to remain curious, like you taught me. I try to hear Mother's trauma, her pain, and realize that it's not my pain, not my trauma. I mostly am able to keep us separate and resist getting enmeshed. But it makes me kind of wish I could skate away on a frozen river, just like in the Joni Mitchell song, even though I realize that river would be called "denial" or "dissociation" or some other psychological term.

Eli has been talking about his own mother. Whenever he mentions her, his face turns red and some awful demon takes control of his brain. You can see it in his eyes. His pupils contract and then the Eli I know—

the good boy who wants very much to become a healthy man—vanishes. He'll pace. Punch his palms and shake his head. You'd think maybe his mother had locked him in a cage for years, like poor Iron John. As I wrote before, it sounds as if Mrs. Hansen did some pretty deranged things to Jacob and Eli when they were little. And when they were teenagers, she infected their minds with words—words like witchcraft designed to bottle up their masculine spirits and make them sick, turning their souls toxic.

"She used to tell Jacob that he was too ugly and lazy to make anything of himself," Eli ranted one afternoon. "She said he'd die a virgin. A million times Mom said that. She started saying that when he was ten years old!"

I asked about their father and learned that both Eli and Jacob were initially told they never had a dad, even though Jacob sometimes claimed to have vague memories of a "hairy man" living with them when Eli was first born. So when they learned about reproduction in school and the need for sperm to produce a baby, they asked again, which enraged Mrs. Hansen, who apparently said, "Why are you so interested in your mother's sex life?"

This, of course, reminded me of what my mother said to me when she caught me kissing Jenna Winterbottom behind the garage when we were in the seventh grade and also how Mom used to call me Sundial whenever we went to the beach because my penis—even when it was limp—stuck out when my swim trunks were wet. The nickname upset me so much, I stopped swimming for a few years, refusing to go to pools or lakes or the beach. And I didn't date anyone again until I started writing letters to Darcy when we were both in college.

And then one July day—between our freshman and sophomore collegiate years—Darce and I went to the beach. I tried to keep a towel wrapped around my waist the whole time, but Darcy kept playfully pulling it off. When she saw me trying to cover my bulge with my hands something flickered in her eyes and I knew that she understood my shame. Instead of saying anything, she led me by the hand into the ocean, where she wrapped her legs around my waist and kissed me until I was hard as a rock. I was so embarrassed but I was also sort of thrilled and on autopilot—instinct completely took over. I was additionally amazed that this beautiful young woman really seemed to be enjoying my body in a way that made me feel proud and desirable and whole.

I remember getting nervous in the middle of the make-out session and blurting out an apology for being hard. I averted my eyes and untangled myself from her. But Darcy swam toward me again and—with so much kindness in her voice—said, "My God. What did your mother do to you?" which scared the hell out of me, because I didn't realize anyone else could see what had happened so clearly. I was shaking and so Darce put her arms around me and whispered, "It's okay," into my ear. She just held me like that for a long time and my erection faded.

I thought I had blown my shot with Darcy but on the way home she asked me to drive into the woods that used to be at the edge of town—where the Caddell Condos now are—and then she directed me to a car-sized rectangle of dirt in a knee-high field of grass. I remember thinking it looked like a freshly covered grave for a recently deceased giant. When I turned off the car, Darce immediately started taking off my clothes and hers. She said, "This is a good thing, Lucas. You're supposed to enjoy your body. Let me make you feel better. You don't have to be ashamed." And she was so gentle that I went along with it and told myself that it was okay and fought like hell against my mother's voice, which was protesting inside my head, calling me perverted and disgusting. And when it was over, Darce put her head on my chest and listened to my heart beating for a long time while I stroked her black hair and wondered what losing my virginity meant. Except for the kissing I had done with Jenna Winterbottom back in seventh grade, I had never before even touched a woman. It was like going directly from a tricycle to a space shuttle without any training, and now I was in zero gravity and wondering how I was even breathing. But, somehow, I knew that I had done all right with the mission and was okay. And that Darcy was satisfied and maybe even in love with me, which might just have been the greatest miracle of my life.

"I love you," I said to Darcy—right there in the front seat of my car— and then regretted it immediately.

It felt uncool.

Premature.

Ridiculous.

And the silence that followed almost turned my heart to stone.

But then Darcy lifted her head and gave me a smile. I looked into her sea-green eyes and saw a different kind of witchcraft—this kind healed and completed and left me feeling more hopeful than I had ever been in my entire life.

"I love you too, Lucas Goodgame," she said, and then gave me a great big kiss on the lips.

But back to my mother.

I just listen curiously to her now during the Sunday calls, while watching the minute arm of the kitchen clock descend from the twelve to the six, at which point, I'll interrupt her and say, "It was really great speaking with you tonight, Mom, but I have to go." She'll protest and accuse me of not loving her and putting her "on the clock." And she'll try to guilt me into listening for longer. But I'll remind myself that I've got a boy to initiate into manhood. And the phallic energy of that mission will make me sit up a little more erect, at which point I'll cut Mother off and say, "Talk next week," before I hang up and resist the urge to answer when she immediately calls back.

Sometimes Jill will be standing there in the kitchen when I finish. She'll always give me an astonished look and say something like, "Someone should give you a medal for calling that woman once a week." I'll shrug and break eye contact. At which point Jill will usually say, "You're a good man, Lucas Goodgame." Then she'll pour herself a glass of wine and leave me to process the call. Sometimes I sit right there all alone at the kitchen table for an entire silent hour, doing nothing but recovering.

I have never felt like a good man after speaking with my mother.

Never.

Not even once.

I've tried to speak with winged Darcy about these phone calls but she isn't talking all that much with me anymore, to be honest. She still wraps me in her wings and holds me nightly. She's still shedding feathers, which I keep collecting in my ziplock bags. I keep those in Darcy's third dresser drawer, where she stacks her neatly folded sweaters. But I can sort of feel Darcy transforming more and more into an angel—meaning she's less and less of a human being, less and less my wife. I'm beginning to understand that my time with winged Darcy is finite and an internal countdown of sorts has begun.

I've been tempted to speak with Jill about this, especially since she keeps saying I can tell her anything and that she absolutely wants me to confide in her. Jill insists she will never betray my confidence, even though she already sort of did, by telling Isaiah about the monster movie before the big reveal at the library. I'll tell you all about that in the next letter, because I'm getting kind of sleepy and still have to spend time with Darcy up in my bedroom with the door locked.

Karl, Karl, Karl.

I thought I'd try once more to make you suddenly appear like Iron John. Maybe it will prompt you to write me back, or call or simply knock on my door one day. You don't have to bring the metaphorical equivalent of a horse and armor and an army of brother warriors, because I am providing those things for myself and Eli too.

I think you should be very proud of me—and yourself too, of course.

But don't you want to see the fruits of your labor firsthand?

Karl, Karl, Karl.

I'm calling.

Can you hear me?

Your most loyal analysand,

Lucas

9.

Dear Karl,

On the night of our pitch meeting with The Survivors, Jill drove Eli and me to the library so that we'd arrive forty-five minutes before the presentation was set to begin. We didn't want to risk any early birds prematurely seeing the monster. Eli was already in costume—booties, gloves, mask, and all—only we'd covered him in a white sheet with two holes cut out for eyes, so that he could see. He looked like a classic little-kid ghost—an easy Halloween costume.

Eli kept saying he was hot. He said sweat was pooling in his booties. And he mused about needing to break in the monster costume some more, asking, "Why didn't we think of that earlier?" And perhaps a million times, he said, "Maybe we can strategically cut in some heat vents—which the feathers would keep hidden, of course—because it's just *brutal* in here."

Jill kept saying that we were going to draw just as much attention with the sheet as we would have with the feathered monster man on full display, but Eli and I argued that it was all about the art of surprise and that we were going to employ showmanship and really sell the pitch, which made Jill say, "Okay," in a way that was more *I'm rooting for you two* than *You two are crazy*. Eli and I both appreciated the positivity, but what really gave me confidence on the ride to the library was seeing Darcy up above in the cloud-filled sky, leading the way to our destiny. Her giant wings were flapping powerfully and gorgeously as she soared above Main Street. I couldn't believe that no one else was seeing her up there in the early evening air, because this was the first time I had ever seen her in sunlight, which I had previously thought was impossible. I wanted to scream at everyone we saw on the streets, yelling, "LOOK UP! IT'S AMAZING! YOU WILL BE HEALED!" And in the magic-hour light, my wife truly was something to behold. But a voice deep within said with great authority, "Winged Darce is for you and you alone," which centered me. And so I somehow kept my mouth shut and soon enough we were there, parked in the Majestic library parking lot.

"Are you absolutely sure about this?" Jill asked, which was when Eli popped a fist-shaped feathered hand out from under the sheet and I gave him a pound.

"Never been surer of anything in my life," I said.

"Me too," said Eli, before mumbling some more about how hot he was in the monster suit, going so far as to compare himself to a pizza in a wood-fired brick oven.

"Okay, Lucas," Jill said, ignoring Eli's repetitive pleas for heat vents, and then smiled at me. "I'll follow your lead."

"You two wait here," I said, and then got out of the truck. As I walked toward the Majestic Public Library, I thought about how it looked like a cross between a hobbit house and something out of a Harry Potter movie, as it was built with cobblestones in a magical Tudor-house-meets-medieval-castle style. There was a thick turret on the left side of the building, which looked like it belonged in an Arthurian legend—as if Merlin were casting spells inside. "Here we go," I said, and then pulled open the heavy, iron-studded wooden door.

Inside, Robin Withers greeted me with perhaps the biggest hug I have ever received from anyone in my entire life. She rubbed my back and said, "It's so good to be with you in this moment, Lucas. You have no idea how we've all missed you." Even though I appreciated the gesture, I remained focused on the goals of the evening, which did not include collecting long hugs and compliments from my fellow Survivors.

So—after what I felt was an appropriate amount of time, enough so that her large hoop earring made a temporary dent in my right cheek—I gently untangled myself and said, "Do you trust me?"

"Of course," Robin said, before adding, "I trust you with my life," which made me feel a little sick, although I'm not exactly sure why.

"May I have your attention!" I yelled across the library. "May I please have your attention!"

Everyone turned and faced me.

"I'm running a very important meeting here in the library tonight. I have to bring in a prop, which I will hide in the meeting-room storage closet. But it's very important that no one sees this prop, so I'm asking everyone to close his or her eyes so that I can move my prop under the cloak of secrecy. I apologize for the inconvenience, but this is of the utmost importance and perhaps it's best to rest your eyes for a few moments anyway after doing so much reading."

Everyone—including Robin—stared back at me.

"It will only take a minute!" I assured them. "Okay. Close your eyes now!"

People looked to Robin, who nodded and kind of patted the air in front of her with open hands, at which point everyone closed their eyes, including Robin.

"Okay. No peeking!" I said, and then ran to collect Eli and Jill, who helped me quickly guide the sheeted monster through the parking lot and into the library. "Please keep those eyes closed! It's very important!" I yelled as a reminder and was relieved when I saw nothing but compressed eyelids.

Once I had Eli safely in the meeting-room closet, I stuck my head back into the general common area of the library and yelled, "You may open your eyes now. Thanks so much for your cooperation, which has aided our important mission!" before closing the door and then arranging my prepared notes on the metal podium.

"You should tell Eli to take off the mask so he doesn't get too hot and pass out in the closet," Jill suggested, which was a good idea, but when I opened the closet door, I found that Eli had already taken off not only his mask but his feather gloves and booties as well. His hair was soaking wet and all of his exposed skin was dripping with perspiration.

"I'm roasting," he said, panting audibly, so I lifted up the springbok backpiece and pulled down the wetsuit zipper, exposing the naked flesh of his sweaty back, which had also turned bright red. "I think," he added, "maybe the suit might be a size too small, because it's really hard to breathe with it zipped up. But don't worry. I can lose weight before the shoot. I've probably already lost five pounds just wearing this suit today."

The wardrobe malfunction was not good news, especially considering how much time and effort and money we had already put into perfecting our monster costume, but there was no time to think about that, because it was almost showtime.

"I'll get Robin to turn up the air-conditioning," I said, and then did just that.

"What exactly do you have planned for us?" Robin said as she tapped the thermostat, dropping the library temperature by seven or so degrees. I didn't spill the beans prematurely, but I promised it'd be worth the wait, and that—thankfully—seemed to placate her.

Back in the meeting room, I found Jill pacing. After I closed the door behind me, she put her hands on my shoulders, looked me in the eyes, and said, "No matter what happens, I want you to know I'm proud of what you're doing with Eli and we'll find a way to continue this work regardless of the reaction tonight."

Before I could respond, Bess and Isaiah entered the room, and then the four of us were holding hands and Isaiah was using his church voice to ask his God to be with us tonight and move the hearts of our neighbors so that we might unite and contribute to the healing of our town, putting hearts back together and lifting up the weary. He went on and on with a lot of beautiful church language that I can't quote verbatim because I was so worried about the presentation that I had trouble listening. But I think it's not so much the actual words that moved me but the genuineness of Bess and Isaiah's belief. When they pray with you, you do not doubt that every fiber of their beings wants the best for you, which is probably why Isaiah is my best man friend and I love him like a brother. I love Bess too. And I, of course, love Jill. I love Eli. And I also love you, Karl, very much.

Isaiah had prayed for quite a long time, I know, because when he said, "Amen," and dropped my hand, I opened my eyes and saw that Tony and Mark had been standing nearby waiting patiently for us to finish. The looks on their faces seemed to say, *Sorry to have been eavesdropping for the past eight or so minutes but—as we're not used to walking in on prayer circles—we didn't know exactly what we should have done.*

And I have to admit that the strange formal intimacy of shared prayer takes a little getting used to, so I was sympathetic, as I hadn't grown completely comfortable yet either, which I tried to tell Mark and Tony with my eyes, giving them an understanding *me too* glance.

Isaiah and Bess didn't mind the eavesdropping, of course, as they'd pray openly in front of anyone, and so we all shook hands and said hello. Here I noticed that Tony and Mark were actively avoiding eye contact with me. With obvious ease, they looked directly into the eyes of Isaiah, Bess, and Jill, but not yours truly, which is when I realized that they felt some sort of responsibility for what had happened in their restored historic theater, so I quickly said, "It's not your fault. I unequivocally do *not* hold you responsible in any way, shape, or form," which made the room go silent for what felt like a few minutes.

When Mark and Tony finally looked in my eyes, their mouths were slightly open and I could see their tongues kind of quivering.

So I tried to seed the future, adding, "Darcy adored the Majestic Theater. It's still one of my favorite places in the entire world. You must reopen. Majestic needs the movies. We need to laugh and cry and cheer together as a community. Don't let the tragedy take that from us. Please. That's part of what I'll be talking about tonight. Reopening the Majestic."

They both swallowed and then Tony took Mark's hand in his, at which point they both nodded at me several times and then took their seats.

I remember noting that mustachioed and stubble-bearded Mark was bulging with daily-gym-workout muscles, while clean-shaven and thin Tony had more of a weekend runner's body. And yet, somehow, they seemed to naturally belong together like clouds and sky.

The other Survivors filed in one by one: Robin Withers, whom I already mentioned, and Jon Bunting, DeSean Priest, David Fleming, Julia Wilco, Tracy Farrow, Jesus Gomez, Laxman Anand, Betsy Bush, Dan Gentile, Audrey Hartlove, Ernie Baum, Chrissy Williams, and Carlton Porter. Everyone from the original Survivors' Group except you know who.

"Should we begin?" Robin said to me once everyone was seated, so I knocked on the closet door twice, letting Eli know that he should begin putting the rest of his monster costume back on.

Robin sat down and I took the podium. Jill winked at me, and Isaiah gave me a thumbs-up, which had me feeling extremely confident, but then Sandra Coyle walked in and took a seat in the back row far away from the rest of us. She crossed her arms in a demonstration of utter defiance. I kindly nodded at her, meaning, *Welcome*, but she glared back at me like she had laser-beam vision—strong enough to melt my flesh, skull, and brains—shooting out of her eyes.

All of the other Survivors looked eager to know why I had called the meeting and therefore seemed more nervously curious than supportive,

WE ARE THE LIGHT

which began to worry me, so I looked back at Jill, who smiled but couldn't hide the fact that she was also nervous, which is when I realized that a long minute had passed without my saying a word.

Isaiah came to my rescue by loudly saying in the friendliest possible way, "So, Lucas, what's up, my friend? Why did you have us gather together tonight? What would you like to say to the group?"

"Right," I said, and then for some reason, I looked out the tall window, which must have been facing west, because the sky was all orange and pink. It took a second, but when my eyes began to adjust and focus on the distance, I saw Darcy making the figure-eight infinity sign up there in the sky as if to say, *I'm still here with you, Lucas. You can do this. The boy is the way forward.* That's when something took over my brain and body and the conscious part of me sort of stepped out of my skin and leaned against the stone wall to watch my physical body and the unconscious part of me deliver a speech so impressive and with such amazing body language that I could hardly believe my ears and eyes.

I told everyone how much I missed Darcy and how I had suffered in silence for months all alone in my house, hardly able to leave, let alone speak with anyone. I talked about my mind-numbing, soul-crushing, and even suicidal pain. The other Survivors were pulling out tissues and wiping eyes with sleeves. Then I apologized for not acting sooner back at the Majestic Theater, saying that if I had reacted more immediately, I might have been able to save more people and that fact keeps me up at night, drills into my mind like a red-hot bit.

DeSean Priest yelled, "You did everything you could and then some!"

And Laxman Anand added, "You should be proud because you did more than any of the rest of us!"

I raised my voice to regain control of the room and asked if the other Survivors ever felt like there was something they should be doing to bring everyone together in a way that was inclusive and didn't cause division.

Which was when I looked toward the back of the room and saw Sandra Coyle shift uncomfortably in her chair. "Ever since the tragedy," I said, "a grieving part of me has felt othered. Like a monster. Like someone infected by an unthinkable fate. Someone whom neighbors can hardly bring themselves to look at for even a few seconds." As I examined the room, I saw flickers of recognition light up many pairs of eyes.

"And, ironically, there are others whom we've all made into monsters as well. Innocents who have been targeted and shunned and who have been made to feel so low they've sequestered themselves. And I'd like to introduce you to one of these people tonight." I pointed at the door to my right. "He's in this very closet right now."

The silence I let hang in the room was palpable.

I saw Jill put her face in her hands. Bess was chewing her bottom lip and Isaiah was tapping his right foot furiously. The rest of The Survivors were on the edges of their seats.

"This innocent has a dream, a vision for bringing the town back together again. A plan for healing! He invites you to be creative! To make a movie with him! To star in this movie, which will be about reclaiming and redeeming the monster within all of us. Reintegrating what has been cast off into shadow. Bringing that back to consciousness." I sounded a lot like my Jungian analyst, aka you, Karl. "We've written the script and made the first costume, which is meant to symbolically represent the aftermath we've all been suffering through. Ladies and gentlemen, may I present to you *the Majestic Prince of Monsters!*"

The closet door swung open, but Eli very dramatically stayed hidden in the shadows within. When I looked around, every mouth in the room was wide open. Then—at an almost glacial pace—the monster lumbered out of the closet and into the meeting room. There was a great collective gasp. When the Majestic Prince of Monsters was front and center and on full display in all his feathered horror, I began to lay out the vision we had for making a feature-length monster movie and then screening it at the Majestic Theater as a way of reclaiming the site of the tragedy for the community, purifying—and maybe even re-sanctifying—the space. I was masterfully building up to the big reveal, at which point Eli would take off his mask and essentially dare The Survivors to accept him as a fellow sufferer, despite the fact that he was linked by blood to the killer of everyone's loved ones.

But then Sandra Coyle stood. "How is this *nonsense*, this *foolishness* meant to help anyone? We need stricter gun control laws! We need politicians who aren't taking kickbacks from the NRA! We need justice! We need—"

That's when the feathered Majestic Prince of Monsters began to tilt backward—stiff as a freshly chopped tree—hitting the back of his head against a sharp metallic corner of the podium as he plummeted to the ground.

Isaiah was the first to reach Eli, and when he tore off the feathered monster mask everyone gasped again—although I couldn't tell if the group was shocked by Eli's identity or the fact that blood was gushing from the back of his neck and pooling on the floor, very much like what we had all witnessed in the Majestic Theater on that fateful December night.

I'm sad to admit that I froze.

"Call an ambulance!" Isaiah screamed as he removed his suit jacket and then pressed it into Eli's wound, cradling the boy's head and trying to stop the bleeding.

Then EMTs were wheeling Eli out of the library on a stretcher—as the newly applied, antiseptically white dressings slowly turned plum red—and Jill was pulling me by the hand to her truck. We followed the flashing lights of the ambulance to the hospital, where the emergency room staff stitched up Eli's cut and declared him dehydrated and suffering from extreme heat exhaustion. Soon enough he was reclining in a bed with an IV drip inserted into his arm and a privacy curtain pulled around his resting body.

When they finally let us in to see him, Eli said, "You really sold the vision tonight, Mr. Goodgame. You were fantastic! But I think we're going to have to make some adjustments to the monster suit."

He went on to say it was ferociously hot in that closet and nerves had forced him to put the suit back on prematurely, so he was sorry that he had passed out and ruined everything, but he thought my speech was so motivating that he was willing to bet this little setback wouldn't hurt us too much in the long run.

"Right?" he said when I didn't respond.

The boy searched my eyes for reassurance, but I'd already spent what I had to give that evening.

Jill elbowed me several times, but I couldn't bring any part of myself to level with Eli and explain that we had most definitely blown any shot whatsoever of enlisting the help of The Survivors and had also most likely retraumatized all of them in the process. Standing there in the emergency room, I believed our presentation couldn't have gone any worse. And our dream of making a monster movie had died before it had even really been born. But I thought it best to gently break that reality to the boy once he was rehydrated and we had gotten him out of the hospital.

When it became apparent that I wasn't going to reply, Jill said, "You just rest, Eli," and then patted his arm maternally before pulling me out of the emergency room and into some dingy abandoned hallway.

"You've absolutely got to make this movie happen," Jill whispered fiercely at me. "After giving a speech like you did tonight, the boy in there is practically exploding with hope. You can't take that away from him *now.*"

"I thought you were against the movie," I countered.

"I'm for finishing what you started," Jill said. "Especially when there's a wounded boy involved. You have the kid's future in your hands now,

Lucas. You're all he's got. And he's pinned everything on this silly dream of making a monster movie and, well, your words tonight moved me—to be honest—and now I, too, am a little emotionally invested."

I was kind of amazed by Jill's sudden about-face and started to worry that the great and powerful version of me that spoke at the meeting would not heed the call the next time I needed him to save me. Because the regular version of me was failing horribly here at the hospital.

"You were absolutely kingly tonight, Lucas," Jill said, before adding, "Darce would be so proud."

"Kingly?" I asked, ignoring the part about my wife, who obviously could speak for herself later that evening, if she wished to. "What do you even mean by that?"

"I don't know. It was like you rode in on a horse to save the day. Like you had on shining armor. I guess I was just really proud to be there with you. Proud for you."

"But the others. They couldn't have been impressed with the way things ended."

"You might be surprised, Lucas," Jill said, which was when Isaiah and Bess arrived and insisted that we pray for Eli's head and the project and everything else, and so we held hands and did exactly that.

Write me back and I'll tell you the rest of the story.

How about it?

Karl, Karl, Karl.

I haven't yet given up on my own personal Iron John.

Don't worry, I'm very patient.

Your most loyal analysand,

Lucas

10.

Dear Karl,

All this time I've been spending with Eli has me thinking a lot about my father.

I know we talked about Dad from time to time during my analysis, but we mostly talked about my mother, didn't we? You did—and I clearly remember this because of the impact it's had—introduce me to the term "father hunger," which resonated immediately with me, probably because I have always had tremendous father hunger. I've been thinking long and hard about what you once said about redeeming the father by healing the self and, therefore, breaking the cycle of pain, which men hand down generationally forever, until a son steps up and actively stops it.

I told you this was why Darce and I decided not to have children, why I got a vasectomy as a way to make sure that we never passed on the worst of what we had inherited.

You shook your head sadly and said that every man in my lineage—going all the way back to the first man who ever lived—was still inside me, trying to free himself from the ever-growing constellation of ancestral hurts. You said that when I healed any part of me, I was healing all of the many fathers and grandfathers who lived on deep inside of Lucas Goodgame. And that when I made love, they all too got to make love again. And when I had a healthy relationship with a son, my ancestors also got to experience that healing joy. And when I ultimately learned to love myself and begin to exist shame free, they also would finally become liberated from shame, at which point they could begin to help as healthy, cured, emancipated ancestors who—when necessary—would rally like a great army within me, lifting my potential and providing me with the hard-fought wisdom of a thousand lives.

Your speech made me sad at first, because I thought you were telling me that I had missed out on gifting my ancestors the ability to father a boy again and initiate him into manhood, but then you told me emancipating my forefathers was what I was doing every single time a young man walked into my office at the high school. You said I was helping the boys, yes, but I was also healing myself and therefore healing the men who came before me in my family tree—the many souls who were embedded in my DNA. I was their redeemer. Their renewed chance at wholeness.

And I began to keep all of that in mind during my work with students at Majestic High School. I took it very seriously. Treated my work as if it were a sacred mission. But I don't think I fully understood what you were saying until Eli set up his orange tent in my backyard.

Darce's parents were older and therefore a bit more settled and relaxed than mine were when she and I were growing up. And my in-laws both died when Darce and I were just in our mid-twenties. Her mother—who was a big smoker—went first. Massive stroke. Her father quickly followed via a coronary that Darcy used to say was literally a broken heart. It was nice to think of my father-in-law loving his wife so much that he couldn't live without her, and that thought got Darce through the mourning period quicker than if she'd focused on the cruel realities of, say, her father's taste for ice cream and red meat and fried foods and the resulting blocked arteries. I guess what I'm trying to get across here is . . . I don't know. The thing that had always felt broken deep inside of me, well, I don't think Darcy had that broken part or that broken thing.

There was this one story I never told you in analysis and I'm not quite sure why. Maybe it just never came up, or maybe I'm only allowing myself to remember it now—perhaps because of all the time I've been spending with Eli—but I'd like to share it with you here, if that's okay.

It happened during my freshman year of college. I've already told you many times that I was an awkward and maybe even strange young man. Because of this, I initially didn't make many friends at the university. Everyone in my dorm was so outgoing and eager to be part of this massive wave that was pushing us all into the future. But I felt an awful longing to return to the past somehow. Maybe I felt like I hadn't accomplished what I was supposed to accomplish in childhood.

I remember walking around the outside of my childhood home the morning my parents were going to drop me off at my new college. The car was packed. Mom was doing her makeup inside. Maybe my father was getting dressed. And I just couldn't stop circling our small house. Round and round I went, dozens of times. Maybe even hundreds. I didn't understand the compulsion until many years later, when I realized that I was moving in a counterclockwise circle. Now I think maybe I was literally trying to turn back time somehow, pushing an imaginary minute hand around the imaginary dial over and over in an attempt to buy another shot to get whatever it was I was supposed to have received during my formative years—exactly what I would spend the bulk of my adult years trying to give to the children of strangers.

The next thing I remember is unloading Dad's car and my parents helping me move my clothes, bedding, and school supplies into my new dorm room—a single, meaning no roommate, which I had requested, thinking I would do better if I had somewhere to be alone from time to time. And then my parents and I were in my new van-sized room and Mom was talking about how much money they were shelling out for something that she herself never got a chance to do—because she had to commute to college—and then my father was shoving a twenty-dollar bill in my hand and, before I knew it, I was alone in my dorm room with the door closed.

I began pacing the seven feet of space I had, listening to all the other young men laughing and yelling and introducing themselves outside in the bustling hallway. It sounded so easy for them. Yet I was terrified of even opening my door, and I wouldn't for days. As I stood there in that first hour—my heart pounding like it was trying to escape my rib cage and bounce its way back to my parents and our little house at the edge of Majestic, PA—I wondered how I alone had failed to acquire the instructions, whatever it was that the other boys had clearly received, the thing that allowed them to look each other in the eyes and slap each other's backs and enter the communal bathroom without feeling as though their heads might explode.

Many of the boys on my floor knocked on my door and tried to introduce themselves, but I kept my head down and said little. I rebuffed as many invitations as it took for everyone to stop extending them to me.

I sat in the back of every single one of my classes and pulled a hood up over my head whenever I wasn't in my dorm room.

I was miserable for a few weeks and I thought an awful lot about killing myself, to be honest, just to be free of the crippling anxiety and heavy depression, although I never settled on a plan and didn't have the guts to even fantasize with specificity.

The pain grew and grew until I asked my parents if I could come home for a weekend, telling my mother that I missed her, which I knew would please her enough to acquiesce, which she did.

When my father came to pick me up on Friday night, he seemed off. Dad was always taciturn and maybe even generally uninterested in me, but on the drive home he was agitated, yelling at the other drivers on the road, mumbling to himself about traffic, and driving erratically. When

I asked what was wrong, he'd only grumble something about his work, failing to use complete sentences, let alone make any sort of connection with his only son. And the longer I was in the car with Dad, the more certain I was that going home was a mistake.

My mother seemed pleased to see me, putting out a nice dinner and even serving her signature homemade apple pie, but when I lay down in my childhood bed that night, I replayed the glances she gave me over dinner—the way she looked at me when I said college was "fine" and that my classes were "fine" and that, "No, I hadn't met any nice girls yet," and I didn't know what I wanted to major in, but, yes, I was grateful for the opportunity to go to college when so many other young people my age had to get jobs. As I lay in bed, replaying dinner, I started to see my mother's grin as something akin to a wolf's smile, and then I was seeing blood dripping from her mouth, which seemed ridiculous to me, so I wiped it from my mind and tried to picture what she had actually looked like.

"Smug" was the word I came up with.

Or maybe "satisfied."

Every time I answered one of her questions, she had smirked, as if she was enjoying my failures—devouring my blunders as if they were bonbons.

When I looked over at my father I didn't see him lift his eyes from his meal even once. There were no words of acknowledgment, let alone encouragement or compassion. When Dad had swallowed his last bite, he immediately pushed away from the table and flicked on the TV in the living room, leaving Mom and me to store the extra food in Tupperware containers before we washed and dried and put away the dishes. During that process, Mom had complained about her work and her friends and the way the food store arranged the aisles and how there weren't enough parking spots at the local 7-Eleven and how my father didn't notice that she had gotten her hair cut. "Lucas," she said, "don't you dare become anything like that stupid empty sack of a man out there on the couch because you're all I have in this world."

I went to bed shortly after that.

In the middle of the night, I woke up feeling panicked and tried to find the bathroom, but my childhood home had turned into a maze, which I frantically tried to navigate like a lab rat in search of cheese. I got the sense that there was no roof above me, and when I looked up, a gigantic version of my mother was sneering down at me, her face as big as the noonday sun. Her hot gaze instantly evaporated all the spit in my mouth. And then it felt like my throat was closing and I couldn't breathe.

I sat up in my childhood bed gasping for air, telling myself it was only a dream. When I finally caught my breath, I exited my bedroom—half expecting to find myself trapped in a maze. The hallway led to the stairs, just like always, so I descended and slipped out the front door to do some counterclockwise circles around the house, which I did until the sun came up the next morning, which is when I asked my father to drive me back to school.

My mother complained bitterly about the cost of gas and my wasting money coming home for less than twelve hours, but soon Dad was behind the wheel and I was riding shotgun, only this time Dad decided to talk to me.

"Lucas," he said, "I'm tired. And you're a man now, so it's time you and I leveled with each other. Your mother has worn me down. I did my best. I kept things together until you left the house, but I can't keep pretending anymore."

He went on to say he was leaving and that I'd have to step up and be "the man of the house," which meant taking care of Mother because he couldn't do it anymore. I was too shocked to speak, because I could tell he was dead serious and relieved to be rolling a massive weight off his chest. I'd always known he didn't love me and here he was finally admitting it, once and for all.

When he dropped me off in front of my dorm, he handed me five crisp hundred-dollar bills and told me to take care.

I managed to make it back to my room before my mind kind of went psycho.

The next thing I remember, I was sitting on my bed punching the meat of my inner left thigh until it turned purple, at which point I set to work, punching with both fists, until there was a complete bruise ring circumscribing my entire upper leg.

Midafternoon, there was a friendly knock on my door. I tried to ignore it, but the person just kept on knocking, so I finally stood up and limped over to put an end to the banging.

When I pulled on the knob, there was a tall, lean, awkward-looking kid standing in my doorway—a wave of red hair crashed down over his left eye. "You're Lucas Goodgame, right?"

I nodded.

"People call me Smithy. I live two doors down."

I nodded again.

"You don't talk much, do you?"

I shrugged.

"That's cool."

I stared back at him, not knowing how to reply.

Then he raised his right hand, in which he clasped an envelope. "Found this in my box. Girly handwriting. Smells girly too. Always a good sign. Got real close to sneaking a peek. But it has your name on it and, well, congrats, Romeo."

He handed the envelope to me, but I didn't look at it right away, because I was too nervous. I needed privacy. I needed this Smithy to leave. But, as he was being so neighborly, I didn't have the heart to say so.

"Listen," he said. "I'm going to be straight here. You don't look so good. Which is cool. No big deal. But I was thinking about ordering a pizza later and maybe sinking a few beers and playing video games or something. You wanna join me?"

When I didn't answer, he said, "Think about it. I'm literally ten feet away. And I'll be there all night. Maybe you can tell me about your lady friend."

Smithy punched my arm in a friendly way, and then he was finally gone, at which point I shut the door and stared at the letter in my hand.

It was from Darcy.

We had worked at We All Scream For Ice Cream together the previous summer, back when it was owned by the DiTullio family. I had mostly done all the scooping, while she charmed the customers—working the register, chitchatting with the moms, flirting unabashedly with any man who walked through the door—and magically filled up our shared tip jar several times a shift. When things were slow, I'd listen to Darcy talk about her hopes and dreams regarding working with special needs children; and how the boys she was dating constantly frustrated and disappointed her; and all of her ill-advised madcap adventures with Jill; and whatever else she wanted to talk about. I could have listened to the sound of her voice forever.

At the end of the summer, when we were saying goodbye, she had kissed me on the cheek and then asked for my college address.

"What for?" I replied.

"So we can be pen pals," she said. "No boy has ever listened to me the way you do. And I have a hunch you write quite the letter. There's just got to be some words in that cute little head of yours."

I had never written a letter to anyone in my entire life, but I nodded anyway and then—with profusely sweaty hands—wrote down my home phone number so that she could call for my new college address later that night, which she did. I read it clearly to her twice over the phone without allowing myself to believe that she would ever use it, even as she read it back to me correctly and with a flirtatious magic that somehow made my new address sound like a ballad.

As I stood in my single dorm room, looking at the first letter anyone had ever written to me—studying Darcy's very feminine loop-de-loop penmanship, which was documented in purple ink, and trying to symbolically interpret the magazine cuttings she had artistically taped to the outside of the envelope, including a young handsome couple kissing—I felt like I had some sort of holy relic in my hand. I didn't have to open the envelope to know that whatever was inside was going to save me, because I had already been saved. Every bone in my body was vibrating beautifully in confirmation of that last statement.

Finally, I lay down on my tiny coffin-sized bed, broke the seal, and then consumed Darcy's words.

Later that night, I stuck my head through Smithy's open door and he said, "Lucas! You made it!" before offering me a greasy pizza slice.

I spent all of Sunday writing Darcy back. I told her about my parents. I told her about playing video games with Smithy, who sure seemed to be fate personified. I said that working with her that past summer was maybe the best experience of my life; and that I loved listening to her; and that she was wonderfully kind and would help a lot of children in the future; and I was thrilled to be writing her. I wrote page after page after page, giving her a glimpse of what had been brewing inside of me for so long, telling her more than I had ever told anyone in my entire life. I bought a cheap rose from a street vender, plucked all the petals, and pressed them dry in a book. Later, I folded them into the pages of the letter so that fragrant red teardrops would fall to her lap while she was reading. I asked around for magazines—talking to many of my fellow dormmates for the first time—and then cut out words and pictures, which I taped to the pages and the outside of the envelope, trying to match Darcy's level of creativity.

On Monday, I bought a roll of stamps from the campus store and applied three to the envelope, just to make sure it would reach her. And when I dropped the letter into the mailbox on the quad, I had this overwhelmingly warm feeling that seemed to be saying my life was about to change in a radical way.

And I was not wrong.

I'm writing you today about that new revived, even life-saving feeling that Darcy's letter gave me at the start of college, because that's exactly how I'm beginning to feel whenever I spend time with Eli, which—happily—happens every day at this point.

When he grins at me over breakfast, it's like I've metaphorically just posted the first letter to him in the mail.

Like I've set something in motion that I don't quite fully understand, but will transform my life powerfully and for the better. Maybe almost in a fated way.

Each day is a glorious new beginning.

Back when she was still talking to me, winged Darcy said my writing you was healthy and I think it truly is.

Besides Darcy, you're the only person I've been this intimate with on paper.

I know you realize the significance of that fact.

Karl, Karl, Karl.

Please write back.

I could really benefit from a couple of encouraging words—just a sentence or two. I imagine it wouldn't take more than a minute or so to scribble and post a few lines.

Minimal effort and yet maximal effect.

I'm sure you have already discovered the self-addressed and stamped envelope, which I've enclosed for your convenience, making the process of responding as easy as possible for you. Sorry for not thinking of that earlier. It was probably inconsiderate, although I definitely meant no offense. I just didn't think of it before. Maybe all the post-traumatic stress. Or maybe psyche is just subconsciously prioritizing Eli at this point and you—of all people—can surely understand why.

Your most loyal analysand,
Lucas

II.

Dear Karl,

I must admit that I wasn't initially convinced by Jill's optimism after the meeting at the library. And I had a fitful night tossing and turning in bed. Winged Darcy watched me with disapproval, digging her elbow into a pillow and resting her face against a closed fist. *Oh ye of little faith*, her pouty expression seemed to be saying, but I couldn't manage to feel reassured and my sleep suffered terribly as a result. But the very next day—while I was cleaning up after breakfast—there was a knock at the front door.

"That's them," said Eli—who never doubted the genius of our plan even for a second, not even when it put him in the emergency room.

"Who's *them*?" I asked, scrubbing bacon drippings from Darcy's cast-iron skillet and wondering how much left-behind grease would qualify as seasoning.

"Whoever we managed to convince!" he said, and then sprinted to find out who was on our porch.

When Eli pulled open the door, Mark and Tony were standing there rather sheepishly in pastel polo shirts, khaki shorts, leather loafers, and light summer sweaters draped perfectly down their backs like capes.

Eli gave me a *told you so* look before inviting our guests to enter and take a seat on the living room couch, which they did with what might be best described as measured hesitation. Mark must have convinced Tony that visiting us this morning was a good idea, I thought, because whenever Tony gave Mark a questioning glance, Mark would nod as if to say, *We discussed this already. We're doing this.* Or he'd squeeze Tony's knee.

Eli plopped down into the recliner and I pulled up a wooden dining-room chair so that I was facing our guests. Then I noticed I was tapping my left foot, so I forced myself to stop doing that and, instead, smoothed out the wrinkles in my linen pants. Darce had bought me those for our trip to Hawaii, which we had taken the year before she got her wings. I've been sleeping in these rather comfortable pants ever since the tragedy, so they are extremely wrinkled.

"That was quite the presentation you boys put on last night," Mark said, only he was smiling kindly and believably. He wasn't making fun of us at all. Then he went on to say that when Eli, Jill, and I left for the hospital, Mark and Tony had stayed behind with the original Survivors' Group to help clean up the blood and disinfect the library meeting room. Once that was finished, The Survivors had another meeting to discuss the merits of what Eli and I had proposed.

"Sandra Coyle gave a big speech," Mark said with a frown, "and, honestly, she did her best to counter everything that you laid out. 'Our emotional and financial resources could be better spent!' she kept yelling. 'Better allocated!'"

"But," Tony said with an edge in his voice, "she was . . . *insensitive.*"

"Especially with Eli in an ambulance headed to the hospital," Mark said.

"I'm fine," Eli said.

Then there was an awkward silence.

"We were both film majors," Tony interjected, refocusing us. "We worked in the industry for years, mostly as producers, until we earned enough to return the Majestic Theater to its original glory."

"We're kind of rehabbing professionals," Mark said. "Buildings *and* personas. Although this might be our first town."

"I have a digital camera," Tony added, warming up to us at this point, "which I use quite often to film shorts. I also have editing equipment. And we both have friends who work in the Philadelphia and New York film industries."

"We're playing the leads," Eli said, leaning forward in the recliner with a protective glint in his eye. "Mr. Goodgame and I will also be codirecting. We insist on retaining control of the script."

"We also absolutely must premier the film at the Majestic Theater," I added. "That's nonnegotiable."

"Of course," Mark said.

"It's the whole point," Tony added. "Why we're sitting here with you this morning."

"We want to . . ." Mark said. "How did you put it last night?"

"Sanctify the space?" I said.

Mark and Tony nodded.

But the tension returned when they insisted on reading the script before they committed. With our fate dangling in the balance, Eli and I pulled up the PDF on my laptop and then gave them the room.

Outside, we threw a Frisbee back and forth in the space between the tent and the backside of our home.

The boy was a bit inflated—as you Jungians would say—by Mark and Tony's flattery and attention. I know because he kept trying to make trick catches—one-hand grabs behind his back and between his legs—which he pulled off about forty percent of the time, but with unending energy and glee and even cockiness.

"Don't worry, Mr. Goodgame. They're going to love it. How could they not?"

"But will they get it?"

"They said they went to film school, right? They own the historic Majestic Theater! If not them, then who?" Eli said, before listing many other facts about Mark and Tony meant to prove that they were film aficionados and therefore our storytelling equals—meaning we'd all surely get along fine, creatively speaking.

But then Eli frowned and said, "You don't think they'll find our script *derivative*, do you? I mean all monster movies follow a basic format, so it's not plagiarism so much as paying homage to beloved tropes. Right?"

He went on for a bit about the genre here, listing specific scenes, plot points, and themes from films I've heard of and some I've even seen—like *Dracula* and *Creature from the Black Lagoon* and *Wolf Man* and *Frankenstein* and *King Kong*—and others I'd never even heard of, such as *Gojira* and *Cat People* and *The Leopard Man* and *The Beast from 20,000 Fathoms*. Eli's monster movie lectures are always interesting and animated by unbeatable passion, but I was growing more and more concerned that Tony and Mark wouldn't pick up on the subtext of our story—what didn't smack you across the face with black-and-white letters on the first read through, but instead buzzed with great life-giving authority in the peripheral.

A complete and thorough grasp of what we'd accomplished surely required multiple reads over weeks and maybe even months. Was it even possible to specifically get—in just one rushed read—that the film wasn't simply about "a monster" at all but was a nuanced exploration of a real human boy's wounded psyche? A boy who *feels* like a monster? And would they understand the subtle complexity of the makeshift father figure who loves the boy monster despite all his shortcomings? Would they get that this unlikely platonic love bond teaches an entire town how to be human again? That the town is embittered by a tragedy that really has nothing to do with the boy monster in question, but on whom they projected all of their hate and shame and frustration anyway? Would Mark and Tony appreciate the level of difficulty required to complete the mission that winged Darcy had laid squarely on my shoulders—what had made my bones hum in glorious vibration?

I knew it would kill me dead if Mark and Tony emerged from the read with mixed emotions and post-read notes about adding more car chases or steamy love scenes or discussions about product placements or maybe even suggestions about elevating the talent level, especially since neither Eli nor I had ever officially acted before. But if completely unknown Ben Affleck and Matt Damon could star in a multi-million-dollar production of *Good Will Hunting*, surely Eli and I could star in our own local production of *The Majestic Prince of Monsters*. Mark and Tony weren't even real Hollywood producers anymore, and there was no world in which I'd sell out the integrity of our film to the first local yokels who came knocking. No, I would stand my ground! And I'd stand it with unmovable dignity and a pride that transcends fame and money and the approval of the local film community!

I had really gotten myself worked up in the backyard, while throwing the Frisbee and awaiting the fate of our movie script.

But then Eli was pointing back toward the house. When I turned around, Mark and Tony were giving us four thumbs-up. And then we were all shaking hands and talking about putting our film together—outlining all the required logistics, most of which I hadn't even known existed, let alone considered.

"The Survivors' Group members will be given first chance to play the roles," I said once again. "That's nonnegotiable."

"Sure thing," Mark said, smiling like a proud father might. Then he added, "This is going to be a really big deal for our town."

"Utterly transcendent," Tony echoed. "Art will win."

And then before I knew it we were all at the Cup Of Spoons sharing the good news with Jill, who made us each a BLT and a cup of tomato summer soup, meaning chilled. The four of us sat there sipping and munching and smiling and talking about the movie and—halfway through the meal—I realized that I had simply forgotten to scan the room for people who might be staring at Eli or me. And when I observed Eli, I saw that he too had forgotten to be self-conscious, even with the back of his head shaved and a huge white bandage stuck to his skull, which was conspicuous as a toilet paper train emerging from the back of one's trousers.

I knew Jill was really excited about the movie when she refused to bill us for the meal, which is when Mark and Tony said they would be counting on Jill to be the film's official caterer, only they called it "craft services." Then Mark declared, "And we'll pay you well too!"

"Well, at least scale," Tony added.

When Eli told them about the budget we had created using his four hundred dollars and the money that Jill wrangled from the life-insurance company after Darcy's alleged death, Mark blinked a few times and said, "You really don't know how the movie business works, do you?"

Eli and I exchanged a glance of admitted naivete before Tony said, "You boys are the talent. We're the producers. Which means we're in charge of securing funding and paying everyone involved."

"We're going to get paid?" Eli said.

"Well, no," Mark said. "But you won't have to put up a dime of your own money."

"In exchange for what?" I asked, worrying about the integrity of the project again, wanting to stay on mission.

Tony reached across the table and grabbed my hand, which he patted as he said, "We want you two to make the movie exactly as you've written it. We want to do this for The Survivors. We're just here to assist you."

"Like fairy godfathers," Mark said, and then laughed heartily, which made Tony shake his head and roll his eyes. "But seriously," Mark said with much more gravitas, "we do need movies to watch together communally. We need to laugh and cry in the same room and this is the perfect way to reclaim our sacred space, as you so eloquently pointed out last night at the library. And we need to heal."

"Boy, do we ever," Tony echoed.

"When do we start shooting?" Eli finally said, ending a pregnant pause in the otherwise lively conversation, at which point we discussed next steps.

Eli and I would distribute hard copies of our script—each copy watermarked with the name of its recipient, of course, so no one could leak our intellectual property without legal repercussions. Tony and Mark said they had a contact who would begin working on wardrobe immediately, including a new heat-shedding and ultimately safer monster costume that they promised would look exactly like the original, which Eli and I had agreed to temporarily surrender to their care. They had another contact who would begin obtaining the necessary props, including securing the help of the police, because we'd written into the script many cruisers with flashing lights and wailing sirens and dozens of men in blue uniforms. At this point, I told our producers to contact Bobby the cop, explaining that he was a former student of mine and would almost certainly be sympathetic to our cause. They made a note of his name on Mark's phone and said they'd get right on it.

"What do *we* need to do?" Eli asked, to which they replied that after distributing the scripts we needed to memorize our lines and get into character, which seemed easy enough, as we had written the lines and based the characters of the monster and his unlikely father figure entirely on ourselves.

"Perfect," Mark said, concluding the meeting, and then we all shook hands.

On the walk back to our home, Eli and I were practically floating. We couldn't believe our luck, especially after the disaster that had befallen us the night before. But when we turned onto my street, we heard a woman screaming at the top of her lungs and we knew our fortunes had changed.

"Hide!" Eli yelled, pulling me behind a bush before leading me into Mr. Underwood's backyard, where we began hopping fences and crouching low to the ground as we snuck our way to our house.

In my backyard, we saw that the orange tent had been trashed. I quickly keyed into my back door. Eli and I slipped inside, turned the dead bolt so that the house was secure, and then slithered on our bellies—military-style—into the living room, where we listened to the crazed woman pounding on the front door with her meaty fists and screaming things like, "You stole one of my sons, but you won't steal two!" and "What kind of a sicko houses a teenage boy not even related to him by blood?" and "I'm going to take you down if it's the last thing I do!"

"Who is that out there?" I asked Eli.

He gave me a long quizzical look.

When he finally said it was his mom, my stomach sank. It felt like someone was trying to pull my soul out of my belly button again, and I wished we were in the kitchen so I could look at the clock minute hand steadily moving its way to the place where I could simply hang up and, therefore, free myself from the sticky web of what you Jungians call "the dark goddess," for at least another week anyway.

"I think the hospital might have called her because of the insurance," Eli explained, and that made a lot of sense, although I wonder why it took her more than half a day to visit our house once she knew her son had been seriously injured.

"Where did she think you were all this time?" I asked.

Eli just shrugged and then said his mom wasn't right in the head.

One of my neighbors must have called the cops because suddenly I was hearing Bobby's booming voice outside and he was telling Mrs. Hansen to calm down and walk away from the house and that he didn't want to have to use force, especially considering all she had suffered—all while the woman kept yelling, saying that she wasn't afraid of him and asking if he was going to shoot her and saying this was exactly why everyone hated policemen these days.

"You really didn't know that was my mom?" Eli said.

I looked through him, unable to make my eyes adjust and bring Eli's face into focus, as we lay there next to each other on the living room rug, which is when Bobby rang the doorbell and said, "Mr. Goodgame, you in there?"

Eli and I remained silent for a long time and then my phone began ringing.

The screen said: Bobby The Cop.

He had my cell phone number from all the times he'd picked me up in his cruiser and also from the investigation the police had done right after the Majestic Theater tragedy. I sent Bobby to voicemail and he left a long message, which I deleted later without listening to it.

The boy and I hung out on the floor for another half hour or so, just kind of staring at the ceiling, and then Eli broke the long stretch of silence by saying, "Mr. Goodgame, can I ask a favor of you?" When I said sure, he said, "Don't ever tell me what really happened the night my brother died, okay?"

My heart started pounding and my throat closed like a clenched fist. I couldn't have spoken if my life depended on it.

"I don't want to know. Like, ever," Eli said before standing up and walking out the back door.

It took twenty or so minutes for me to calm my heart rate and slow my breathing.

When I went into the kitchen and looked through the window over the sink, I saw that Eli's tent had been re-erected to its original shape. Somehow, I knew that Eli was inside, recovering from his mother's assault on whatever sanctuary it was that we were building. And—as a person who often finds refuge in the medicinal qualities of solitude—I also knew it was best to leave the boy alone out there.

Best for Eli.

Best for me.

Best for our film.

Bobby must have gone to the Cup Of Spoons, because he soon returned with Jill, who let him into our home and then made me sit down across from Bobby at the dining room table. He asked a lot of questions regarding how Eli came to be living with Jill and me. At first, Jill tried to answer all the inquiries on my behalf, but Bobby said he had to hear my version of the story, which let me know Jill had already told hers. When I finally spoke, I was honest about everything, telling him exactly what I have already told you here in these letters. And when I finished speaking, he said, "The boy is eighteen and therefore officially an adult. But I'm going to need to speak with him. *Alone.*"

We led Bobby out through the back door and then scrambled back into the kitchen to watch through the window over the sink. Our favorite cop crossed the lawn and made his way to the tent, calling Eli's name the whole time. When Eli didn't answer, Bobby bent down and slowly unzipped the front flaps. He squatted like a catcher for a minute or so, before disappearing into the orange fabric.

Jill started talking too quickly, guessing what Eli might be saying to Bobby and also reassuring me that neither she nor I had done anything wrong. "Quite the contrary!" she declared, working herself up into a heightened emotional state. "After what happened to Darcy, we should be given medals for taking in that boy." As she went along like that, her face turned deeper shades of red and her voice got louder and more agitated, until I was worried she might actually go out into the tent and try to physically remove Bobby from our property, which was when I reminded Jill that I had helped Bobby when he was just Eli's age. Then I said, "He's one of the good ones," meaning Bobby truly does seem to want to protect and serve his community. You can see it in his eyes whenever he talks to someone while he's in uniform. It's almost like he's trying extra hard to say, *Yes, I have a badge and a gun, but I will only use it for good and never to make you feel lesser than anyone else.*

Bobby emerged from the tent twenty or so minutes later and made his way back to us.

"What were you talking about out there?" Jill asked with a frigid bite in her voice that I knew was meant to protect me, but made me wince a little on Bobby's behalf.

"Just needed to make sure Eli was here of his own free will," Bobby answered, which was when Jill got even more upset and started using words like "ridiculous" and "invasive" and "humiliating."

Bobby humbly absorbed Jill's tirade, allowing her to spend all of her energy as he nodded and maintained eye contact with a natural ease that would make even the best mental health professional envious. Even you, Karl, would have admired his ability to cultivate what you call the objective ego.

When Jill finally finished giving Bobby a piece of her mind, he said, "The boy says you two are literally saving his life," at which point he took off his policeman's cap. Then he said, "I have to follow up on all calls and accusations no matter who they come from. We realize that Mrs. Hansen is grieving in her own way and it can't be easy when the only child you have left won't speak to you. I'm sure you understand."

That seemed to take all the bad steam right out of Jill, who quickly shifted to asking Bobby if he wanted an ice tea, which he graciously accepted.

We all took a seat at the kitchen table, at which point Bobby said, "What's this I hear about a monster movie? And a need for police participation?" I realized that our new producers were working quite speedily. Bobby confirmed that by saying Mark and Tony had left him a voice message. Turned out that Bobby had already pledged his help to Eli in the tent.

I couldn't stop myself from smiling like a little boy with two fists full of candy.

Then Bobby said pretty much all the cops in town would jump to get some positive press—given that the collective is being rather tough on the police these days—especially since Eli assured him that everyone would admire the men and women in blue for not taking themselves too seriously while participating in the making of Majestic's first feature film.

When Bobby expressed concern regarding our movie's depiction of local cops, I was surprised to learn that Eli had told him so much about the plot. Then I felt a great need to reassure Bobby, who had been so kind to me.

"No one in our movie is good or bad," I said, and then went on to explain that even the monster isn't either-or but *both-and*. It felt important to make sure Bobby understood there is no good-bad splitting in our cinematic universe. Just true depictions of whole people, each with both a shadow and a light side. When he nodded back at me, I added that the story is deeply rooted in Jungian psychology and is a tribute to you, Karl. Well, my contribution is anyway. Does that make you proud?

Bobby smiled politely and thanked me for staying away from your house, because he hadn't caught me walking past it recently. And then we all sipped our cold, sweaty glasses of tea in silence for a minute or so before Bobby said he had to keep patrolling the streets of Majestic. He excused himself, putting his cap back on in the process.

Jill went back to the Cup Of Spoons and I went out to the tent, only I didn't talk to Eli about what he had said to Bobby or even our attaching the entire local police force to *The Majestic Prince of Monsters*. Instead, I lay down next to Eli and said, "Do you want to talk about your mom?"

When he didn't answer, I started talking about my own mother, telling him many of the things I have already told you in analysis and also in these letters. I didn't look over at Eli's face because I was worried I wouldn't be able to keep talking if I did, but I could feel him listening, drinking in all I had to say. And there was something deep within my soul that assured me I was nurturing the boy—saying exactly what he needed to hear at that moment—and, ultimately, making Eli feel less alone.

When I finished, Eli said, "Why don't they love us? Our moms?"

"You can't give what you don't have," I said, and then we just lay there under the heavy truth of that statement.

Then Eli said, "Other kids have loving moms. Most people seem to have at least decent moms. Were we just unlucky?"

I wasn't sure how to answer that one, so I kept quiet.

"Mom used to make Jacob wear a dress and lipstick when we were kids. Only in the house, where no one else could see. As punishment," Eli said in a way that let me know his mother had, of course, done similar things to him. Then he said, "I'm not like Jacob," but there seemed to be a question hidden in the spaces between the words.

So I answered that unspoken question, saying, "No, you're the exact opposite of Jacob. His shadow."

I could tell Eli didn't know what I meant by shadow, because he didn't have the benefit of talking with you for two hours every Friday night for fourteen months. But since he didn't ask for an explanation, I didn't offer one.

Eventually, we transitioned to Darcy's office and started watermarking scripts, which took us a surprisingly long time as we had to individualize dozens of copies and my old laptop became glitchy. But that business kept our minds off the heavy topics of dark mothers and homicidal brothers.

And before we knew it Jill was back with a pesto pasta dish and we were all gathered around the dining room table digging in.

After dinner, we realized that we didn't have enough paper, so we had to wait until the morning to get supplies. Next we ran out of ink. Then we realized we needed manila envelopes, so we were running back and forth to the office-supplies store for the better part of two days. Once we finished everything, we assigned each Survivor a manila envelope, on which we wrote their name, before stuffing inside the corresponding watermarked pages.

You should have already received a copy of the script watermarked with your full name. It's not that I don't trust you with our intellectual property—I obviously do, especially given all I've already told you—but I can't go playing favorites in the film world, which is much different from and squarely outside of our analytic container. No one will be able to accuse me of nepotism, I assure you of that. Since you haven't contacted me yet, I'm assuming you haven't actually read the script. I'm pretty sure it would have motivated you to finally reach out. Especially since I was moved by the creative Muses to write one of the roles with you specifically in mind. I'm also pretty sure you'll know which that is once you get around to reading. (Hint: it's the father figure's Jungian analyst.) We aim to cast ASAP, as we'd like to premiere this before summer ends, if only to speed along the healing that the town of Majestic so desperately needs.

I hope you didn't mind me hand delivering the script, sliding it through the mail slot in your front door. I didn't look in your windows and won't ever again. Promise. Eli and I don't want to risk our work being delivered to the wrong addresses or getting lost in the mail altogether. We hand delivered all of the other watermarked scripts as well, so you didn't get special treatment, nor was I using this as an excuse to spy on you or anything creepy like that.

So if you called Bobby the cop on me, it wasn't necessary.

But don't worry. I'm a resilient man.

And the best of my soul still loves the best of your soul.

Psyche continues to say, *Reach out to Karl. Include him. Liberate him. Heal him.*

Analysts are people too.

Please join us.

Your most loyal analysand,

Lucas

12.

Dear Karl,

Maybe we should get through the bad first, before we get to the good?

Bobby brought your manila envelope back to Eli and me, saying that I wasn't supposed to be within so many yards of your house, even though I haven't been peeking in any windows these past few weeks, respecting your privacy, which I explained to Bobby, who said that didn't matter. Eli even tried to say he alone had delivered your script and my last letter, which wasn't illegal at all—because there was no restraining order or anything like that taken out on the boy—which was when Bobby said there was video of *both* Eli and me standing on the porch and me sliding the manila envelope into the mail slot.

When did you put up recording devices on your house? And why?

I didn't see any lenses, but Eli says they make them so small these days, and maybe it was a doorbell camera, which he says we could have easily missed, especially because we weren't looking.

I don't know why you're so afraid of me lately—because I would never in a million years hurt you—but I have, once again, agreed to "stay far away from the property." I've sworn over and over again to Bobby, who says he could get in a lot of trouble if I keep "breaking the law," because he just doesn't have it in his heart to arrest me. Jill emphasized the severity of the threat to Bobby's career, which is why I'll be sending this letter—along with your original watermarked copy of the script—via the U.S. Postal Service.

As you will soon see below, casting is complete except for the analyst role, which I'm keeping tentatively reserved for you, should you come to your senses. Isaiah has, however, graciously volunteered to be your understudy. He read your lines at the first table read and—dare I say—he's rather convincing as a Jungian analyst. Must be all his religious training and his personal connection with the numinous.

Jill played the part we wrote for Sandra, which admittedly is kind of thin. We made her the mayor of Majestic, trying to appeal to Sandra's ego, but the character only says things like, "This town is worth saving!" and "God save Majestic!" when everyone still thinks the monster is evil, and then, "You are the true sons of Majestic," at the end when she places medals around the necks of the boy monster and his father figure during the ceremony of honor. Jill really isn't officious enough for the role, but she gave it her all during the reading. The mayor character's name is Sara.

So bad news part one is that you have some serious competition. Even after a single rehearsal, the other actors—including Eli and me—have gotten used to Isaiah playing the Jungian analyst, whose name is Carl with a *C* rather than a *K*, by the way. Isaiah now has some sweat equity banked, but there's still a chance you could swoop in and reclaim the role if you act quickly. Maybe you'll want to use one of the phone numbers listed on the last page of the script. You can talk to Mark or Tony if you're more comfortable dealing with producers, rather than fellow actors or directors.

But you really don't want to miss this once-in-a-lifetime chance to play a part written specifically for you while helping to heal your traumatized community. The rest of The Survivors seem to be getting something worthwhile from the project so far. That good feeling's bound to multiply once we get into costume and makeup and start shooting.

Haven't you ever wanted to see your face up there on the Majestic Theater's big screen, beautifully framed by the parted red curtains?

Ticktock, Karl. Ticktock.

The second bit of bad news is that I haven't seen winged Darce in a few days. The first night she failed to fly in through the window—I'm sad to say—I didn't even notice. It was after the first read through, which I'll tell you about below. Afterward, Mark and Tony met with Eli and me in our living room to discuss any possible last-minute role swaps and to tweak the script where necessary after hearing everyone actually saying the lines aloud. And I couldn't believe it when Tony said it was almost three a.m. and we hadn't even finished all that we had set out to do. We all agreed to continue in the morning over breakfast at the Cup Of Spoons. And then I was climbing the stairs to my bedroom. The second my face hit the pillow, I was unconscious. It wasn't until the next morning that I realized I hadn't seen winged Darcy the night before, and then I began to feel hollow inside.

I told myself that maybe my wife really *had* been standing there in the corner when I had come to bed, only I was too exhausted to notice. Because she absolutely wanted me to make the film with Eli, I knew she'd be understanding, so I kind of shrugged it off as a weird hiccup in our otherwise healthy numinous relationship. But Darce didn't show up the next night or the night after that and now I'm starting to worry that maybe she could no longer resist flying up into the light. I'm pretty sure she wouldn't leave without saying goodbye, but I have to admit I'm a little terrified of that possibility too. I don't think that angels can get hurt or sick or—God forbid—killed here on earth. But wasn't the devil once an angel? And look what happened to him!

I've been telling myself that maybe winged Darcy is testing me. Or maybe she's helping me build up a tolerance for being apart from her, because I knew from the start that she couldn't stay with me here on earth forever.

Maybe she'll show up tonight and all will be well?

Let's just go with that, shall we?

Moving on . . .

All of the original Survivors' Group members—except you and you know who—immediately agreed to be in the movie. But DeSean Priest said he didn't want to play the doctor who—as a by-product of the drug he's trying to invent to cure his young daughter's stage-four cancer—accidentally develops radioactive neon-green sludge that he tries to get rid of by dumping the runoff into a sewer grate, not knowing that a local teenager has been using the town's underground pipes as a secret hideout, where he also raises mourning doves to honor his deceased brother who was a big fan of birds. The radioactive sludge combines the DNA found in all the feathers on the sewer floor with our hero young Earl's DNA, which spontaneously makes feathers shoot out of every inch of his skin and, ultimately, turns him into the Mighty Mourning Man.

Since DeSean is the town's local pediatrician, he worried that his being seen on-screen experimenting with non-FDA-approved substances—even under the mask of fiction—would send the wrong message to his patients. Eli and I tried to convince him otherwise, but he wouldn't budge and eventually talked Ernie Baum—everyone's favorite local butcher—into trading roles with him. We had cast Ernie as a butcher named Eddie, thinking he could bring a lot of realism to the part. But it turns out that Ernie liked the idea of playing a "mad scientist" and had even brought a copy of Mary Shelley's *Frankenstein* to the table read. Robin Withers had given him the classic when he came to the library asking for something to help him prepare for acting in the movie. Ernie promised to train DeSean in the fine art of butchery so that his knife-fighting scene might look realistic. We reluctantly agreed to allow the switch. To be honest, Eli and I didn't feel great about having our casting questioned, but when we saw how much energy the newly placated Ernie and DeSean brought to the table read, we knew we had made the right call. Sometimes you have to bend to not break, as they say.

WE ARE THE LIGHT

The table read brought us back once again to the library conference room, only this time it was Eli who made the speech. After saying "full disclosure," he explained that our film would officially serve as his high school senior project, which he needed to complete in order to graduate. He said he hadn't walked in the graduation ceremony with his class for obvious reasons—meaning no one wanted him there. I could tell all of The Survivors felt a little bad about that reality, which provided a lot of extra motivation for what we were all about to begin doing.

Eli said he hoped to submit the final cut of our monster movie to film schools so that he might gain admittance for the winter semester. His goal was to leave Majestic by January.

I hadn't heard that before.

He had his hands shoved deep into the pockets of his shorts and his voice was shaky. There were a lot of "likes" and "ums" sprinkled throughout his speech, but no one really minded.

The number of times people looked over at me, however, was disconcerting. I was seated directly to the right of Eli, and everyone was sitting in a large circle, so, at first, I thought maybe the angles were playing tricks on my eyes and everyone was really looking at Eli, because he was the one who was speaking. But the more I observed, the more I understood that people were looking at me and smiling like they were proud of yours truly, but I really couldn't understand why.

When everyone thought Eli was finished, the room gave him a polite round of applause, but it turned out he actually wasn't done.

Over the clapping, Eli blurted out, "I'm not like my brother, Jacob," which made everyone stop clapping.

The silence was intense.

I don't think Eli had meant to say those last six words out loud, because he looked over at me with a fresh panic in his eyes, and then he burst into tears before running out of the room. Isaiah instinctively jumped up out of his seat, but I was already chasing after the boy and so I raised a hand in the air, meaning *I got this*.

I followed Eli out of the library and into the woods beyond the parking lot. When I finally caught up to him, he had picked up a fallen branch and was beating an oak tree with it, using both hands to swing the dead limb back and forth like a giant's baseball bat.

He was screaming that he knew about the guns and should have told someone and now all those people in there were smiling and helping. And he could have prevented the tragedy if he had said something to someone about his brother's ever-increasing weapons-and-ammo collection, and the fact that Jacob had grown dark; and was talking about disturbing things; and was listening to depressing music; and had been spending a lot of time in the forest an hour or so away from Majestic illegally shooting animals; and had a growing collection of raccoon and fox skulls; and was always bragging about how good of a shot he had become, even literally saying he "could take a life without feeling a thing" and—

When Eli really started to spin out of control, I wrapped my arms around the boy, forcing him to drop the tree branch, which thudded down on the forest floor. Then I said, "You are not your brother. You didn't do anything wrong."

"But I could have said something! I should have called the police! How can I ask those people to help me now?"

As his tears and snot dampened my chest, I told him that we weren't asking those people in the library for anything. No, we were giving them a chance to be part of an artistic endeavor, which offered the possibility of communion and healing and transcendence.

"They want to be here," I said with my hands on his shoulders and our eyes locked. "I want to be here. You know what happened to my wife. And I'm still here. *I'm here*."

"Why?" he said.

"Well, I've just always wanted to star in a monster movie," I said, trying to lighten the mood. "And this might be my only shot."

The boy broke away from me and started kicking sticks and rocks. "They're all going to think I'm unprofessional now. No one wants to work with a drama-queen director."

"Are you kidding me?" I said. "All the best directors are emotionally unstable."

He smiled and listed a bunch of film directors who'd had mental breakdowns on movie sets, saying he'd send me YouTube clips later that night, which he did.

We got him cleaned up as best we could in the library bathroom and then were surprised to see that Bobby and two of his colleagues had joined the read-through circle while Eli was having his first official director meltdown in the woods and was, therefore, on his way to becoming an auteur.

"Everyone down at the precinct loves the script," Bobby said when we walked into the room, "but we can only spare three officers for this read through. You'll have the full Majestic force when the cameras start rolling. That's a promise."

Then Bobby winked at me, which was strange, because I believed he really was going to bring the entire force to the shoot.

Without missing a beat, Mark said that—as the producer—he needed to get this read through started, because babysitters were on the clock and people had real jobs to work in the morning.

And so Eli and I took our places, slipping down into the much safer fictional world of monster movies. There were the expected first-read-through jitters, but everyone really got into their roles and whenever Eli looked up after performing his lines, all the adults in the room nodded and shook triumphant fists in the air, which puffed the boy up in a good way.

The aggregate of all the above made my innards burn hot enough to incinerate all the darker thoughts that had been turning secret internal parts of me black, pretty much ever since you sent back your personally watermarked script and then winged Darcy stopped flying through the bedroom window every night.

I kind of really need consistency these days.

If you actually ever read through the script, which I've once again enclosed for your convenience, you'll see the monster's father figure is named Louis and—in order to remain sane—he needs to speak with his analyst once a week, and therefore, his sanity deteriorates rapidly when Carl is abducted by the feathered Mourning Man, who forces Carl to listen to all of the monster-boy's mad radioactive-induced ramblings. But in a surprise second-act twist, Carl helps the Mourning Man to see that he isn't really the monster he thinks he is. He does this by listening and replying when necessary, saying a kind word here and there, as well as giving the Mourning Man a Jungian lens through which he can view and begin to make sense of his new strangely fractured world. Then the bird boy and Carl rescue Louis from his madness before they all save the day.

Of course, the script isn't so on the nose. Most of the above is subtext, which you'll surely get right away when you eventually read it.

It's going to be a fantastic movie.

A real crowd-pleaser.

And wait until you read the third-act surprise.

There won't be a dry eye in the house.

You won't want to miss that.

Your most loyal analysand,
Lucas

13.

Dear Karl,

Even though Darce transformed herself into an angel at the beginning
of last December, I purchased and wrapped Christmas presents for her
anyway. The bulk of my holiday shopping had already been completed by
the time Jacob Hansen opened fire on all of us who were in the Majestic
Theater that fateful night. But on one of my many epic post-tragedy
December walks, back when I was clocking eighteen or so miles a day
between all those funerals, I happened to walk past Majestic Books and
right there in the window was the perfect gift for my wife.

I went inside and told Maggie Stevens that I just had to have it for
Darce, at which point she put my selection into a paper bag, handed it
to me, and said, "No charge." I, of course, tried to pay for what I was
taking, pulling out cash and extending it toward her, but she kept waving both her hands and saying, "I can't take your money, Lucas," and
"Merry Christmas," and "Thanks for what you did," and even "You're
a hero."

That last one made me feel as though she had sunk the pointy end of
a steak knife into my Adam's apple and so I turned around and exited the
store, and—as I made my way home, hoping to wrap winged Darcy's gift
before she might see it—I began swallowing repeatedly in a desperate
attempt to make the awful feeling disappear.

Like every night back then, winged Darce visited me on Christmas Eve. I had all of her presents arranged in a little pyramid in the corner of our bedroom where she often stood watching over me as I tried to sleep through the night. Every gift box was wrapped in white paper and tied up with gold bows. When Darce flew in through the window, she looked down at her pyramid of presents and smiled sadly. That's when she told me angels weren't allowed to accept gifts from human beings—even if said angel had been married to the gift giver when the winged one was alive.

I argued with her, saying, "What harm could possibly come from it?"

But she kept shaking her head no. I couldn't believe it, especially after all the work I had put into the wrapping, even measuring all the boxes with a ruler and making all the necessary cuts and folds. Her pyramid of gifts could have appeared in any glossy, glamorous magazine or in any fancy Manhattan storefront window—it was that perfect of an offering.

"Give these to Jill," winged Darce said.

When I searched her eyes, they seemed to say, *Jill gave up her trip to see her parents in North Carolina on Christmas, just so you wouldn't be alone. She's been looking after you, like a best friend should. Keeping your mother at bay even. Don't let her wake up to no presents on Christmas morning.*

I asked if we could open just one together. Maybe the least of them. Then I gently pulled a flat white square—what Maggie Stevens had given me at Majestic Books—from the middle of the pyramid. "Here," I said. "I got this gift for free."

Winged Darcy frowned, but I unwrapped her present for her anyway, revealing the Angelic Cats calendar, which features twelve different cats dressed as angels—one for every month of the coming year. I flipped through all the different photographs depicting harps and halos and clouds and grand sets of feathered wings and, of course, cats. We had been forced to put Darcy's beloved geriatric calico, Justin, down the previous summer. As Darce hadn't yet emotionally recovered enough to make room for a new kitten, I thought the calendar was the perfect stepping-stone placeholder. My wife smiled at each month's offering, but there was something new and maybe even alien in her face, which was when I realized that she most likely no longer had a need for earthly calendars—let alone pets—and was therefore humoring me so I wouldn't feel too bad about my silly human motives and reasonings and need for people to like whatever I might gift them.

"I'll hang it in the kitchen," I finally said, trying to save face. "It'll remind me of you. You always loved a cute animal calendar."

When she opened her gigantic wings, I fell into them, at which point she wrapped me tight as a newborn baby.

Jill already had Christmas music playing when I woke up late the next morning and followed the smell of coffee down the steps and into my living room. She had somehow managed to set up and decorate a small tree that definitely hadn't been there the night before, because I had specifically told Jill numerous times that I did not want to celebrate the birth of Christ this year in any excessively extravagant ways. As I stood there halfway down the stairs, taking in the newly festive atmosphere, Jill came out of the kitchen and observed me carefully, as if I might explode into a rage. And I was tempted to, because I didn't want any of this. But then I remembered what winged Darce had said the night before, so instead of yelling at Jill and throwing the small Christmas tree out the front door and into the street, I went back up to my bedroom and began to transport the pyramid of gifts down the stairs. I placed each present around the tree, making a complete O of wrapped gifts, which is when Jill said, "I didn't get you anything except the tree," so I explained that I had bought these for Darcy, who would surely want her best friend to have them.

Jill bit her lip and then turned her back before disappearing into the powder room. When she reemerged maybe twenty minutes later, she served me breakfast for lunch, because it was already noon. She had made sausage and waffles, which she topped with powdered sugar, strawberries, and cream. I didn't feel much like eating, but I forced as much of the food down as I could. Not because it was delicious—which it certainly was—but because I realized that this was Jill's Christmas gift to me and I remembered how awful it felt when winged Darcy had rejected mine.

While Jill was cleaning up the kitchen, I called my mother, just to get it over with. She didn't ask about what I was doing on my first Christmas without Darcy. In fact, Mom didn't ask me a single question. Instead, she talked about how lovely their waterfront gated community had looked with all the boats lit up for Christmas Eve. Then she went on and on about the "breathtaking" diamond tennis bracelet her boyfriend, Harvey, had purchased for her along with the "many-carat-ed" matching earrings. Next, she waxed on about how much fun they were having with Harvey's son and grandchildren. Apparently, they all were going for a sunset cruise on Harvey's fishing boat. After fifteen minutes or so, Mom said she should get back to the party before adding that it was a real shame I hadn't made the journey down because Harvey's son, Hunter, was a remarkable human being and perhaps even a man I could learn a thing or two from.

"Merry Christmas, Mom," I said, and then hung up the phone.

In the living room, I managed to convince Jill to open up most of Darcy's presents, which she reluctantly did. Jill said she would wear the leather jacket I bought but the matching shoes were a size too small. Luckily, I had kept all of the receipts, I told her. She confirmed that the facial and hand creams could be put to good use along with the bath bombs and soaking salts and the gift certificate for a massage at Majestic Zen. And then there were the smaller gifts, like pink razors and lady shaving cream and a jumbo family-sized pack of Twizzlers, which is Darcy's favorite movie snack. But then Jill opened the little box that contained the plastic gift card that got the owner into the Majestic Theater for an entire year, which made Jill go white and ask why I had wrapped that up.

I could tell she was really uncomfortable because her eyes were wide open and her whole body had started to tremble.

"For when they reopen the Majestic," I explained.

Darcy loved going to the movies. We went practically every weekend. Always got our money's worth and then some out of the yearlong pass. We gave movie passes to each other every Christmas. It's an unbreakable tradition. And Jill also loves the movies. She'd gone with Darce and me to the Majestic a thousand times. Maybe more. So I knew she would definitely use the pass, even if she didn't appreciate what was painted on the Majestic Theater's Grand Viewing Room ceiling as much as Darcy and I did. Which oddly gets me thinking that there's some detail I'm just not remembering about the Majestic, something important and maybe even divine.

Jill just sat there quivering with the annual movie pass in her hands and her mouth ajar.

I began to realize that I had somehow ruined Christmas for her, but I really wasn't sure how or why. Did she really think Mark and Tony were going to raze a historic building just because there was a single tragedy? Canceling the movies and losing such a sacred space would be punishing ourselves twice over. It didn't make any sense. But Jill's facial expression made it clear that she was never going to see the logic in the argument I just made. And for some reason, that realization made me very angry.

So I stood up, grabbed my coat, and walked right out the front door.

I punched my fists deep into my pockets and walked so fast I was practically running. All of the Christmas lights and decorations blurred together in my peripheral vision, creating these blindingly long unbroken streams of electric joy, none of which I could find a way to metabolize. I felt like a starving man separated by unbreakable glass from a steaming succulent feast masterfully laid out on the grand table. I could punch and kick and headbutt that glass all I wanted, but I would never be granted permission to taste the food on the other side. I was only permitted to stare and drool.

I banged on your door, Karl, but, of course, you didn't answer. And I walked past the Hansens' home many times as well.

I don't know how many miles I logged that day, but by the time Bobby the cop pulled up alongside me in his cruiser, the sun had long ago set.

"Nice and toasty in here, Mr. Goodgame," Bobby said after he rolled down his window. "Hop in."

My ears were chips of ice at that point and I was beginning to worry about the more permanent aspects of frostbite, so I did as I was commanded and without protest.

As he drove me home, I couldn't stop shivering, and at one point, Bobby reached over and placed his hand on my left shoulder. I wasn't sure if he was trying to warm me up or if he was just trying to say everything was going to be okay. Regardless, I reached across my body with my right hand and placed it on top of his. I think I was trying to say, *Thank you.* Somehow, we ended up driving the rest of the way home frozen in that position.

When we pulled up to my house, I asked Bobby if he wanted to come in for a cup of coffee, but he said he had to get home to his family, which is when I realized he was off duty and had just been doing Jill a favor. I didn't want to take up any more of his holiday, so I nodded and made my way into my house. He waited until I was inside before he shifted back into gear and we exchanged a wave as he drove off.

There was no more Christmas music playing and the wrapping paper we'd left on the living room floor had already been disposed of. The circle of gifts was also gone and I never did see any of them again, so I'm not really sure what happen to those presents. But I found Jill seated at the kitchen table transferring all of the important dates Darce and I tried to remember every year—birthdays and anniversaries, when to change the heating and air-conditioning filters—from last year's Beach Dog Lifeguards calendar to the new year's Angelic Cats calendar. It was weird, because I didn't remember bringing the new cat calendar down from my bedroom, which probably meant Jill went into my private space while I was gone and found it. I hadn't given her permission to do that. I hadn't given her permission to transfer all of the dates either. And my skin began to tingle like it sometimes does whenever someone is touching something of mine without my permission.

"What are you doing?" I asked when it became obvious that she wasn't going to look up from the task at hand.

When she didn't answer, I went up into my bedroom and stayed there for the night. Later, when winged Darce arrived, she told me to give Jill time, saying she had been through a great shock and didn't have an angel to guide her through all of the confusing aftermath, which made sense. And the next morning, the Christmas tree in the living room was gone and everything went back to normal with Jill and me. Well, until we went to Maryland later that spring, but I've already told you about that.

Here's the reason I told you that Christmas story: to explain how Eli knew that Jill's birthday was early in July. It was the Angelic Cats calendar in the kitchen that clued him in. After he turned from June's winged tabby kitten playing a harp to July's winged tuxedo adult cat soaring through the sunlit clouds, Eli said, "Did you know Jill's birthday is next week? July seventh." When I said I did but had forgotten, Eli added, "You've got to do something for her."

"*Me?*" I said. "Don't you mean *us?*"

"Look," Eli said, shaking his head, "Jill's always cooking for us and everyone in Majestic so why don't you take her out to a nice restaurant in the city or something? Give her a night off. Let someone cook for her for a change."

"You don't want to come along?" I asked, which is when he asked what exactly was going on between Jill and me, to which I replied that we had been very good friends for many years. Then I told him that Jill and Darcy and I had all gone to the same high school he had attended, where Eli and I had met, back when I used to help troubled teens.

Eli didn't seem to care that all of us had the same alma mater. Instead he went on a rant about how much Jill had been doing for both of us, pointing out that she did all the cooking and cleaning and laundry and now she was doing the catering for our monster movie production, all in addition to holding down a full-time job. "So," Eli said with finality, "you're going to take Jill out for a nice fancy dinner on her birthday."

Before I knew what had happened I was dressed in khakis and a button-down shirt and riding shotgun in Jill's truck, which was pointed toward Center City, Philadelphia. Jill was wearing a white sundress that showed off her well-toned legs, leather sandals that showed off her recently painted nails, and large golden chandelier earrings that bulged through the two curtains of blond hair that framed her face, which she had made up special for our evening.

We parked in a garage near Rittenhouse Square and then walked to a restaurant called 215, which Eli had found on the internet, saying it was "the hot new place."

When we entered, Jill told the hostess we had a reservation under "Majestic Films Incorporated," because Eli had given them our corporate account and even our corporate credit card, which Mark had supplied for occasions such as this.

"Right this way," the hostess said, and then led us toward a prime seat in the corner, where we'd have privacy. After giving us our menus, she said, "It's not often that we have Hollywood types in here," and then she winked at Jill, although I'm not quite sure why.

This was a tapas place, meaning you were supposed to order many small plates, which Jill took care of for the both of us, shortly after which food started arriving and didn't really stop for more than an hour. Jill was in heaven and kept saying, "Can you believe how *good* this is?" She asked our servers so many specific questions about the food that the head chef finally came out and offered Jill a tour of the kitchen, which she happily accepted. I could tell that this chef, who was maybe ten or so years younger than us, was attracted to Jill because he kept looking at her backside whenever Jill's eyes were focused on one of the many boiling pots or the hissing pans or trays baking in the large silver ovens. He also kept touching Jill's arms lightly as he moved her around his work space and never once made eye contact with me. I followed the two of them like a forgotten tail. I started to get the strangest feeling in the pit of my stomach—it felt like I had swallowed a ball of fire—and then I was sort of angry with Jill although I'm not sure why.

After we paid for our meal, Jill asked if we could walk around the city. It was a hot night, but not too hot. Just hot enough to make your skin feel alive and your lungs feel a bit heavy with the moist city air.

In the Rittenhouse Square Park, we sat down on a bench and Jill said, "Forty-nine. How did that even happen?" When I shrugged, she added, "I wish Darcy were here." Then she took my hand and held it in her lap. When I gave her a questioning glance, she said, "It's okay," and then she just watched the people pass as she lightly stroked the back of my wrist. It almost tickled, but I found her touch mesmerizing. I sat there unable to move a muscle for what felt like a half hour.

Then Jill turned and looked into my eyes for a long moment before she said, "You and me, Lucas, we're going to be okay. Eli's going to be okay too. You understand that, right? Because that's what I want for my birthday—for you to know that the three of us are going to be okay."

When I didn't say anything, she kissed my right cheek and then led me back to the parking garage by the hand.

On the drive back—riding shotgun in Jill's truck again—I was sweaty and nauseous. It felt like I had done something unforgivable, when all I had done was follow Eli's instructions, taking our Jill out to dinner on her forty-ninth birthday, thanking her for all she had done for Eli and me, letting her know that she was appreciated.

But the night just didn't sit right with me.

When Jill pulled her truck into our driveway, Eli's tent was glowing orange as a jack-o'-lantern again. I was glad that he didn't come out to see how our evening had gone.

Inside the house, Jill looked at me for a long time as we stood there in our tiny vestibule, before she said, "Do you want to come up to my room?"

I swallowed hard and felt the blood drain from my face. When I started to shake, Jill hugged me and—in a very different sort of voice—said, "It's okay, Lucas. It was a really nice birthday. Thank you."

When I finally stopped shaking, Jill kissed me on my left cheek this time and then she climbed the stairs and disappeared into our guest bedroom.

I stood there in the vestibule, trying to puzzle together what had just happened. It was like my feet were cemented to the floor and my fists weighed five hundred pounds each. Only when the spell wore off was I able to climb the steps. And then I was in my room again with the door locked. I opened the windows wide, but winged Darcy never came.

I'm really starting to worry about her.

Do you think I did something wrong, Karl?

Was it wrong to let Jill hold my hand on the park bench?

Was it wrong to sort of like and maybe even need the touch of another woman?

Have you touched a woman since Leandra left the planet?

Knowing how you'd answer those questions might really help me.

Your most loyal analysand,
Lucas

14.

Dear Karl,

Right before the most recent full-cast read through of the script, something called the "Wardrobe Mobile" pulled into the Majestic library's parking lot. In essence, the Wardrobe Mobile is a mini–tractor trailer, only the back has been modified into a storage container–slash-workshop packed full of fabric and sewing machines and costumes and props.

Mark and Tony had huge smiles on their faces when they introduced our entire cast to the driver and owner—a woman in a denim skirt and cowgirl boots whose name is Arlene. She had apparently volunteered to be our costume designer and manager. Arlene smiled as she introduced her assistant, River, a young, brown, androgynous-looking man with a headful of long braids.

"We're really digging the vibe of what y'all are doing with this project," Arlene said from the back bumper of the mobile.

"And we dig the script too," River said. "Kind of Lovecraft-ish. With the perfect dash of early forties Jacques Tourneur."

I didn't know what or who those things or people were, but the comment lit up Eli's face like a fireworks finale.

And then before we knew it all of The Survivors—along with Jill and Isaiah—were taking turns going into the back of the Wardrobe Mobile, only to emerge completely transformed minutes later.

They put me in jeans and a sweatshirt that read "The Majestic Magicians." I told them our local school mascot was the Mavericks, but River argued that "Magicians" was hipper and kind of more accurate as we were obviously trying to pull off some magic with the project. "Trust me," River said, and so I did, especially when I stepped out of the Wardrobe Mobile and Eli nodded his approval.

They dressed up Isaiah in a white linen suit and a straw fedora, which didn't really scream "Jungian analyst" to me, but as my best man friend was so pleased with the outfit—going all Hollywood, if you will—I didn't say anything about the lack of authenticity.

Jill was hilariously dressed in a robin's-egg blue pantsuit that made her look like a much more beautiful version of a middle-aged Hillary Clinton. Jill can pull anything off, so she, of course, looked movie-star gorgeous and got a big cheer as she did a little catwalk across the bumper of the Wardrobe Mobile.

Arlene and River saved the best for last. When Eli emerged from the mobile covered head to toe in pheasant feathers, everyone applauded like we had just won a sports championship. The monster even looked tiger-striped, which meant our new wardrobe designers had lined up all the feather markings properly. Somehow, Arlene and River had managed to perfectly re-create our vision of the creature, aka the Majestic Prince of Monsters, aka the Mourning Monster. *It even had a springbok backpiece!* But their superior sewing skills made it possible for them to use a much more pliable and breathable lightweight spandex base layer.

"I'm agile and cool as a bird," Eli yelled as he used the Wardrobe Mobile's bumper as a springboard, launching himself high into the air, where he flapped his feathered arms and spread wide his feathered legs.

We returned to the library conference room for our second read through and the costumes really seemed to elevate our performance. No one got up to use the bathroom or answered a cell phone call or seemed distracted in any way as we read through the entire ninety or so minutes of the script. And when we finished, there wasn't a dry eye in the room—well, besides the pair on my own face—even though everyone had, obviously, already experienced the last act.

River and Arlene, who were sitting with Mark and Tony at the head of the circle, were bawling their eyes out.

"I don't know how you people are doing this after all you've been through," Arlene said.

"I just can't even," River said.

Jill, Eli, Mark, Tony, and I stayed behind to help Arlene and River get the costumes back on hangers and deodorized and arranged according to scenes and all the rest. I didn't realize how much time and effort went into wardrobe preparation and maintenance.

At one point when I was alone with River, he said, "So you're the real hero around here, hey?" which made me feel like he was trying to suck one of my eyeballs out of its socket. I froze, which I guess he took for modesty, because he added, "I don't think I could have done what you did or what you're doing."

Instead of replying, I turned around and started walking, which I realize was rude, especially after all River and Arlene were doing to make our movie successful, but it was like I was on autopilot or maybe I was a puppet and my arms and legs were connected to strings controlled by something I couldn't see or understand. I was three doors away from home when Jill and Eli pulled up next to me in Jill's truck.

"Hey," Jill said through the open window. "Did something happen?"

I shook my head no.

"Whatever was said, River couldn't stop apologizing. He felt terrible."

I nodded, meaning, *It's okay.*

I think maybe Jill sent Eli to his tent, because he didn't follow us inside. When I sat down on the couch, Jill plopped down next to me. She let a lot of silence stack up before she said, "What do you need?"

"I want to reach out to Sandra Coyle one last time," I said, which surprised me.

"You don't think I can pull off the mayor role?" Jill answered, half joking and half serious.

Which is when I said Jill would most definitely make a much better Sara than Sandra—I went on a little about Jill's table read performance, which really was excellent—but then I told the truth, adding, "It's just that you weren't there in the theater that night. And, well . . . Sandra was."

"Okay," Jill said, and went up to the guest room, leaving me alone on the couch.

I pulled out my cell phone and went through all The Survivors' Group numbers I had programmed in after the first meeting back in December. When I found Sandra's entry, I pushed it and then held the phone up to my ear.

It rang five or so times before Sandra picked up and said, "Lucas Goodgame, do you know what time it is? *It's almost midnight!*"

"I didn't realize it was so late," I said truthfully, and then there was a long pause before Sandra asked what I wanted.

It was here that I felt my average self step outside of my body again. The mundane version walked over to the opposite side of the room and then leaned a shoulder against the wall, where I watched a superior Other Lucas field Sandra's question.

I told Sandra we wanted her to be in our movie. That we knew she thought it was a waste of emotional and financial resources. I described the read throughs with an intensity that was almost poetic. How we had all been laughing together in the library conference room—so loudly that Robin said we were practically shaking the books off the shelves. I let

Sandra know everyone except me had cried communally on multiple occasions. So the monster movie project really was therapeutic. It miraculously seemed to be helping The Survivors. And maybe it would help Sandra too if only she'd join us. Because it wasn't good to hole up and exclude oneself. And art could most definitely be medicinal, which was probably part of the reason why she went to the Majestic Theater with her husband, Greg, that night in the first place. Because she knew the unifying and soothing powers of the silver screen. I was tapping into the great transformative passion that is sometimes hidden within my shadow. I thought I might be winning Sandra over. So I wasn't surprised when she asked me to visit her house in the morning at eight o'clock, which I, of course, immediately agreed to.

But when I hung up the phone, I began to feel as though I had stepped on a psychological bear trap. The steel-toothed mouth had crunched down on my leg bone, and my bloody stump was now chained to a giant stake from which no amount of pulling could free me.

Upstairs I opened the windows like always, but winged Darcy didn't make an appearance. It's been an alarmingly long stretch since she's held me in her wings. And as I lay on my bed, I thought about Sandra and you excluding yourselves from the project. I tried to be curious about your reasons. I attempted to neutrally look at things from your point of view. I could have understood not wanting to participate if you two hated movies, but you were both there with all the rest of us in the Majestic Theater the night of the tragedy. And I have countless other times seen you both at Mark and Tony's cinematic cathedral. Remember how I'd always wave from a respectable distance and you'd nod back once in acknowledgment, in a way that wouldn't let anyone else know you and I had a clandestine alchemical relationship? Regardless, I know you and Sandra at least *like* movies. So I just really can't make the pieces fit. If you want to end your part of the mystery, I'm all ears. Or maybe it's more appropriate—given the present mode of communication—to say I'm all eyes.

Around five a.m., I realized I wasn't going to sleep, so I got up and showered and then caught Jill just before she walked out the door on her way to yet another day of cooking at the Cup Of Spoons.

"What are you doing up so early?" she asked with her truck keys dangling from her right hand.

"Couldn't sleep," I said.

Jill examined my face for a beat before saying, "Sorry, but I'm late," and then rushing out through the front door, which is when I knew she was still hurt by my wanting to recast Sandra in her role. But psyche was telling me I needed to reach out to Sandra and you taught me to always listen to psyche.

I wanted to go for an incredibly long walk but worried I would get too sweaty and smelly to meet with Sandra, so I instead made a coffee and sipped it as I watched the early morning light sweep away the last tiny bits of the previous night's darkness.

When the kitchen clock said 7:20, I took a deep breath and left the house.

As I made my way across Majestic—leaving the smaller-house section, passing through the medium-house section, and then finally entering the large-house section—I tried to mentally clarify what exactly I hoped to accomplish when I looked Sandra in the eyes.

Did I merely want to complete the set—meaning make sure all seventeen Survivors' Group members participated simply for the sake of being whole?

That wasn't it, I thought, especially since I was pretty sure I wouldn't have your participation anyway.

Did I want to exert some form of control over Sandra to fill a narcissistic need?

No.

The icy edge in her voice—what seemed to make everyone want to look down at their shoelaces—motivated me. So did the pain I felt radiating off her whenever she was within ten feet of me. I thought maybe I could relieve Sandra of that discomfort.

I told myself it was a worthy pursuit as I opened the iron gate in front of the Coyles' gigantic house, moved through the rose gardens that lined the walkway, and then rang the doorbell.

A young, well-dressed woman with cropped auburn hair and perfect makeup answered and said, "Mr. Goodgame, Sandra is expecting you."

As I entered the house, I realized that this young woman was most likely the assistant I had once spoken with on the phone when I had called to invite Sandra to the first movie meeting in the library, so I said, "Are you Willow?"

"I am," she answered almost melodically. Then she pointed into a sitting room of sorts and said, "Sandra will join you in a moment," just before she took her leave.

I paused there in the hallway and listened for the sounds of Sandra's children, but the house was all but silent. I wondered whether Sandra had sent her kids away to live with relatives, or maybe to boarding school, the idea of which made me frown. Maybe they had slept over at the houses of local friends, I thought.

When I entered the room, I saw a grand piano, a beautiful stone fireplace, several paintings of otherworldly looking landscapes I couldn't place on a map, a gold Victorian-era fainting couch, and two bulky leather-and-wood mission-style chairs. But what really caught my eye was the gigantic picture of the deceased Greg Coyle situated on a wooden easel so that he was staring at you—maintaining eye contact—no matter where you moved in the room. A confident and yet somehow humble smile revealed impossibly white teeth. His nose was long and pronounced, but attractive in a regal way. And small salt-and-pepper curls sat on his head almost like a hat, as he had kept the sides clipped close to the skin. Greg was a handsome and rather accomplished golfer who'd had a reputation for being kind. He often donated his time to our student athletes on the high school golf team, among whom he was very popular.

Sandra entered wearing a pin-striped business suit and sipping hot tea from a china cup and saucer. She sat on the gold fainting couch and so I sat on one of the mission thrones.

"Hope you've said hello to Greg?" she said.

It was a strange question that I didn't quite know how to answer, so I kept quiet, which made her smile.

"Listen, Lucas," she said, placing her teacup and saucer on the coffee table that separated our shinbones. "You've impressed me. The speech you made in the library and what you said last night. Never again call me at that hour, by the way."

I nodded and apologized because I really hadn't realized it was so late when I called the night before.

"You're very good at moving people. I'd go so far as to say you have a gift."

My skin started to tingle in a bad way at this point.

"I want to let you in on a little secret. I'm running for office and I've actually managed to secure quite a bit of funding," Sandra said, before going on to list the specific position and the famous names of her financial backers, all of which impressed me to say the least. Then she said, "How would you like to join my team, Lucas? You could help my speechwriters. Who knows, I might even bring you up onstage with me from time to time. And then, should I win, I'm sure I could find more work for a talented man such as yourself. And I'd compensate you well, of course." She listed the amount she was willing to pay me to be her consultant for a minimum of one year and it was quite a bit more than I had ever been paid by the town of Majestic to help its troubled high school students in an equivalent amount of time.

"What I'm aiming for," Sandra said, "is *real* power. The power to make a significant difference. The power to make sure others never experience what you and I experienced last December. You'd like that, wouldn't you? Protecting others from the heartbreak and horror we've been enduring these past several months?"

I found myself nodding, completely forgetting my original goals for this conversation.

"Then join my team, Lucas. Let's accomplish something real. Push policy in the right direction. Get stricter laws on the books. Save lives!"

When I failed to reply, Sandra said, "You're not getting this. Okay. Let me put my cards on the table. You're a bona fide hero, Lucas. There's political currency in that. But not if you ruin your brand by making monster movies with the brother of a psychopath. A kid who's—let's just be honest here—he's probably a psychopath himself. If you want to be part of a *real* solution, if you want to *really* honor Darcy, you've got to put childish things aside and be a man. I know you mean well, but you need to trust me when I tell you that Sandra Coyle will be driving the real response to the Majestic Theater tragedy. And I'm offering to let you ride shotgun. What do you say?"

I blinked several times—somewhat stunned by this strange offer—before I said, "Eli's not a psychopath."

"It's kind of you to want to save the boy, but can you really undo whatever it was that his mother did to those kids? Can you change DNA? He's obviously a lost cause. Everyone knows that. And a distraction, politically speaking. We don't want him to become sympathetic to the public eye. We need a clean narrative, which is also why I need you on my team."

I looked over at Greg's gigantic head for a second before I returned my gaze to Sandra and said, "But I came here to convince you to be in our movie. A lot of people are getting involved. It's been a positive experience for everybody."

"That salary number I quoted you before," Sandra said, "what if I double it? I hear you haven't been able to set foot inside the high school since the tragedy. You're surely too young to live off whatever retirement they're giving teachers these days."

It was true. According to Jill, I didn't have enough money to last two years, let alone the rest of my life. But I hadn't come to Sandra's to discuss money. So I said, "Is there any sort of compromise we could make? Any other ask you might have? I think you'd really like being in our movie."

Sandra stared at me coldly. It was like she was analyzing me—trying to figure something out before she made her next move. But then her eyes narrowed and a heaviness began to suck all the oxygen out of the room.

"After what happened in December," she finally said, "I don't ever want to think about the movies again. I don't even want to smell popcorn."

Her gaze cut through me. And I could feel the hate in her heart when she said, "That Hansen boy is going to disappoint you. Mark my words. Apples don't fall very far from apple trees."

I wish I could say I delivered a snappy comeback or at least stood up for Eli, but I just showed myself out of Sandra's house as she yelled, "Think about my offer, Lucas! It expires in forty-eight hours!"

As I strode home I knew I didn't need another second to decide anything. I would never align myself with a politician who could label a teenaged boy—with whom she'd never exchanged a word—a psychopath. My answer was a unanimous no. A billion times no.

When I arrived home, Eli wasn't in his tent, nor was he in our house. I found a note from him on the kitchen table explaining that he was spending the day with Tony, who had agreed to teach Eli how to use the digital camera and also give the boy a crash course on film composition, blocking—which, apparently, is where all the people stand in a shot—and various other camera techniques. Tony had called it "Film Class 101" the night before, which had made me smile. It sure seemed now like many adults were eager and ready to mentor Eli toward a brighter future. I'm not really sure how Jill and I had made that happen, but I felt relieved nonetheless, because it took a lot of pressure off me, as I was no longer solely responsible for Eli.

Since I hadn't slept the night before, I was feeling pretty tired, so I went up to our bedroom, lay down, and passed out.

When I woke up it was pitch-black, but I could feel a steady pulse of wind fluttering against my face, which is when I realized Darcy had returned for a visit and was flapping her wings to keep me cool as I slept. I couldn't see anything, so I tried to turn on the light, but nothing happened when I flicked the switch. So I called Darcy's name. She didn't answer. But the pulses of wind kept hitting me. I followed them to the corner of the room, where something grabbed me, and then all the air was slowly being crushed out of my lungs. And I could feel the soft tickle of feathers everywhere on my body.

"Darcy?" I said with the last breath I had left in me, but the feathers only squeezed me tighter, until I lost consciousness, which, ironically, is when I woke up.

The sun was streaming through my bedroom windows in a way that suggested it was late afternoon. I lay there for a long time trying to catch my breath, while the day's dust motes danced in the sunbeams. Then I began to wonder where Darce could be. The separation anxiety was more intense than anything I had ever experienced before. It fluttered heavily in my gut—like I'd somehow swallowed a crow and it was flapping its wings and trying to peck and rip its way out. Its trauma pumped poison through every vein in my body until I couldn't lift my arms or legs or head up off the mattress. I couldn't command a single muscle in my body until somewhere around sunset, when the antidote arrived in the form of Eli bursting through the front door down below and screaming with joy, "Mr. Goodgame! I have so much to tell you!"

With the dark magic broken, I sat straight up and yelled back, "Can't wait to hear! *Coming!*"

And then we were on the living room couch and Eli was showing me how Tony and he had sketched out every single scene of our movie in an oversized notepad. It was like looking at a massive cartoon strip, seeing the story unfold one frame at a time. Eli was talking a mile a minute and waving his hands and occasionally karate chopping the throw pillow that lives in the corner of the couch. And as he went on and on, I thought, *How could anyone not love this boy?*

"Mr. Goodgame, are you okay?" he said, which was when I realized that I had zoned out a little bit, so I smiled and nodded.

The boy smiled back and then resumed his monologue, which he repeated in its entirety when Jill arrived home with chicken parmesan over linguini for dinner. After washing and drying the dishes, the three of us threw the Frisbee around in the backyard before Eli decided to "chill out" in his tent while Jill and I swung side by side in Darcy's hammock, where I told Jill she'd officially be playing Sara.

"So Sandra turned you down?" she asked, which is when I told Jill that I had felt compelled as a human being to try to give Sandra the medicine our film was offering. But as an artist, I was relieved to now have such a smart, talented, and beautiful woman as Jill playing the mayor of Majestic. I could tell my friend was pleased because she immediately began scissor kicking the bottom halves of her legs over the side of the hammock.

When Jill started to yawn a half hour or so later, I told her I was also tired, which was when I retired to my bedroom and wrote you this letter.

In closing, I must inform you that your window for being in our movie has sadly and officially closed, as we begin shooting tomorrow and it would be unfair to take the role of Jungian analyst away from Isaiah at this point, being that he's already been fitted for his costume and has attended all of the table readings and meetings and all the rest. He's also always pulling me aside—away from The Survivors. In quiet alone places, he'll touch his forehead to mine, look me in the eyes, and say he's proud of me.

Then he'll slap my back really hard while yelling, "Thank you, Jesus, for men like Lucas Goodgame! *Ahhh-men!*" which always makes me laugh, because he sort of sings his amens in a way that lets you know he's truly as happy on the inside as he appears to be on the outside.

I feel pretty lucky to live in the town of Majestic among such kind people.

Your most loyal analysand,
Lucas

15.

Dear Karl,

I want to tell you about the first few extremely eventful days of our movie shoot, but before I get to those amusing anecdotes, I feel overwhelmingly called to share a dream I had. I suspect your analytic insight would really help my psyche stabilize.

Unfortunately, I have to admit that after the tragedy I stopped updating the dream diary you require me to keep. I mostly failed because I was forgoing sleep to be with winged Darcy and you can't dream wide-awake. My wife is still, unfortunately, MIA. And now I'm losing sleep worrying about her whereabouts. You can't find an angel who doesn't want to be found, so there is little I can do, right? I'm trying very hard to be patient, while remaining calm, trusting that Darcy's and my love will transcend all.

But back to my dream, which the unconscious gifted me the night before the first day of our monster movie shoot, right after I finished writing the last letter I sent to you.

In the dream, I'm in the third grade. We're taking a math quiz, and I'm worried because the answer to every problem is thirteen. I check my work over and over, but I always come up with thirteen, which seems terribly improbable. I wonder if I'm being tricked or if I received a different, personalized test designed to catch cheaters who might copy from my paper, because none of my fellow students seem alarmed. I begin sneaking peeks at my classmates' answers. I can't find a single thirteen written down anywhere else in the room, which makes me worry I'm failing the test.

"Lucas Goodgame!" my teacher, Mrs. Falana, yells. "Get your eyes off your classmates' work and bring your test up to me right this second."

The rest of the students begin taunting me in unison, like a Greek chorus, singing, "EwwwwwwWWWWWW!" as I trudge, test in hand—head hung in embarrassment—to the front of the room.

When I reach Mrs. Falana's desk, I extend my paper full of thirteens toward her, but when I look up, she's turned into a naked skeleton. You'd think my dream self would be terrified, but it's not. The skeleton says, "Report to Mrs. Case immediately."

Then I wake up.

You always ask what feelings are associated with the dream, so I'll list those here. I felt a deep sense of shame. I felt as though I was all alone. Maybe even like I had been given something I didn't want.

For context, I should probably tell you about what I think I remember happening to me in the third grade.

One fall day, right around Halloween, Mrs. Falana pulled me aside and said, "You're going to spend Friday mornings with Mrs. Case, down the hall."

I remember thinking I had done something wrong, or that I had flunked some sort of test and was, therefore, being sent to a remedial class.

That first Friday morning, as I walked the empty hallway toward Mrs. Case's room, I remembered the strange exam Mrs. Falana had given us a few weeks back. There were no spelling or math or geography or reading comprehension questions on this particular test. Instead there were just rows of strange pictures. We were asked to pick three images from the many columns and then explain why we had made those particular selections. I had never taken a quiz like that before. All of my classmates also found the experience quite odd. Stranger still, after discussing it at length in the lunchroom that day, all of us simply forgot about the bizarre test and no one ever spoke of it again.

When I entered the classroom at the end of the hall on that first morning with Mrs. Case—whom I'm not sure I had ever seen in the building before—I saw a woman with long black hair and pale skin. She was seated at a round table. I see Mrs. Case in my mind now wearing a dark green dress and many silver rings on her fingers. She also has a long silver chain hanging around her neck, at the end of which—right between her breasts—hangs a silver ball that reflects your warped image back at you, only upside down.

"Enter, Lucas," she said. "And take your rightful seat at the table."

"Am I in trouble?" I asked.

She laughed and said, "Quite the opposite."

"Then why am I here?"

When Mrs. Case said I had been added to the elementary school's Gifted & Talented program, I protested, saying, "I never get As. I'm not smart. This is a mistake."

"There are different types of intelligence," she said, and then spread out a deck of cards before me on the table. She asked if I knew what the cards were and—after I shrugged—she said, "These will help me understand you better. Take a look."

I remember thinking they looked medieval, although I wouldn't have known that word back then. But there were kings and queens and towers and magicians and angels and suns and moons. They looked a little like the Led Zeppelin album covers I'd seen in Dad's record collection.

Then Mrs. Case scooped up all the cards and thoroughly shuffled them before spreading them out facedown on the round table.

"Pick one," she said.

When I asked, "Which one?" she smiled knowingly and said, "That *is* the question, isn't it?"

I remember scanning the cards, feeling as though I had absolutely no idea what was going on. But then my skin started to tingle and, suddenly, the card closest to my left hand caught my attention. When I flipped it over, I saw a skeleton using a scythe for a walking stick. At his feet were two decapitated heads—a woman's on the left and a crowned man's on the right. At the bottom I read the number thirteen followed by the word "death" and a strange symbol.

"Is this bad?" I asked.

But Mrs. Case was smiling. "Nothing in this deck of cards is bad or good."

"What does it mean?" I asked.

"It means you have very good bones." She scooped up all the cards once more and put them into their box.

And I never saw her tarot deck again. In my memory now, I see myself seated in the classroom at the end of the hall, reading strange stories with Mrs. Case every Friday morning. Fairy tales, I guess you'd call them. She and I would take turns reading aloud to each other—about witches and trolls and princes and giants and sorcerers. After each story, she'd ask what it had meant to me and I'd do my best to answer honestly. I never knew if I was giving the right answers or not, but Mrs. Case said the point was to think about the stories and let them get into our bones, where they would stay for the rest of our lives and maybe even help us through the worst of times.

"How can a story help me?" I'd ask.

And she would always answer, "You'll see. A million times before you die, the answer will pass right before your very eyes."

There were two other students in Mrs. Falana's class who would leave once a week to spend time with Mrs. Case. I asked them what they did with the strange teacher at the end of the hall. Jason Bachman always scored highest on the math tests Mrs. Falana gave us and so, with Mrs.

Case, he did nothing but math problems. Carla Naso was our best speller and she studied the dictionary when she was in Mrs. Case's room. They asked me what I did and I said, "Reading comprehension," even though whatever I was doing with Mrs. Case didn't much resemble Mrs. Falana's reading comprehension tests, which I often failed.

"What card did you pick when she spread out that weird Led Zeppelin–looking deck?" I asked Jason and Carla.

But they just stared back at me blankly, before saying, "What are you talking about?"

I described the tarot deck in more detail, but they only shrugged and then looked at each other as if to say, *Lucas Goodgame is such a dweeb!*

I couldn't figure out why I had been selected to work with Mrs. Case, but I liked spending time with her, so I just sort of stopped asking questions.

I don't remember when I ceased seeing Mrs. Case once a week. I want to say our meetings continued all through elementary school, but the truth is I only remember the initial few times I was taken out of class and the few conversations I had with Jason and Carla before I realized that they were having radically different experiences. After that I stopped talking about Mrs. Case with anyone else at all and maybe my brain stopped recording memories regarding any of the above.

I broke the Sunday-only rule this past week and called my mother, who immediately launched into another of her monologues. It took me almost a half hour, but I was eventually able to interrupt her long enough to ask what Mom remembered of Mrs. Case. My mother laughed and said there was no Mrs. Case at the Majestic Elementary School.

"I'd certainly remember if you'd been pulled out of Mrs. Falana's class once a week for remedial instruction, because I'd have been thoroughly mortified," Mom said. *"I was the president of the PTA."*

I told Mom that Mrs. Case and I hadn't been doing remedial work, but when Mom asked what exactly this alleged Mrs. Case had taught me, I went silent. Part of me didn't really remember what I had experienced and another part of me felt like the teaching had been private—for my ears and eyes only. I began to worry I'd even lose what I remembered if I shared any of the above with the wrong type of person. And every bone in my body knew Mom was definitely the wrong type of person.

Karl, I remember you saying in one of our analytic sessions that the Death card was associated with spiritual rebirth and the Scorpio sign, under which I was born. It can represent the end of one thing but also the beginning of something new, which seems apropos, here at the start of our movie shoot, which I will tell you about in a second.

There's a part of me that isn't sure if the above is a memory of what really happened to me when I was a child or is something I dreamed up. I feel as though I would have told you about my time with Mrs. Case in analysis if it had really happened. And yet, it's in my memory now as I write to you. Regardless, why do you think I'm having these dreams and thoughts and imaginations? What do you make of this? I know you have studied tarot and Jewish mysticism.

There's no one else in my life with whom I feel comfortable having these sorts of conversations. Not even Jill or Isaiah. And it wouldn't be fair to Eli, who has enough of his own psychological baggage to process these days, not to mention the weight of his current creative project, which has quickly outgrown our wildest expectations.

Maybe you know this already, but you don't film a movie chronologically. You film it according to the schedules of the actors in each scene, making sure everyone is available. And sometimes you film according to weather, meaning you shoot outdoor scenes when mother nature is cooperating with the script and save the indoor scenes for when she has other plans. Eli and Tony ranked every scene in the film according to logistical difficulty and then aimed to film the trickiest ones first, thinking that if anything should go wrong, we could always move to an easier scene and bump the harder to the next day.

I didn't really understand any of the above until I started asking questions on day one, mostly because I was surprised to be shooting the last scenes of the film first. Eli explained that getting the entire Majestic police force and all of their cruisers involved was the biggest logistical nightmare. Then he pointed to the sky and said, "Weather's perfect for filming the car chases. We can't do those in the rain. And we have to get everything done between the morning and evening commuter traffic, because we need to block off the road. Also, we're grabbing the drone footage today."

"Drone footage?" I asked.

Which is when Eli explained that Mark and Tony had hired a drone cinematographer to capture the aerial shots. Then later on a rainy day or in the middle of the night they'd set up a green screen, maybe in the YMCA gym, suspend Eli in his monster costume from the ceiling, and film his flight scenes.

"When did we write in flight scenes?" I asked, which was when Eli explained that he and Tony had been tweaking the script while I had taken some time to get my head together, which made me feel like I wanted to step out of my body again, especially since Eli had said I needed to get my head together so matter-of-factly. When I thought back on the previous two or so weeks, I realized that I hadn't been spending as much time with the boy, but had let all of our new colleagues step up. I didn't know a whole heck of a lot about making movies, truth be told, and I tried to make myself feel better by thinking of it not so much as *stepping down*, but rather as *stepping out of the way*. Mark and Tony were great people. The boy was happier than I had ever seen him. So why did I feel so dark inside—and like maybe I was kind of disappearing a little bit?

Luckily, there wasn't much time to dwell on these bad feelings, because soon we were filming Bobby and all of the other police officers driving around Majestic slightly above the speed limit. Tony and Eli explained that they could speed up the film in postproduction to make it look like the cops were driving faster than they really were because Bobby said they couldn't break the speed limit if there wasn't a real emergency, which there wasn't. It was interesting to see Tony and Eli setting up cameras on the streets and inside the police cruisers and even filming from tree branches and the roofs of stores. We spent all morning shooting flashing cop car lights and wild hairpin turns and recording sirens and police talk. And all of the cops did a great job of acting, especially since Eli, obviously, wasn't literally up in the air flying around Majestic, so Bobby and his colleagues had to point at clouds and stare up at the blue sky with an intensity one reserves for the supernatural. They did such a good job I started to believe that the feathered monster might really be up there if I only tilted back my head and took a look for myself.

Eli kept giving the actors notes, saying things like, "This isn't something you see every day. It's a flying feathered man! You're terrified, but you're also intrigued. Like the cops at the end of *E.T.*"

It was heartening to see how everyone—even passersby in the street—respected the instructions Eli gave. Whenever the sound guys Mark and Tony had hired would get their microphones in position, Eli would say, "Quiet on the set," and then it was so silent I could hear my own heartbeat.

Next, we filmed my character—the monster's father figure—running through the woods with Eli in costume.

"Just fly away!" I yell at the monster as we slalom through the trees with cameramen and sound guys following us.

"My power of flight isn't strong enough to carry us both!" the monster yells back.

"I'm an old man. You have so much ahead of you. And there has to be a place for young men like you. Somewhere in the great big world. There must."

"I'll never leave you. *Never!*"

When we get to the stream, it isn't exactly the raging river called for in the script, but Eli had assured me they'd touch it up in postproduction to make it look impassable.

With our backs to the trickling brook that will look like a fearsome river in the final movie, the monster and his father figure face all eight members of the Majestic police force, who are pointing very real-looking fake guns at us.

Here Bobby says, "This is the end of the road for you two. The CIA said shoot to kill all human targets. But they'll want the monster for testing and experimentation. After which, they'll want to dissect the bird boy to advance science and prevent anyone else from spontaneously growing feathers, God forbid. Bullet holes might destroy important scientific information. *Got it, everyone?*"

"Hey, species traitor," Betty the cop says, while pointing her fake gun at my face. "Come on over here so we can make it look like suicide."

Just like the script called for, Eli's character says, "Nooooooo!" and begins running toward Betty, who reflexively takes aim at the monster and fires her pretend gun, only my character steps in front of the feathered boy, taking a bullet right in the chest. I actually dive through the air, spreading my arms and legs wide, which—in postproduction—Eli and Tony will depict in very hip slow motion. We cut here, so that the makeup-and-special-effects team Mark and Tony had hired could get me into the bloody bullet-pierced version of my costume and make me look like I'm about to die from a gunshot to the chest.

At our read throughs, several Survivors brought up the triggering effect of having a gunshot wound in our film, given all that we had experienced during the Majestic Theater tragedy. I had argued in favor of keeping the pivotal scene, saying, "How can we transcend something we won't even face in fiction?" I championed artistic freedom and the medicinal power of story. "Medicine tastes bad," I said, "but it heals!"

With my character all bloody in the grass by the riverbank, the police—with their fake guns still trained on the monster—begin to close in around us.

"Remember," Bobby yells, "the scientists need the monster alive for their experiments. Do not shoot to kill! And try not to shoot at all."

At this point the monster screams at the top of his lungs, tapping into a deep reservoir of strength and talents he didn't even know he had, and thrusts his hands out in front of him, which sends the cops flying backward into the trees.

Our special-effects team had put camouflaged ropes around the waists of the cops. Teams of people yanked on these ropes, sending the cops flying back onto mattresses hidden under piles of forest debris.

Then the monster lifts me to my feet and says, "Hold on, Father. I'm going to get you help."

"But you aren't strong enough to fly with me in your arms," my character says.

"I am now," he answers.

Then Eli and I both jump into the air, but the rest of our flight will be recorded later in front of a green screen.

The monster flies my character all the way to Mayor Sara's house, which in real life is Mark and Tony's house. As I mentioned before, Jill plays the mayor, who is horrified to learn that the CIA has illegally coopted our local police force. She quickly secures medical treatment for my character, who almost dies on the operating table, but is ultimately saved by the trauma surgeon who is expertly played by Survivor Julia Wilco. Eli says—in postproduction—we'll insert some stock footage of

WE ARE THE LIGHT

open chest surgery, cutting from "the glistening internal organs" to my sleeping face with oxygen tubes up my nostrils.

The next day, we filmed the remaining hospital scenes, in which Isaiah and I have our big emotional post-operation bedside scene. He plays your role, my Jungian analyst—Carl with a *C*—who, when I wake up from surgery, says, "I really thought we were going to lose you," before going on to say he's proud of me "for making friends with the shadowy monsters of the world," because, "like Jung says, 'There's gold in our shadows.'" When you see the film, you will immediately spot all the Jungian references peppered throughout. I hope it makes you smile proudly.

That aforementioned scene where the monster and my character receive medals from Jill's mayor character, Sara—kind of like the end of *Star Wars*—was in the bag by day three of filming, which happened a few days ago. Today was actually the sixth day of shooting already.

With the notable exceptions of you and Sandra, all of The Survivors—regardless of whether they are in the day's scenes or not—have been hanging around our movie set, encouraging whomever is acting that scene and also helping with the setup and breakdown of each set, as well as all the other lighting and sound and wardrobe and camera requirements. People are even using their work vacation days to be there.

It's funny because winged Darcy was the one who pointed me in this direction, saying, "The boy is the way forward," so many times, but I haven't seen her flying in the sky even once during filming. I'm making this film for her, which it will say right at the beginning: Dedicated to Darcy Goodgame. There will also be an in-memoriam section listing the names of all eighteen people who were killed at the Majestic Theater, including Jacob Hansen. I got a lot of pushback for wanting to include Jacob's name, but when I threatened to shut down the entire production and then started screaming again in the library conference room—even knocking over the podium at one point—The Survivors acquiesced. And maybe it was good that Sandra Coyle had decided not to participate in the film, because there's no way I could have gotten Jacob's name on the in-memoriam list if Sandra had a voice.

Everything for a reason, maybe.

Eli has been living with Mark and Tony lately, because that's where all the editing equipment is located and the boy wants total control over the final cut, which I understand. I asked Eli if my not being involved with the editing was okay, saying starring in the film was maybe as much as I could handle these days. He immediately agreed to take over my end of all that, saying, "Tony's been incredible. I'm learning so much. I can't even believe it."

Before I came inside to write you this letter, Jill and I were swinging in Darcy's hammock for an hour or so. We were mostly silent for our hammock ride, since we had both put in a long day of moviemaking. But toward the end, Jill said, "Lucas?" and when I said, "Yes?" she said, "Are you okay? Because you've seemed a little off lately." She didn't say it in a mean way, but in a loving, concerned way, which was more like, *What can I do for you? How can I help?*

But I couldn't think of anything that Jill could possibly do for me. She didn't have the ability to find angels. And I don't think she would have wanted to speak to me about my strange dreams. I know she would have listened. Jill would listen to anything I ever wanted to tell her. But I wasn't sure she had the ability to hear what I needed to say. I didn't think she would be able to understand. And there is perhaps no greater pain than the suffering that comes from speaking plainly but failing to make any sort of meaningful connection with the people who care about you.

So instead of answering Jill, I took her hand in mine and held it as the last swipes of red and orange sunk below the western horizon.

"You've been very convincing as the monster's father figure," Jill said. "Especially when you got shot."

So I told her no one had ever played a mayor better than she had, even though she still had a few scenes left to shoot.

"Don't make fun of me," she said.

"I'm not," I said, and then sat up a little in the hammock so that I could assess her facial expression.

When she bit her lip and lightly poked my ribs with her index finger, I realized she was just teasing me, so I smiled, relaxed my body, laced my fingers together behind my head, and then searched for the night sky's first star.

"I'm not going anywhere," Jill said. "I'm going to see this through. All the way. No matter where it takes us."

I wasn't exactly sure what she meant by "No matter where it takes us"— which seemed kind of dark—but it felt good to have her there next to me in the hammock and so, when she leaned her shoulder into mine, I didn't move away. We stayed in that position until a few stars popped through the sky above and winked at us all at once, rather than one at a time.

When I said I was tired, Jill nodded, and then we were inside climbing the stairs to our bedrooms. I wondered what had happened to Jill's house. Was anyone living there now that she'd moved into ours? Not knowing the answer to that question kind of frightened me, but I put it aside and began writing you this letter, which has calmed me considerably.

I really think I could benefit from a session.

If you're embarrassed by your initial need to take a break from analyzing analysands, you should know that I would never shame you for needing a sabbatical. I'd only be so grateful for your return. We don't even have to mention your hiatus, but could simply pick back up where we left off and never speak about our pause again.

I'm worried that I was only using Eli and the film as a sort of distraction from the darkness that might be chasing all the light out of me. I'm starting to really worry about myself, Karl.

To be one hundred percent honest, whenever I stop thinking about Eli and the film, I get so terrified I can hardly breathe. You're the only one who knows this about me. I'm trusting you. I forgive you for needing a break from my neuroses, but please don't let me down now. You're kind of my only hope.

Thanking you in advance.

Your most loyal analysand,
Lucas

16.

Dear Karl,

Sorry I haven't written in a long time. I haven't been feeling well. Finishing Eli's monster movie took all the remaining strength I had. It's only now—weeks after we wrapped the shooting—that I find myself able to sit down and compose another letter for you.

Eli and Tony had been editing everything as we went along, the whole time we were filming. The movie is officially in postproduction now, and—for reasons not entirely clear to me—there's suddenly an extra big push to have the premiere before summer officially ends. As a result, the orange tent in my backyard no longer lights up when the sun goes down. Eli lives with Tony and Mark seven nights a week. Jill and I hardly see him at all anymore.

I don't know why but I've been humming "Puff, the Magic Dragon" in my head over and over again, and I can't stop no matter how hard I try. My father had that Peter, Paul and Mary record and used to play it when I was little. The song always made me so sad. It still does. But at the same time, I also love "Puff, the Magic Dragon." I thought maybe winged Darcy would be Puff and I'd be Jackie Paper, the boy who befriends the noble dragon. But then I realized that I was Puff and Eli was Jackie Paper, because, lately—ever since Eli's disappeared from my life—it's felt like I've slipped into a psychological cave of sorts. I definitely don't frolic so much anymore. I find it hard to be brave. And, these days, I don't really have a cherry lane to play along.

Whenever my father put on his Peter, Paul and Mary album and the aforementioned song started playing, I'd wonder if I'd ever find my Puff. Oh, how I yearned for a magic dragon to be my best friend—to the point where I'd tear up whenever I heard the lyrics, maybe because I was so lonely all the time.

It's okay that Eli is with Tony now.

Jill's still here with me.

To be honest, I've lost the ability to match Eli's excitement about our creative project. I haven't been able to summon that other stronger, more confident Lucas to cover for me. And I'm pretty sure winged Darcy has flown up into the white light without even saying goodbye. I don't blame her. I mean, the sixteen other victims couldn't resist for a single moment, let alone the months that Darcy made it through, just to make sure I was okay.

I don't know if I ever told you this before, but every night, just before we'd fall asleep, in the safe darkness of our bedroom, Darcy and I would talk about the things we were grateful for. Our cat, Justin, would often be curled up between our heads, purring out his gratitude as well. Darcy was always grateful for her students, saying they gave her purpose and hope for the future. She was a speech therapist, so she helped kids get their tongues and lips around slippery vowels and hard consonants. She'd talk about these little guys and girls all the time, and with so much enthusiasm that you couldn't help falling in love with my wife. I've often wondered who is helping Darcy's students now and whether he or she loves those kids with as much generosity as my wife had. I've thought about going to Majestic Elementary just to let the new speech therapist know how important the job is, but I've only ever made it to the elementary school's parking lot. It's like someone's put a force field around all the schools in Majestic—a force field that keeps me out.

Lying in bed at night, during our gratitude sessions, I'd tell Darce I was grateful for my students too, because it felt good to help them through their problems, just like I was grateful for the chance to help Eli when no one in this town was paying him any attention.

Darcy always said she was grateful for her empathetic husband and I always told her I was thankful for my kind and wise wife.

We'd both list things like food and shelter, and the names of our friends, and the ability to take long walks, and living in a safe and loving community, and the medicine that Darcy needed for her diabetes, and the contact lenses that gave me the ability to see. And we always said your name, Karl, because you were helping me so much with my mother and father complexes and my childhood wounds. Your healing me, of course, benefited Darcy as much as it benefited yours truly. You were initiating me into the world of men because my father didn't know how to do that. And so, shortly after we started working together, Darcy began saying your name every night when we made our gratitude list there in the dark, with Justin the cat purring between our heads.

As I sit here writing you this letter, Jill's in the next room. Only six inches of wall separate my wife's best friend from me. Maybe two inch-thick pieces of drywall sandwiching some insulation. I could punch my way through with my bare hands. And yet I feel so painfully alone, which I realize is ungrateful, especially considering how many people in Majestic have rallied around Eli's monster movie.

Before we started shooting, Tony gave us a warning, saying, "The first few minutes you're on a movie set are very exciting. The following weeks will bore you to tears." I didn't understand how that could be possible, but once I experienced how long it took to set up even a thirty-second shoot—blocking and lighting the scene, getting the sound guys in place, deciding on camera angles, making sure actors are dressed correctly and are wearing the proper makeup; and then shooting the same scene over and over, saying the same lines a million times in a row—I began to understand that making movies was a lot of hard work and not at all as glamorous as you'd imagine it to be.

A funny thing began to happen too. Everyone was cooperative and kept a good attitude and seemed happy to have something to take their minds off the tragedy that we were all still mourning. And so this intense sort of bonding kept breaking out everywhere on set. People hugging, laughing, even singing and dancing. It was like we had all become children again and were eager to please some unseen version of our parents, if that makes any sense. We were all being good boys and girls, taking instructions and directions from Eli and Tony with good cheer in our hearts. And Jesus Gomez even had these white T-shirts made with the words "Reclaiming the Majestic Theater" written in gold across the chest. Everyone wore them whenever they weren't in an actual scene, which required wearing the appropriate costume from Arlene and River's Wardrobe Mobile, which dutifully followed us around Majestic as we filmed. And even people who hadn't been in the Majestic Theater on the night of the tragedy came out and watched us respectfully and curiously. Some began offering to help, while others gave Tony and Mark cash donations to offset the growing cost of the film.

But the more people started showing up for Eli, the more the town began to heal, the lonelier I began to feel, and then it was like I was really disappearing again. I started avoiding mirrors because I was afraid I would no longer be able to see my reflection. Thankfully, everyone was so busy with the shoot that they didn't notice my withdrawal. The only one who said anything about this was Jill, who started asking me questions every night on Darcy's hammock. Somehow it became our nightly ritual to swing out there, shoulder to shoulder.

"Are you really okay, Lucas?" Jill would say.

"Yep," I'd say.

Then she'd grab my hand and squeeze it, as if to say, *I know you're lying, but that's okay, because I got you.*

But it wouldn't make me feel any less alone.

Jill put her kitchen assistant, Randy, in charge of supervising all the cooks for the film crew. So many people from Majestic volunteered to help shop and cook and serve food that Jill was able to make me her number one priority, especially since the Cup Of Spoons had closed for the duration of our creative endeavor.

"Jill will see you through," Isaiah would say to me whenever he caught me hiding in the shadows of the sprawling movie production. Then Isaiah would slap my cheek lightly and add, "That woman's got you, my friend. And God's got you."

But Isaiah's praying and Jill's handholds on the hammock didn't do much for me. I know that sounds ungrateful and ugly, but it's the truth.

It's funny, because lately I've been thinking a lot about my dad and this one spring when he volunteered to coach my Little League baseball team. We had pine-green uniforms and hats and were called the Centaurs, which, now that I think of it, is a strange name for a baseball team, although I don't think my dad chose the name. The other teams had regular names like the Lions, the Bears, the Tigers, but we were the half-man-half-horse team for some reason.

I wasn't a very good baseball player and my father had never really seemed all that interested in the sport, so I was surprised when he told me he would be my coach. The first thing he did was take me to a sporting goods store to pick out a bat and a glove.

"Choose wisely, because you need to look the part," I remember him saying.

I didn't know which specific glove and bat would make me look like a baseball player. Wouldn't any and every glove or bat do that? I remember feeling extremely nervous as I looked at the great walls of baseball equipment in what used to be Majestic Sports but is now a Starbucks. A black glove with gold letters caught my eye, so I pointed to it, but my dad frowned and said, "Baseball gloves should be brown, Son. Only a show-off wears a black glove." Dad plucked a brown glove off the wall and handed it to me. "See if it fits," he said. It was tight and hurt my hand, but when he said, "Fits like a glove," I did not protest.

We repeated the scene above, only standing in front of the wall of bats this time. I guessed that a metal bat would send the ball farther away from home plate, which was technically true, but Dad said, "Real men use wooden bats," before picking out the one he wanted me to use, which was too heavy for me to swing properly. "After a week or so of push-ups, it'll be fine," Dad said.

That afternoon Dad and I tried to have a catch in the front yard. He had an old first baseman's mitt from back in the day when he played for Majestic High. I remember being surprised when I saw his well-worn glove, because we had never before had a catch. For some reason, I got really nervous and every inch of my skin began to tingle unmercifully. Plus, the new glove was killing my left hand, squeezing all the blood out of my fingers, which I had jammed into the small holes.

I had no problem throwing the ball to the other boys in my grade. I could hit their gloves pretty much every time, but when it came to my dad, no matter how hard I concentrated, the ball always sailed over his head. He tried to jump up and catch it, but I'd accidentally throw it so high, he had no chance. When he'd land, he'd scream, "What's wrong with you, Lucas? I'm not getting that. *Go!*" With my heart pounding, I'd run through the neighbor's front yard and into the street to retrieve the ball and on my way back, Dad would say, "Just because you have my last name doesn't mean I'm going to play you. You have to earn your position on the team. And you're off to a terrible start."

I remember thinking if I could only hit my dad's glove consistently, I'd never wish for anything again as long as I lived. I had never wanted anything as much as I wanted to make the baseball travel directly from my hand to the webbing of my dad's first baseman's mitt. But every time I tried, the ball left my fingers early and flew twenty or so feet over Dad's head.

"Lucas!" Dad screamed after the fourth or fifth time. "I'm done!"

Dad stormed into the house and wouldn't make eye contact with me for a week.

When the season started, I noticed that Dad was much more patient with my teammates, who actually seemed to like my father. He was nice to all of their parents too. And he never yelled at me in front of any of the people involved with Majestic Little League. Dad didn't encourage me as much as he encouraged the other kids, but I didn't mind. Not being yelled at was nice enough. It was always better when Dad's attention was focused on other things.

Dad played me in left field, because almost everyone on the other teams batted right-handed and no one could pull the ball to the opposite field, and so the action never came to me, which was wonderful. I could stand out there in left field and sort of disappear. And in the dugout, Dad would make everyone stand and clap and cheer on whomever was batting, so I could hide behind all of that noise too. The only time people really saw me was after everyone else had batted and the ninth hitter was called to the plate. I always batted last because I almost always struck out. Everyone in the dugout would clap and cheer me on, but my dad never said a word until we were in the car driving home, at which point he'd lecture me in a yelling voice about my "potential as a baseball player" and "wasting opportunities" and "grabbing life by the throat." He'd say he was only trying to inspire me right after he'd told me I was embarrassing him.

I remember sort of retreating inside of myself that baseball season, and when we won the championship game and Mr. Minetti sprayed Dad with champagne and all my teammates were throwing their hats and gloves in the air, I started to worry that there was something very wrong with me. Dad later said winning the Little League playoffs was one of the greatest moments of his life. And many of my teammates wrote him heartfelt thank-you letters with pictures of them in their Centaur uniforms enclosed, all of which Dad hung up in his study, where they remained until he left Mom and me during my freshman year of college. I don't know if Mom threw those pictures away or Dad took them with him, but if I had to bet, I'd say the latter.

During the movie shoot, no one treated me like my father had during the one season he coached my baseball team. No one yelled at me. No one shamed me. I had a starring role in the film, so no one had put me in metaphorical left field or had metaphorically batted me ninth. But I just couldn't cheer as loud as my teammates at the end of each scene or when we wrapped. And I never felt like I was truly part of the team. Perhaps I put myself outside the circle, because I was definitely all alone in left field again, dreading the moment when they'd call me to the plate to strike out, even though Eli and Tony were always so happy with my acting. At one point Ernie Baum literally said, "Lucas, you just knocked that scene out of the park. *Home run!*"

We were winning the championship again, and although I was on the team, I wasn't worthy of the celebration somehow. I didn't want to be disappearing. More than anything in the world I wanted to connect with my fellow castmates, my neighbors, the people in my life, but everything was suddenly quicksand and I couldn't manage to grab hold of any sort of lifesaving vine. And maybe no one else realized I was rapidly disappearing into the suffocating unknown below.

This is turning into a bummer of a letter and I feel like maybe I should apologize for that. If Darcy and Justin the cat were here tonight, I'm sure they'd find many things to be grateful for. Justin would purr and Darcy would remind me of all I have, how lucky I am to have so many friends and neighbors willing to make a feature-length monster movie with me. So many people who want to help us reclaim the Majestic Theater for the forces of good, uniting everyone through a shared sense of humanity and purpose.

There's something else I need to say and it's hard.

I'm kind of shocked that you haven't answered a single one of my letters. I've put off saying anything about this for a long time. I thought maybe I didn't want to hurt your feelings or put unfair expectations on you. But lately I'm beginning to wonder if I'm not mad at you.

Sometimes I think it cruel, what you did. Getting me to open up and really trust you. I showed you so much of what I had previously kept hidden from everyone, even Darcy, and then in my greatest time of need you send me a cold, heartless letter that ended my analysis without giving me any chance for closure. I realize that your wife was murdered, but so was mine. And all of the other Survivors showed up for me and each other in a pretty big way, which makes me wonder if all the Jungian stuff was as powerful as you claimed it is.

I remember you telling me that you had your own wounds, your own demons. That every healer is a wounded person first. And that the goal was to manage the pain, make it meaningful enough to carry on in a way that might be beneficial to others, which in turn helps to heal the self. "To make suffering meaningful," you had said so confidently. I really believed you. Bought in. And everything I've written to you in these letters demonstrates that clearly, I'd say.

So what's your excuse?

Why haven't you responded even once?

Why did you abandon me?

I'm afraid the darkness inside is winning.

A response—even a few words—would do so much to help me hold on. And maybe if I can hold on for a little longer, the light will make a comeback?

I thought making the movie with Eli would fix all of this, but apparently it didn't.

I don't know what else to do.

I'm scared.

And I feel all alone.

Please help me.

Your most loyal analysand,
Lucas

17.

Dear Karl,

Jill's rented me a tuxedo for the premiere of our monster movie. Apparently, she's purchased a fancy dress and matching shoes, but I'm not permitted to see those until the big night, which—like the ads plastering every inch of town say—is this upcoming weekend. Jill's also put up a sign in the Cup Of Spoons' front window saying the restaurant will be closed the day of the premiere and the day after because of the big catered after-party at Mark and Tony's. Jill thinks that will keep us out too late for her to get up in time to open for breakfast. She's even scheduled a pre-premiere hair-and-makeup appointment, which seems a bit extreme to me, even though we're going to arrive by limousine—donated free of charge by Michael's Limos—walk a red carpet, have our photo professionally taken in front of our official movie posters, and maybe be interviewed by movie-industry reporters and local TV-news personalities.

Mark keeps saying he's used his contacts to get "our narrative" onto the radar of "people who matter," and therefore, our movie premiere is going to be "a very big deal." I have a hard time imagining all that, but then again, the media came after the tragedy and didn't stop bothering me for many months. Mark insists I will not be asked any "inappropriate questions" and even got one of his movie promoter contacts to agree to "handle" me the night of, which I gather means that this person will make sure no reporters try to make me look bad or bring up topics that might take me to a dark place.

Mark says that Eli will also have a handler to protect him from the press. I think all of The Survivors will have handlers, which probably makes everyone feel okay about the whole red-carpet deal, but I don't know for sure because I haven't been talking to too many people lately.

We still don't see Eli as much as we used to, but he's dropped by for a few dinners with Jill and me and we sometimes go to Tony and Mark's, where the boy now lives full-time. Everyone keeps saying how proud I'm going to be when I see the final product. Mark and Tony offered to screen it for me early, but I decided I wanted to experience it for the first time with the other Survivors and the rest of Majestic. Go full circle—reclaiming the Majestic Theater, like Jesus Gomez's T-shirts suggest—in unison with everyone who was there that night.

We've sold out the Majestic's Grand Viewing Room—which is massive—even though Mark and Tony listed floor tickets at $250 a pop and balcony seats at $150. All of the proceeds will be donated to a national charity that helps the victims of gun violence. We all voted on which one we thought was the best and it was nice that the vote was unanimous because it meant that no one felt bad about where the cash was going. The Survivors got tickets for free, of course, and I've enclosed your pair within this envelope.

When I attempted to drop off Sandra Coyle's tickets, her assistant, Willow, wouldn't invite me inside. She was nice enough and even somewhat apologetic as she said, "Sandra says your clock expired," whatever that means.

When I explained I only wanted to give her boss complimentary tickets, Willow said, "I can't accept them on Sandra's behalf."

After some quick thinking, I asked if Willow could accept the tickets on her own behalf, which made her puff out her cheeks for a second before she said, "I like you, Lucas. I like what you're trying to do. I like how nice you're being to Sandra. But she's my boss."

Finally, I extended my hand like I wanted to shake hers in defeat. But when she reached out, I pressed the envelope into her palm and then darted away before she could give the tickets back. As I was shutting the iron gate, I glanced back and the young woman was covering her mouth with her free hand and clutching the tickets to her chest with the other, which made me think I'd won her over a little.

Who knows?

Maybe she and Sandra will show up at the premiere out of curiosity or FOMO, as my students used to say. (Fear of Missing Out.) I think attending the premiere would be good for Sandra Coyle's soul. I'm pretty sure her deceased husband, Greg, would agree.

Fellow Survivor Tracy Farrow organized meetings with a behavioral psychologist who volunteered to help all of us prepare to reenter the Majestic Theater, aka the scene of the trauma. Everyone met at the library again. I went to the first session, thinking it might help, but it was pretty much cognitive behavior therapy, which I know you look down on because it treats the symptom without really getting at the root problem. You'll be pleased to know I left halfway through the meeting and didn't go back, even though the rather kind psychologist had volunteered her time and therefore it didn't cost The Survivors any money to attend. They've been meeting every night and will continue to do so until the premiere. Some of The Survivors tried to talk me into rejoining their therapy group, but I kept declining politely until they stopped asking.

Jill was upset when I told her I wasn't going back. She kept insisting that reentering the Majestic Theater for the first time since last December could be psychologically difficult, but Jill has never been exposed to Jungian analysis, and therefore doesn't know that it is superior to all other forms of psychological treatment.

At one point, during what seemed like our first real argument, Jill said, "If Jungian analysis is so healing, where has Karl been?"

I didn't have a good retort in the moment, but after reflecting a bit, I've told myself that you will reengage at the appropriate time and that maybe your sudden withdrawal was even part of my treatment. I mean, it forced me to write all these letters, which have definitely been therapeutic and medicinal. The town of Majestic probably wouldn't even be having a movie premiere if you had simply resumed my analysis after the tragedy. Sandra would have gotten her way and The Survivors would be obediently working on a political campaign instead of happily and therapeutically making art.

I have to admit that I didn't understand your genius at first, but I see it today. So, mission accomplished. You can come out of hiding and attend the premiere now that I've learned what you were trying to teach me.

Just now, in the middle of writing this letter, someone banged on my front door. When I went downstairs and answered, I was surprised to see Tony, because it was close to ten at night and Jill was already asleep, or at least she didn't come out to see who was knocking, which she most likely would have done if she were still awake. Because he had walked in the rain, Tony was soaked to the bone, so I invited him in and gave him a few towels from the powder room. When we sat down on the couch, I noticed that his eyes were red, which seemed to indicate that he had been crying.

I asked what was wrong, but in a nice way, leaning in toward him, using all my natural listening skills that I have often employed with troubled teens. Tony resumed crying right there on my couch, so I reached out and patted his shoulder, meaning, *It's okay; I'm here.* That released a great river of words, which rushed forth fast and furiously.

He talked about how he and Mark had considered selling the Majestic Theater after the tragedy and had even begun negotiations with a local dramatist who wanted to convert the historic movie hall into a playhouse for live performances.

"There were serious money discussions," Tony said. "But then you guys hit us with your crazy monster movie idea. And, well . . ."

He went on to say that the tragedy had initially put a strain on his relationship with Mark, because Tony was angry and wanted to leave Majestic, PA, altogether. Tony took the shooting as a sign that people were evil at heart. And that maybe it was best to leave the suburbs, where there were "so many angry young white men." Mark saw the moment as an opportunity to prove that a historic movie theater could make a difference in a community, being what you Jungians call medicinal, although Tony didn't use that exact word.

"Our disagreement was an additional, smaller crisis because we had such different responses to the tragedy. I wanted to cash in and he wanted to double down . . ." Tony trailed off here for a moment. I felt compelled to acknowledge what he'd said so far with a reassuring nod, which seemed to help him continue. He went on to say, "But then you brought us Eli. I was suspicious at first because he was Jacob's brother. But somehow you convinced everyone. You did that, Lucas. And working closely with Eli these past few months . . . he's such a remarkably good kid. It's like he's the polar opposite of . . ."

Tony started coughing a lot here and the tears were flowing hard enough to darken the collar of his jade-green polo shirt even more than the rain had.

Something deep within me activated, and before I knew it, my arms were around Tony and he was crying into my shoulder while I held his back.

That's when I noticed Jill watching from halfway down the staircase. I got the sense that she had been there for a while and, therefore, had heard much of what Tony had said. But as soon as Jill and I locked eyes, she turned back upstairs and disappeared into her room. I know because I heard the guest bedroom door close behind her.

Tony must have heard her too. He pulled away from me and began wiping his eyes with the backs of his wrists as he said, "I'm sorry, Lucas. I shouldn't be here. I mean, if anything, I should be comforting you. I just felt . . . well, I felt *compelled*. I know that sounds ridiculous. Just to . . . to thank you."

Then he stood up and walked out the front door and back into the rain, which had gotten worse rather than better.

I just sat there on the couch thinking about the last conversation I'd had with Eli, which happened a day or two previously when he came to officially take down his tent. As I helped him stuff everything into the storage bag, he talked about how Mark and Tony were using their contacts and our movie to try to get Eli late admittance into an undergrad college with a filmmaking track.

Apparently, Isaiah had already signed off on Eli's graduation, even though I hadn't yet submitted an evaluation for Eli's senior project. Eli told me that Isaiah had taken it upon himself to get all that done, which is when I realized I had begun to shirk my responsibilities as an educator. I wondered when that had started, but couldn't deny that I was no longer keeping Eli's best interests first in my mind. The boy didn't seem mad or resentful—instead, he seemed sad and kind of worried about me, although he didn't directly express the sentiment.

After we had Eli all packed up and ready to go, he looked at his flip-flops and said, "You did so much for me, Mr. Goodgame. It's amazing. All that we made happen. But I've started to think that maybe you did all this monster movie stuff for me instead of doing whatever it was that you needed to do for yourself."

I remember the sun was hitting my eyes with an intensity that made me blink repetitively.

"I'm really sorry about your wife," Eli continued. "But I think you might need more help than I can give you. I'm only eighteen."

He swallowed hard and when I finally looked into his eyes, he threw both of his arms around my neck and pulled me close. After a second, I hugged him back. Then he held me for a long time like that, just sort of rocking me back and forth from left to right and right to left and back again.

"I'm really sorry about your brother," I said, which made him push his face into my chest the way that Tony would just a few days later—what I described above. Eli and I stood like that for a few minutes before he let go and then walked away without looking back at me or offering any more words. I haven't seen Eli since and have confirmed in my mind once and for all that I am indeed Puff, the Magic Dragon, and Eli is Jackie Paper.

Calling me the best public speaker in town, Mark asked me to make a speech at the premiere—right before the red curtains part and the movie begins. I'm really hoping that the strong, eloquent version of me will resurrect himself at least one more time. I think being back inside the Majestic will make Other Lucas rally. There will be so many people there who will need him to inspire them toward healing and general well-being.

I also have this fantasy about winged Darcy showing up to support me. Even if she has already flown up into the great white light, maybe she can return to earth one last time. Angels probably need closure too. Maybe all of The Survivors' winged loved ones will be in the air between the Majestic Theater's red seats and the Grand Viewing Room's ceiling, which is wonderfully painted to look like the sky—fluffy white clouds set against a sea of robin's-egg blue and even a sun. It's quite breathtaking. Darcy and I used to go to the movies early just to look up at the beautiful artwork. Regardless, they never play pre-movie ads at the Majestic Theater and only screen one or two previews before the feature starts. Mark and Tony always pipe in opera music, which never fails to make Darcy and me feel like we are in a different, more ancient world whenever we sit in the red seats with our heads tilted back and look up at the artwork.

"Majestic's answer to Michelangelo," Darcy used to say.

During our last night together, just before the movie began, I remember holding my wife's hand and staring up at the Grand Viewing Room's ceiling, only instead of opera, it was Christmas music playing. When I think about it now, I hear Ella Fitzgerald singing her version of "Angels We Have Heard on High." Darcy always loved the First Lady of Song. I remember my wife's warm lips lightly touching my cheek. In my memory now I smell peppermint, because that was the flavor of lip gloss Darce was wearing when she was transformed into an angel.

During our nightly swings on Darcy's hammock, Jill keeps saying I don't have to attend the premiere if I don't want to. Even though—like I said before—she already bought a dress and rented me a tuxedo.

"We could go away. Book a place somewhere. Disappear for a bit," she'll say, and there's a part of me that wants to do exactly that, even though I realize I owe it to everyone to rise to the occasion and lead the charge to reclaim the Majestic Theater.

"I have to make a speech," I say to Jill.

"No you don't," Jill says. "Especially if you're not ready."

"Ready for what exactly?" I'll say, and that always makes Jill go silent.

What do you think, Karl?

Am I ready?

When I get really honest with myself and drop down deep within—this often happens when I meditate or try to go back into my dreams and continue them, like you taught me—I hear a very soft noise that I can't identify. Sometimes it sounds like wind rushing through trees, only it's far away. When I concentrate and try to listen harder, the sound will rise up and get closer, until I'll begin to make out what exactly it is that I'm hearing. I'll get closer and closer to mentally placing the sound, but just before I do, some defensive part deep inside hauls off and kicks me in the metaphorical psychological nose, bringing me right back to the everyday humdrum, where I can no longer hear anything within me at all.

And I can't shake the feeling that I'm going to finally hear whatever this noise within me is when I walk into the Majestic Theater's Grand Viewing Room and sit down next to the black sash that will mark the last seat in which the human version of my wife ever rested. I've been told that Mark and Tony replaced the upholstery of every chair in the theater, so there is no possibility of anyone being retraumatized by bloodstains or anything like that. But when I try to visualize reentering that space, every centimeter of my skin begins to tingle and every cell in my body starts vibrating. Then I'll start worrying about hearing that mysterious noise locked deep within me.

When I'm being honest with myself, I kind of know that the hidden sound—whatever it may be—is powerful enough to kill me dead, only I don't think I'll grow wings and turn into an angel and fly up toward the white light. It's more likely that the earth will begin to quake and the ground below my feet will open up and I'll fall down into the glow of lava and magma and smoke and a hell that I've never been able to imagine before.

There's a part of me that's hoping for that, again, if I'm being honest, and why not at this point? There's a part of me that feels we deserve some sort of eternal punishment.

Is that strange?

Or is that just part of the human condition, Karl?

What would Jung say?

Maybe Other Lucas really will show up again and win the day?

Wouldn't that be nice.

I'd like you to be there if Other Lucas makes an appearance, but I wouldn't want you to see me fall deep into damnation.

I feel like there are things that I haven't been able to tell you in these letters. I've wanted to tell you. I just don't remember everything. There. I've told you part of it. That's a first step. But how can I tell you more, since I can't exactly remember what happened?

I have nightmares now.

Jill rushes in to wake me up whenever I start screaming in the middle of the night, but I can never remember what I was dreaming about, no matter how hard I try.

I kind of feel like this might be my last letter to you, Karl. Especially if you don't attend our monster movie premiere. If you haven't noticed, I've written you one letter for every person killed at the Majestic Theater last December—except for Jacob Hansen. This is the seventeenth letter. I had planned on writing eighteen, but I don't believe I'll have the time or emotional energy to accomplish that before our big night. And I also don't really think you're going to attend our premiere. Or maybe it's more accurate to say, *I'm not allowing myself high hopes.*

If my letters were the least bit worthy, you would have written me back by now, right?

Enclosed with the tickets is a photo of your wife's name as it appears in the in-memoriam section of our monster movie. I had Tony take it. You'll see I made sure they spelled it correctly—L E A N D R A J O H N S O N—which is the least I could do for my favorite Jungian analyst.

In closing, I want to say that no matter what happens at the premiere—or to me afterward—you've really helped me. I looked forward to our Friday-night analysis sessions more than you probably ever realized. They made me a better educator, friend, son, and husband.

I often didn't see my progress. And I'd even sometimes say things like, "Am I being taken for a ride, Darce? I don't know. Is it worth all the money we're paying?"

My wife used to look me dead in the eyes and say, "Since you started analysis, you're so much lighter, so much more fun to be around. It's like you're a completely different person. Not that I didn't love the old you. But it's nice to see you finally enjoying your life for a change."

And I really was starting to enjoy my life—maybe for the first time.

That's quite a fact.

Just in case I never talk to you again, please know that you helped me. Even after you stopped allowing me direct access to your medicine, you still kept helping. Just the idea of you helps. Writing these words here tonight helps. I definitely wouldn't have made it this far without you.

So thank you, thank you, thank you.

You're a wonderful man, Karl Johnson.

Your most loyal analysand,

Lucas

THREE

YEARS

AND

EIGHT

MONTHS

LATER

18.

Dear Karl,

It's been quite some time.

Buckle up, because this will most likely be an extremely long letter written over multiple sittings.

It will also be the last batch of words I ever compose for you.

When I sign off again, it will be forever, although I will, of course, continue to honor our very important relationship in other less immediate ways.

I suppose we should begin by acknowledging the two massive purple elephants here with us in the metaphorical room—or whatever you want to name this container I've somehow created. I honestly have no idea what to call it. A trove of love letters? A diary? A painfully slow confession? The ramblings of a grieving madman? All I know is that writing you buoyed me through an incredibly dark period of my life. Without at least the idea of you reading or listening, I know my resolve would have eventually failed. I would have been pulled down into the murkier psychological depths below and surely drowned.

Gigantic Purple Elephant Number One:

It feels somewhat creepy—and maybe even unstable—to be writing you now that I've unequivocally accepted the fact that you are dead and were the whole time I was sending you letters. You were dead while I was walking past your home over and over—and even when I was knocking on what I thought was still the front door of your residence. I couldn't accept what I had seen back then, mostly because I still so desperately needed you to be alive. I guess I made you into a psychological mirage of sorts, just to keep myself moving forward through whatever lonely desert I was in. My unquenchable thirst for you made my mind boil.

Thankfully, today I'm not as sick as I was back then. I'm no longer dissociating. I've reclaimed all of my ugliest memories and have been working very hard to bring them permanently to consciousness, integrating everything. And I'm also trying very hard to forgive myself, even though no one else thinks I did anything wrong.

I feel as though I've now processed both traumas—the Majestic Theater massacre as well as finding you the way I did after all the funerals ended. And maybe I've healed enough to write this last letter, concluding whatever I started when I was so ill. For many reasons, it feels important to bring that dark chapter to its natural conclusion. To honor it. Hold it up to the gods in appreciation, as you might have once said.

So, yes, I've accepted that both you and Darcy and all the others are really gone from this world forever.

I remember you saying once—and I'm surely going to misquote you here, so please forgive me in advance—that Jung believed neuroses are the psyche's best response to the crisis at hand and, while we always want to work toward healing and stabilizing psyche, we should also honor, or at least acknowledge, its valiant attempts to protect us.

I've read through all the mad letters I sent to you. I still have them on my laptop. Initially, I was worried about who had the physical manifestations of all those rambling confessions. What would these unnamed people do with my ravings? Would someone be so cruel as to post the product of my illness on the internet? And if so, would I ever be allowed to continue my work at Majestic High School? I'm not sure I'd want even

Isaiah or Jill to read the words my dissociated self wrote to you. I've lost sleep thinking about this.

A young couple with two small daughters lives in your house now. When I happened to walk by a year or so ago I saw carpenters converting your consulting room into what now looks like a cross between a greenhouse and an enclosed patio. Through the large glass plates, anyone wandering by can now see tall green plants and outdoor furniture, all of which I think you'd actually like. In a royal-blue bathrobe and white slippers, the mom often takes her morning coffee out there. The rising sun lights up her face as she does her emails on her tablet. I can tell she loves living in your house. Sometimes I see the girls playing on the front lawn and they look happy too, completely oblivious to the last thing you did inside their idyllic home.

I've worried that my letters were piled up on the floor behind the front door when this family purchased the property. Did the young mom and dad read through all my intimate thoughts? And if so, what did they think? Did they label me crazy? Did they even make it past the first letter? Would they have looked at the postmarks and read them in order or would they have read randomly? Or did they immediately throw all my letters in the trash? I've seen the young family in town. When I wave and say hello and smile, they always return my pleasantries without any hesitation, which seems like a good sign.

Maybe Bobby the cop grabbed all my letters. It also could have been Jill or a kind and discreet Realtor, many of whom I know through my decades at the high school, because I've worked with their sons and daughters. For some reason, I feel like other people have read the letters I've written, but—so far—no one has said a word to me about them. Like I've said many times, we live among kindhearted people.

Gigantic Purple Elephant Number Two:

I'm cheating on you.

I've been seeing another Jungian analyst for more than three years now. We do three sessions a week. Tuesdays and Thursdays at eight a.m. As well as Sundays at nine p.m. His name is Phineas and he's told me that you and he were well acquainted through the many conferences and professional gatherings that all Jungian analysts attend. That's as much as he would say about his relationship with you, claiming it would be inappropriate to go any further, which I sense he could.

Phineas is more willing to talk in general about Jungian analysts and has told me that a common mistake analysands make is thinking that their analysts have everything figured out and, therefore, are not vulnerable to the darker forces of this world, which obviously isn't true. He and I have discussed the concept of the wounded healer at length, which sort of applies to me as well. I have many childhood wounds, many broken places inside, but that allows me to feel and understand the pain of high school students in a way that many of their less broken—or maybe less conscious—parents cannot.

Phineas has read the letters I've sent you and—full disclosure—I've agreed to let him read this one too, once I've finished it. He says reading my letters to you made him admire my psyche's creativity and resilience, which made me feel a little less embarrassed.

"We are all capable of the miraculous," Phineas often says.

I think it's important to state right away that I'm not angry with you or disappointed by what you felt you had to do, because knowing you as I did, I'm pretty sure you didn't make that decision in a fit of passion. No, I believe it was a deliberate, measured choice that you made after thinking through all the options very thoroughly, even though Phineas says we can't ever know for certain what was in your head and heart when you did what you did. I resented and even hated you for a stretch, but that ugly time has passed. I still miss you, of course. But Phineas has said many times that there is an inner Karl currently living within me and that my inner Karl will be with me forever. And in that sense, the letter writing I was (and I guess still am) doing was/is an attempt to integrate that inner Karl and to commune with the eternal you.

Phineas has been trying to get me to write this last letter for more than three years. From the very start of my treatment with him, Phineas has been adamant about "closing the Karl circle," finishing what psyche commanded me to start, back when I was so unbelievably sick. Phineas believes this will be "soul medicine." While, right from the beginning, I very much wanted to heal, I don't think I could have written these words before now. I truly believe that I'm finishing this letter-writing business just as fast as I psychologically can. It's been a rocky few years to say the least, which you will see for yourself below.

You're probably wondering how the movie premiere went, right?

The short answer: it's taken Phineas and me three and a half years of three-sessions-a-week analysis to fully unpack what happened. I'm not sure I actually remember all of it, because I started to dissociate pretty extremely. Perhaps it's best to write exactly what I do remember and then you can allow your great sense of intuition and piercing insight to fill in the blanks.

On the afternoon of the premiere, Bess and Jill went to the hairdresser and nail salon, while Isaiah took me out for eighteen holes. Neither of us is a very good golfer, but Isaiah has a membership at the Pines Country Club—where the very kind Greg Coyle used to be the golf pro—and so I'll ride around on the cart with Isaiah every so often and do my best not to break any nearby windows. On that particular August afternoon—which I remember was hot enough to keep summer's last cicadas screaming—I couldn't really concentrate and asked Isaiah if he wouldn't mind if I just kept score for him rather than play a round myself. After briefly trying to convince me to continue on, saying it would "clear my head," Isaiah finally relented, and by default I became his caddie—driving the cart and cheering his good shots and writing down his strokes. Isaiah was unusually quiet, focusing on his game, until somewhere around the fifteenth or sixteenth hole, when he said, "Lucas, I have to say I'm more than a little worried about you."

Isaiah went on to list a bunch of weird things I had done, like disappearing from the movie set when they needed me and walking around Majestic in the middle of the night and not eating and the obsessive scratching of my arms until they scabbed and a few other things. Then he said, "If tonight is too much for you, no one would blame you. I can skip it too. We can hang out at your house or wherever you'd like. Maybe drive down the shore or something. Just get out of town."

"I owe it to Eli to be at the premiere," I said. "And I have to make a speech."

"You actually *don't* have to do that," he said as he used a red towel to wipe a clump of dirt off the face of his five iron.

"But I really think I do."

"Why?"

I couldn't answer Isaiah because I just felt like I had to go back into the Majestic Theater and I really hoped winged Darcy would be there waiting for me. I also wanted to know what the sound deep inside me was. But I was still sane enough to realize it would have been bad to say any of the above, so I said nothing.

"I just don't think you're ready for this, buddy," he said. "I don't know if any of us are fully prepared, but you, Lucas, in particular seem . . . I don't know."

"Isaiah, I'm right as rain," I said, and then tried my best to maintain eye contact, but the pressure built in my eyes again and I ended up looking away before he did.

I'm sure Isaiah didn't let me off the hook that easily, but in my memory now, I only see me silently helping my best man friend finish his round of golf, after which he and I showered and changed in the locker room. Then he treated me to an early dinner, saying he had to spend his monthly minimum.

During all of that, I remember sort of not really being there with Isaiah and his sensing that I had drifted far away, but at the same time I could tell he didn't know what to do about any of it. I was the person who helped people with their mental health problems. Isaiah was the guy who ran the high school and trusted his God to do the rest. Before we ate our early dinner, he prayed, asking Jesus "to help get the brave and good-hearted Lucas through the premiere," but this particular prayer didn't seem to work as well as his previous prayers had. My skin didn't tingle. I didn't start shaking. I didn't really feel anything at all. I also didn't eat any of my food, which seemed to upset Isaiah. He kept saying, "You have to eat, Lucas."

Back at my house, Isaiah and I changed into our tuxedos and sat in the air-conditioned living room watching the Phillies on TV while we waited for Bess and Jill to return from their day of pampering and beautification. When they finally walked through the door they were almost unrecognizable because they had on so much makeup and their hair was done in ways I had never seen before, but Isaiah and I were smart enough to tell them they looked fantastic as they rushed up the stairs to put on their dresses.

"Last chance to back out," Isaiah said to me, but I shook my head and then that was that.

When the limousine pulled up out front, Jill and Bess were still getting dressed, so Isaiah yelled up and told them we had to go, which we did, because Mark and Tony and Eli were waiting for us. And then before I knew it we were all in the back of a stretch limousine. Tony was pouring everyone a glass of expensive champagne. Eli was grinning like a little kid on Christmas morning. Bess, Isaiah, and Jill were marveling at the luxury of our vehicle. And Mark was congratulating everyone over and over again, until Tony said, "Just how many glasses of champagne have you had already?" which made Mark's face turn red.

"Can we open the sunroof?" I asked, thinking maybe Darcy might already be with us, only flying up in the air above.

Mark said it was a little hot to open the sunroof, but Tony yelled for the driver to "crank up the air-conditioning and let the sunshine in!"

I stared up at the sky for the rest of the ride, but I never saw winged Darcy. I tried very hard to paint her with my mind, but it didn't work. I started to feel so lonely I thought I was going to burst into tears, so I began to pinch the loose skin between my left thumb and forefinger, digging in with my nails so hard I wondered if they'd cut through the skin and actually touch. The pain was just enough to keep my emotions at bay.

Then Jill was whispering in my ear, saying I didn't have to do this if I wasn't ready, so I said, "I'm ready!" only I yelled it—I know because everyone's face went white and then it was very quiet in the limousine. When I saw that Eli was frowning, I kind of pulled myself together enough to say, "This is a lot for me, but it's also really special and important."

Everyone nodded back reassuringly, but I could tell I had ruined the limousine ride for my friends, which made me feel lower than I already did.

When we pulled up to the theater, the Majestic Police Department had everything blocked off. There was a heavy police presence—officers in uniforms everywhere. There was also a real red carpet roped off by smiles of red velvet that were connected by shiny gold posts. I could see many of The Survivors lined up to get their pictures taken as reporters yelled questions and tried to get them to pose.

As we exited the limousine and joined everyone on the red carpet, I was pleasantly surprised to see Sandra Coyle. She was dressed in an elegant black evening gown and matching black gloves, accented with dangling diamond earrings and a diamond choker. Willow was there carrying the large headshot of Greg Coyle—the one that I had seen on the wooden easel in the Coyles' sitting room. When we finally got within earshot, I heard Sandra pontificating on the transformative power of the movies. And how she was a hundred percent behind our monster project from the very beginning. And she was honored not only to be here but to have helped fund the project.

"Sometimes we vote with our dollars," she said while staring directly into a camera lens, just before flashing a blindingly white smile. The reporters seemed to be hanging on her every word, which they diligently captured with the small recording devices that they were extending toward her.

I gave Mark and Tony a questioning glance.

"Sandra was a late financial backer," Mark said.

"Like late *last night*," Tony said, elbowing my ribs.

"Everyone loves a winner," Isaiah said.

I know that reporting all of this sounds cynical, but I was truly happy to see Sandra at the premiere because it meant that every member of The Survivors was in attendance, making us whole again.

But I had started to sweat profusely. I thought it was the August heat, even though there were large fans set up to keep us cool. But there were so many people taking my picture—flashes of light everywhere—and a young woman was ushering me through the media section, telling reporters that I unfortunately was unable to answer any questions that evening; and then we were bypassing the photo ops that I knew Jill was looking forward to; and then Jill was saying she'd be waiting for me in our seats—which were right next to the black sash Mark and Tony had put on the chair in which Darcy had been shot—and then I was locked in Mark and Tony's private bathroom staring at myself in the mirror and wondering if it was really still me that I was making eye contact with.

I don't know how much time passed before my handler started banging on the door and yelling that it was time for my speech, but it was enough for me to sort of lose touch with reality. Suddenly, it was like I was in an early Spike Lee film and I was gliding forward without moving my feet, riding on some invisible skateboard. And then I was behind the great red curtain, stage right, watching Mark and Tony and Eli discussing the redemptive and uniting power of the movies and how remarkably resilient our town of Majestic, PA, is and will always be.

Suddenly they were talking about me without using my name, saying things that I wasn't sure were any longer true. When Mark finally said, "Ladies and gentlemen, I give you Lucas Goodgame!" everyone in the Grand Viewing Room rose to their feet and applauded loud enough to crack the plaster walls. My handler gave me a little push and then I was in front of the red curtain, gliding across the stage, once again without even picking up my feet, let alone moving one in front of the other. When I was center stage, Eli handed me a microphone just before he and the others exited stage left.

The applause went on for some time, but eventually everyone stopped clapping and took their seats, creating the distinct sound of several hundred people sitting down in unison. Then it was deadly quiet. There was a spotlight hitting my eyes, so I couldn't make out any faces in the audience, which made it impossible to search for winged Darcy. I started to worry, until I remembered that she wouldn't be seated in a chair, but would be hovering above, if she had come at all. I knew that I should be trying to summon strong Lucas to give the required speech, to honor the dead, and to lift up the community, but—selfishly—I was totally consumed with a need to see the angelic version of my wife, if only one last time.

Tilt your head back and lift your face up, said some strange, suspicious voice deep within me.

It's what I most wanted to do, and yet I was suddenly terrified, almost paralyzed with dread.

Look up! Do it! the voice commanded, which is when I began to shake uncontrollably.

"It's okay, Lucas!" I heard Jill yell from the audience. "I'm coming."

I could hear people making room for Jill to pass as she made her way from the center of the Grand Viewing Room to the stage on wh..ch I stood. I could hear her footsteps and then I could hear that she was running. I knew I didn't have much time.

End this! the dark voice said. *Now!*

I felt something grab the hair on the back of my head and pull down, so that my face tilted up and I was forced to stare at the ceiling—at what Darcy always called Majestic's answer to Michelangelo; at what she and I had gazed up at in wonder before every movie we ever watched in this building. I saw the sun and the blue sky and the clouds. But what I also saw forced me to my knees. Then I was screaming. And punching myself in the head and the chest and the thighs. And trying to scrape the skin off my face with my fingernails. I got in an impressive amount of damage before the good people of Majestic subdued me, all while Jill kept sobbing out that she was sorry.

Soon after that, I was in restraints and riding in the back of an ambulance with two young EMTs telling me I was going to be okay. I wasn't going to be okay anytime soon, and I knew it—so I just kept screaming.

Having been to the Majestic Theater many times yourself, you already know what I saw up there on the ceiling painted so beautifully—what psyche had brushed out of my memory. A host of angels soaring majestically, with wings spread wide. Seeing them again broke whatever spell my unconscious had put me under immediately after the tragedy, when I looked down at my bloody hands. And so on that stage, staring up at the painted angels frozen forever on the ceiling of the movie house—when I was supposed to be giving my speech—I was also down in the aisle seats the previous December. And the life was rapidly draining out of my wife as—up on the giant screen—a black-and-white Jimmy Stewart exclaimed, "Merry Christmas, movie house!" And then I was desperately trying to make the blood stop coming out of Darcy. But my hands couldn't keep all of that purple liquid inside of her skull and throat and I could plainly see that the life had already exited her eyes, which were reflecting the movie light like two tiny cold mirrors. I heard my neighbors screaming and moaning through the obscene *POP! POP! POP!* of Jacob Hansen's guns, as he raised and pressed the barrels into heads and throats, executing every other person with what I have since learned are called "contact shots."

In our early group-therapy sessions, many people theorized that Jacob wanted to make the people left alive suffer even more than he wanted to kill our loved ones. Through discussions with various mental health professionals we also learned that the extreme violence combined with the disorienting darkness of the movie theater froze some people in their seats while others ran for the emergency exit, which Jacob had barricaded with his car minutes before. It was easy for Jacob to execute the movie patrons frozen in their seats. The mass of bodies pressing forward into the blocked emergency exit—with their backs turned toward the killer—were even easier prey.

I'm not one hundred percent certain, but I believe Darcy was Jacob's first kill, as I don't remember hearing any gunshots or screaming before Jacob ended my wife's life. Like many others, Darcy always loved sitting with her feet stretched out into the aisle that separated the front block of floor seats from the back. We got there a little later than usual that night and had to settle for the last two center aisle seats closest to the entrance hallway leading to the lobby, from which Jacob first emerged.

Just when I thought my mind was disintegrating—back during the early December tragedy, as Darcy's soul was first leaving her body—that strong and sure version of me rose up and took the wheel. I ran toward the muzzle flashes and the *POP! POP! POP!* Then I was flying through the air, driving the entire weight of my body through the young killer's spine. When we both hit the floor, I grabbed a fistful of his hair and began slamming his face into the concrete below us—over and over and over—feeling his skull caving in a little more with each downward thrust of my right hand. It was like I was outside my body watching a man possessed by demons, because that Other Lucas couldn't stop and didn't until—ten or so minutes later—Bobby the cop finally pulled me off of Jacob's limp, blood-soaked body.

Somehow back on the night of our monster movie premiere, as I was kneeling alone on the stage in my tuxedo, screaming and punching myself and reliving the trauma in front of a sold-out crowd, I was also looking through the various first-floor windows of your house, Karl.

It's three or so nights before Christmas. All the funerals are over. Maybe it's right after the last one. And then I'm seeing your body suspended in midair. Your dining room table has been pushed to the side. A single chair below you has been knocked over. And when I make my eyes travel up the length of your limp torso, I can see the orange extension cord wrapped multiple times around your neck and anchored to the chandelier above. And then I'm kicking in your back door and the neighbors are calling the police and I'm trying to get you down, but it's a two-man job, so the best I can do is sort of hold up your stiff, cold body so that there's no more tension on your windpipe as I scream for help. I supported your weight until my back and leg muscles cramped and gave out. I yelled until I had no more voice. I really did try to save you, Karl, because I loved you more than you probably realized.

Phineas says it's okay to love your analyst and that maybe it's even a sign that the alchemical process—the reparenting of one's self—is succeeding. I know you didn't do what you did to punish me, but because you most likely couldn't live without Leandra or deal with the aftermath of what all of us who were in the Majestic Theater that night suffered. As someone who has had an extreme and largely involuntary response to the tragedy, allow me to say, I understand how the mind can break. I won't ever judge you for it. But I wish I had looked in your window a little earlier that day. Maybe I would have seen what you were about to do.

In my fantasies, I always catch you in the act, usually while you're wrapping the cord around the chandelier base. When I rush into your dining room, you fall ashamedly into my arms. I pat your back and tell you it's okay and that we can get you help.

Maybe even Phineas could have helped you make it through, who knows?

After my very public breakdown at the movie premiere, the EMTs took me to a mental health facility, where—against my will—I was shot up with enough drugs to make me sleep like the dead. Just before I lost consciousness, I distinctly remember realizing that the wind-rushing-through-barren-trees noise hidden deep inside me was the sound of my soul screaming. The last thing I remember before I blacked out was knowing with great certainty that I never wanted to hear the life-sapping sound of my soul screaming ever again.

For this reason, I took all the pills that the medical staff offered me while I was staying at the mental health facility. The meds put me into a stupor that made me drool and fall asleep sitting up in the TV room, where I first began to see the TV ads for Sandra Coyle's political campaign. She's the governor of Pennsylvania now, so I've become used to seeing her talking head on the television and her face on billboards. But back then it felt like I had been transported to an alternate universe. And I remember wondering how Sandra had been able to so quickly transform the screaming of her soul into political gold, while I had ended up unable to lift my body from a plastic couch in a lockdown unit.

There were many people locked up with me, but I was unable to engage with any of them. To be fair, most were also unable to engage with me. The few who seemed relatively normal were given special privileges and spent a lot of time in the open-air square of grass that anchored the common room, which was kind of like a box comprised of four large panes of glass designed to keep the less sane from entering the atrium's cube of sun without permission. I'd see the normal people in there all lit up like gods about to be beamed up to the heavens. I kept thinking, *If only I could enter the gleaming cube, this would all be over,* but the drugs made it virtually impossible to stand, let alone navigate the hierarchy of this new mental health ecosystem.

I'm sure Jill and Isaiah tried to get me out of that place or at least attempted to see me, but I was told that I wasn't allowed visitors for at least five days and I couldn't remember anyone's cell phone numbers, as I had them all programmed into my phone, which had been confiscated when I first arrived. So the anachronistic pay phone on the wall was useless to me.

Daily, I'd meet with social workers and psychologists who asked me a lot of pointless questions like: *What were my mental health goals?* and *How did I plan to pay my bills in the future?* and *Did I have a reliable support group?* and *Had I properly mourned my wife's passing?* I thought I had previously known how much I missed you, Karl, but it wasn't until I got locked up that I truly felt the full weight of my grief.

"I need a Jungian analyst," I kept telling them. I'd say I wasn't picky. I didn't require that they'd studied at the C. G. Jung Institute in Zürich. But I adamantly refused to be treated by a non-Jungian, which I think greatly insulted everyone at this particular facility. At one point, this one social worker—a young woman who looked no older than Eli—rolled her eyes at me. But mostly I just sat in the TV room falling asleep sitting up and drooling all over myself as Sandra Coyle's head kept popping up on the television screen to outline the dangers of unregulated gun ownership. I kept telling myself that it was okay to sleep—that I was emotionally and psychologically exhausted and that I could try to make friends with the people around me tomorrow, when I'd be more rested.

But then Isaiah and Jill were there saying it was time for me to leave, which I said couldn't be right because it had only been a day or two at most. But they insisted it had already been three weeks, which I found hard to believe even as I was actually walking out of the building and toward Isaiah's sedan. I remember noticing that the leaves were changing colors, which frightened me a bit, if only because it seemed to prove that I had lost a significant amount of time. Jill sat with me in the back seat while Isaiah drove, and that's when I realized I would never make it into the atrium's magical cube of sunlight and that I wasn't going to be beamed up into the heavens, which made me feel so low and sad I almost couldn't stand it, even though it was obviously much better to have been freed by friends.

The next thing I remember is waking up with my head in Jill's lap and my body curled up in the fetal position on the back seat. Jill was running her fingers through my hair. She and Isaiah were talking in whispers, which made me realize that they thought I was still asleep, so I closed my eyes and pretended to be.

"I don't know if we're doing the right thing here," my best man friend said from behind the wheel.

"Well, we're not leaving him in that place," Jill said.

"You won't be able to restrain him if he has another breakdown."

"He's not going to have another breakdown."

"How do you know?"

I think I might have fallen asleep again here because I don't remember anything else from that car ride.

Then Jill and Isaiah were helping me out of the sedan and—when I looked around—I was surprised to see my front yard had been completely covered with signs and cards and flowers and stuffed animals. It looked like several hundred people had left personalized messages of support. There was a big banner hanging like a smile on the face of my home. It was white with gold lettering, which made me wonder if it had been Jesus Gomez's doing, since it matched the T-shirts he had made for everyone. It read: "Majestic's Got You, Lucas!"

Two weeks later, right before the first of our now weekly Sunday-morning soccer matches—in which I have somewhat miraculously started as our team's goalie for the better part of four years—Jesus gave me a brand-new pair of white-and-gold goalie gloves. When I thanked him, he said that the gloves were the absolute least he could do for me.

"I'm going to do more, my highly esteemed friend," he said through a toothy smile. Then he drummed on my chest with his fists, as though my right pec were a boxing speed bag, while adding, "Your objective is easy. Keep the ball out of the net. But don't worry too much if the bad guys score on you today because we're going to keep doing this every Sunday forever and ever, and so you and me, Lucas Goodgame, we're going to get better. *You understand?*"

When I nodded, he used my left pec for a speed bag. When he had finished pounding my chest, he raised two fists high in the air and yelled, "I love Sunday morning!" as he sprinted to the center of the field for kickoff, because Jesus is our center forward as well as the league's leading scorer.

But back in my front yard when I first was released from the mental health facility, I wanted to take in every single message, and as I looked around, I began to worry about the amount of thank-you cards I would have to write, thinking I'd need to buy supplies and stamps and figure out everyone's address, which is when Jill said, "All this love should make you smile, not frown," so I forced the ends of my mouth to curl upward as we made our way inside.

My home was spotless. The windows had been cleaned. The carpets still had vacuum cleaner marks. And everything smelled like fresh linen and pine. The fridge and freezer had been stocked with dozens of meals, each in a different Tupperware container with a different Majestic sur-name written across the lid in magic marker. All of The Survivor mem-bers' names were accounted for as well as others. "I had to start turning away food," Jill said, and I nodded in acknowledgment, because there was literally no more room in the fridge.

Suddenly I was overcome with exhaustion, so I went into Darcy's and my bedroom and collapsed into the bed, where I instantly fell asleep and dreamed of nothing.

It was dark when Jill woke me up, saying Isaiah wanted to speak with me. Thinking we were about to have a phone conversation, I was surprised when Jill handed me my laptop with Isaiah's and Bess' faces lit up on the screen. They were beaming.

"Aliza had her baby," Bess said just before a river leaked out of her left eye and ran down her cheek.

"A girl," Isaiah said. "And they're calling her Majestic. Maj for short. How about that?"

"Seven pounds, two ounces of joy and completely healthy."

"I wanted to tell my best friend in the whole world first."

"We'll FaceTime you when we get to California."

I'm pretty sure I managed to say congratulations and that I loved them, but I can't be certain as I was still so exhausted, and when I closed my eyes again, I slept for fourteen hours straight. I know because Jill kept saying, "You slept for fourteen hours straight!" as she made me lunch.

That afternoon, a tall man with a pointy beard and shoulder-length salt-and-pepper hair sat down across from me on my couch, introduced himself as Phineas, and then said, "Do you want to start an alchemical process with me?" which let me know he was a Jungian analyst and I was, therefore, back in good hands.

Phineas gave a little speech, saying we were going to treat the root problem, not just the symptoms, which made me feel like I was finally about to get some medicine that would actually heal me, rather than just put me to sleep. But I couldn't resist asking if he wasn't afraid of me, given that Jill had surely told him everything I had done to myself and others.

He asked if I had ever physically harmed anyone who wasn't actively trying to kill my friends and family.

Of course, I told him I hadn't.

Then he asked how many times I had committed acts of self-harm in the three years prior to the Majestic Theater tragedy.

When I honestly said, "None," he nodded affirmatively and then asked if my self-abuse during the lead-up to the movie premiere could have been a symptom of withdrawal, since my analysis had been stopped abruptly and without any plan for managing my mental health in the aftermath.

I admitted that extraordinary circumstances had produced my violence, and could see what he was driving at, before ultimately saying, "But regardless of circumstance, regardless of intent, regardless of motivation or the fact that I may have even saved lives—by definition, I'm a murderer, Phineas. I've killed a human being."

"Everyone has a murderer inside of them," Phineas said almost dismissively, as if he wasn't fazed by what I had done. He didn't even break eye contact. "I certainly have an inner murderer in me. So does Jill and Isaiah and everyone else you've ever met. Our inner murderers have been keeping us safe for thousands of years. They've fed us meat. They've kept our families alive. They've defended our countries whenever psychopathic authoritarians have tried to pummel us into submission."

I understood what he meant, but, suddenly, I couldn't make eye contact with him.

Then he said it might be more charitable—and accurate—to call the force inside of me "an inner warrior." A "brave and noble" inner warrior. He said that's how everyone else in Majestic saw me. And that maybe it was time to shake my inner warrior's hand. Maybe even thank him for what he so heroically did. All that he'd sacrificed to save the lives of others.

When he got done saying all of that, I could hardly breathe.

At the end of that first introduction to Phineas, he told me we'd be having three sessions a week for the foreseeable future, which prompted me to admit that I probably couldn't afford his hourly rate at that frequency.

"Been taken care of," Phineas said as he made his way out the front door. "See you tomorrow. And start writing down your dreams, no matter how insignificant they seem. I want to know what the unconscious is saying."

When I turned around, Jill was coming down the steps and asking how it went.

"Who's paying for my analysis?"

"You still have health insurance through the high school. Did you like Phineas? I think he's fantastic. And perfect for you."

"The school's health insurance package doesn't cover analysis three times a week," I said.

Jill rounded the newel at the end of the handrail and tried to escape into the kitchen, while casually saying, "What should I make for dinner?"

"Who is paying for my analysis?" I said at a volume that was almost yelling, which surprised me.

Jill turned around and looked at me. "I am."

"But you don't have that kind of cash just lying—"

"I sold my house," she said, and then sucked the bottom left side of her lip into her mouth. "So I really hope you don't mind me living here. Now what do you want to eat?"

Jill went through the refrigerator calling out the names of preprepared meals that were already unfrozen, but I didn't really hear any of what she was saying, mostly because I was still trying to process the fact that she and I were now living together permanently. I didn't mind, at all. But I knew how long it took to build up house equity—especially by feeding all the residents of Majestic, PA, breakfast and lunch. And I also knew how much analysis cost, how rapidly it would eat up Jill's gains. And yet I really needed analysis. I went back and forth in my mind, trying to untie the Gordian knot.

Finally, I decided to keep precise track of how much money we were paying Phineas, so I could reimburse Jill once I got better and could therefore start working again, because I had no idea if I'd be getting a biweekly paycheck now that school had started back up again and my position had surely been filled by someone saner than me.

When I asked about Eli, Jill told me that Mark and Tony had indeed gotten him late admittance into some college in Los Angeles that had a film track and often got students internships at the various moviemaking studios. The boy was already in California, courtesy of Survivors' Group member Tracy Farrow's frequent-flier miles. Just like Aliza before him, Eli would go on to make California his full-time home, building various indie film sets during his summer breaks. Once in a while I'd get a bit of news from Mark and Tony, but the boy didn't try to contact me directly. I figured he now most certainly knew exactly what I had done to his brother and, therefore, would never speak to me again. While his sudden absence hurt, I really couldn't blame Eli and wished him all the best.

Sometimes, whenever she'd catch me feeling blue, Jill would say, "Eli will get back in touch when he's ready. Give him time." I'd nod in response, but I never allowed myself to believe her. Every cell in my body said he was gone forever—that, in addition to killing his brother, I had ultimately let him down when he needed me most by ruining his premiere and Majestic's big chance at reunification and healing.

After a few weeks, Jill felt I was stable enough for her to get back to full-time work at the Cup Of Spoons. She arranged for me to be adult-sat by various Survivors' Group members. Like I already told you above, Jesus Gomez and his soccer team had me on Sunday mornings. And we trained most Sunday afternoons after the a.m. games. Jesus is the only adult-sitter whom I don't think I'll outgrow after my mind and soul get better. Under Jesus's tutelage, I've miraculously become the top-rated goalie in our over-fifty men's league. With Jesus's four sure-footed cousins lined up in front of me, I've got an impressive defense—which deserves the lion's share of credit—but I have gotten much better at keeping the ball out of the net. If you can't tell already, I'm pretty proud to have unearthed such an unlikely latent skill.

On Mondays, I volunteered all day at the library, putting books back on the shelves under the watchful eyes of Robin Withers. Tuesday mornings were reserved for games with Betsy Bush, Audrey Hartlove, and Chrissy Williams. Betsy was the queen of Uno. Audrey liked playing nickel-ante poker. And Chrissy's favorite was Scrabble. I spent Tuesday afternoons with Bobby and his cop friends playing pickup basketball at the YMCA. On Wednesdays, I'd help file paperwork at Laxman Anand's law firm in the morning and we'd lift weights and play racquetball at Majestic Fitness in the afternoons. On Thursdays, Carlton Porter and I volunteered at a homeless shelter in Philadelphia, where we mostly cooked and served food when we weren't sorting through clothing donations, all of which we'd wash before distributing. On Fridays, I'd go running with Dan Gentile in the mornings and then I'd go to pottery class with David Fleming in the afternoons. And on Saturdays, Jill turned over the Cup Of Spoons to Randy so that she and I could get into her truck and go exploring. She'd always have a spot picked out and a picnic lunch packed. Sometimes we drove to the Jersey shore. Sometimes we'd go hiking. We might go to an arboretum or a flower show or a pumpkin festival or skiing or to a concert or dozens of other events and places that Jill had found when she researched possibilities on the internet.

In this way, years passed, and—thankfully—I didn't have any more violent episodes, not a single one.

Oh, I forgot to tell you about Aliza's baby, who is, of course, beautiful and perfect. Bess filmed her husband holding newborn Maj and kissing her forehead and making raspberries on her belly, and I had never seen my best friend so proud or happy. My heart almost couldn't take how wonderful that scene was. "I'm a grandfather, Lucas! Me! Pop Pop Isaiah!"

Late one night during Isaiah's first of many visits to California, Aliza video chatted with me. I hadn't seen her face in quite some time. Lying in my bed, I lifted my phone and was shocked to see a lady in her late thirties staring back at me instead of a young woman.

"You were right," Aliza said to me in the middle of our chat.

"About what?" I asked.

"That things would get better. That I could be the true me and my dad would eventually come around. That he'd forgive me and even accept who I am."

"He's a good man, your father," I said.

"*You're* a good man, Mr. Goodgame," she said, and pointed her index finger at me.

Even though I could tell she meant it, I couldn't allow myself to believe it. So I averted my eyes and started asking questions about baby Maj, which seemed to make everything okay, because Aliza lit up and didn't stop talking for forty-five minutes after that. Everything about her daughter was a miracle to this first-time mother—everything was new and wonderful and full of hope.

Somewhere in that initial year—maybe it started a month or so before the tragedy's first anniversary—Jill and I started visiting Darcy's grave. And that became a weekly tradition that we maintain to this day. I didn't notice this before visiting with Jill, but there are angel wings spread across the top of Darcy's marker—wide enough so that you can see every feather clearly and skillfully delineated. Jill says I had insisted on the angel wings, which apparently cost a lot of money because they were hand chiseled by a sculptor, but I have no conscious memory of even going to pick out a stone.

During those first few years, Jill and I would usually bring a blanket and sit down on the grass right above Darcy's belly, and we'd take turns telling my deceased wife about what happened to us during that week—all of Jill's culinary ups and downs at the Cup Of Spoons, all of my experiences with my adult-sitters, and all of our Saturday adventures. Even after more than three years, Jill breaks down crying at the end of each graveside visit when she tells Darcy that she misses her and is doing her best to take care of me. And I'll pat my lips with my hand and then touch my wife's cold headstone, transferring the kiss.

We religiously leave a fresh batch of flowers, which are never there when we return the next week. On the drive home from the cemetery—maybe as comic relief—Jill and I like to make up stories about what happens to our bouquets. Our favorite is a running one about a graveyard keeper named Gary who collects all the cemetery flowers for his wife, Gertrude, who requires massive amounts of store-bought flowers before she will make love to him. Gary's graveyard pay is meager, which requires him to steal whenever he is feeling hot to trot, which is always. Often, Jill and I will get really creative and the stories become quite elaborate. Sometimes we'll be so into the week's version that we'll sit parked in our driveway with the engine off just to finish telling the latest episode.

Woe is the horny henpecked Gary, who must steal all of the graveyard flowers to earn love and affection!

That's how we always end each chapter.

At some point in the game, we brought Darcy in on the joke, telling her that Majestic's mourners are now buying the flowers specifically for Gertrude instead of our deceased loved ones, just to ease poor Gary's suffering. It makes Darcy laugh, if only in our minds.

That first Christmas, Isaiah and Bess returned to California to spend the break with their granddaughter. Like I already mentioned, Eli still hadn't been in contact and was rumored to be staying permanently in the

Golden State. Mark and Tony resumed their yearly Christmas tradition of screening *It's a Wonderful Life* and I heard that it was a sold-out event with a large police presence. But I had decided I would never again set foot in another movie theater, let alone the Majestic, even though Mark and Tony had given all Survivors lifetime free passes. Most of the original group members have resumed their usual moviegoing habits, which Phineas says is a form of immersion therapy.

When I first asked Phineas if I should make myself go to the movies, he said, "You'll go when you're ready."

And while we had dozens of holiday invitations from all of The Survivors, Jill and I decided to leave Majestic for the month of December, driving south with the goal of ultimately spending Christmas with my mother and her boyfriend's family in Florida, if only to get as far away as possible from the Majestic Theater. Phineas also thought it might be good to face my lifelong biggest fear (my mom), saying, "That dragon has your gold!"—meaning that if I could metaphorically slay the metaphorical dragon that was my mother, I could reclaim what she'd stolen from me. I wasn't sure what precisely my mother had stolen from me, but facing Mom felt significant, especially in the early shadows of Darcy's murder. So Jill deputized Randy once again, touching each of his shoulders with her favorite Cup Of Spoons spatula, before handing him the keys to the restaurant. Shortly after that ceremony, we hopped into her truck and hit the road in search of psychological gold.

By December first, our hometown was already lit up with strings of Christmas lights and plastic Santa Clauses and reindeers and snowmen and gigantic silver snowflakes, all of which depressed me. When we officially left festooned Majestic by turning onto the highway, I felt a wave of relief wash over me. I was anxious about being away from Phineas for the first time, even though we agreed to chat by computer screen once a week. But mostly I just felt an overwhelming desire to get very far away from the Majestic Theater before the one-year anniversary of my wife's murder.

When we got to Jill's parents' woodsy cabin outside of Brevard, North Carolina, it was late and we went right to the guest room without even seeing Mr. and Mrs. Dunn. Jill slept in the queen-sized bed and I slept on a love seat in the corner, but it was the first time we had spent an entire night in the same bedroom since that time I told you about in Maryland by the lighthouse. Even though I was tired, I had a hard time sleeping. Apparently, Jill did too, because in the middle of the night she whispered, "Lucas? You awake?" When I confirmed I was, she said I could sleep in the bed with her if I thought it might be more comfortable. The love seat wasn't long enough for me to fully stretch out my legs, but I wasn't sure I should get in bed with Jill on account of wake-up sex. The best love-making I had ever experienced in my life happened whenever I had unconsciously started making love with Darcy in my sleep. We would both wake up in the middle of sex—going full speed—with no idea how it had even begun. I was worried about having wake-up sex with Jill, but I didn't want to say that, so I said nothing and just stared up at the darkness until the sun rose hours later and began to cast long shadows on the bedroom walls, which were celery green.

I hadn't seen Jill's mom and stepdad since the day Jill married Derek. They looked like smaller, more wrinkled versions of themselves, despite the fact that they were avid hikers and ate vegan. As we ate breakfast together—bananas and peanut butter on raisin bread—I couldn't help noticing how at ease Jill was around her parents, who both smiled at their daughter and listened to her and often touched and hugged and kissed her. I kept thinking that if I'd had parents even half as nice as Jill's, I would never live so far away from them.

Later, when Jill and I were alone together on a walk through the Pisgah National Forest, I asked why she allowed so many miles to separate her from her parents. She said it was so that she could live close to Darcy and me. When I asked why again, it was with a little more emphasis in my voice. She said that Darcy had been her best friend and that she could never have left her. Then she said Darce had helped her through a rough patch with her biological father, back in middle school. The way she said it made me understand that I wasn't supposed to ask any additional questions, and I didn't. Darcy had once told me what Jill's real father had done to her, saying that's why Jill had married Derek, because she had been hardwired to tolerate abuse. And it was Jill's current stepdad who had helped her mom get them away from Jill's biological father, which is why Jill considers Mr. Dunn to be her real dad, and even uses his last name to this day. I think Jill understood that I knew all of the above already. I could just feel it. So I kept quiet.

"Besides," Jill added as she kicked a pine cone off the trail, "Majestic's my home. It will always be my home."

Jill cooked fabulous meals every night for her parents. The food was so good you didn't even realize it was vegan. We did jigsaw puzzles together. And Mrs. Dunn and I teamed up against Jill and her father for several epic games of pinochle by the roaring woodstove. Toward the end of our stay, the temperature plummeted and the four of us bundled up and went in search of frozen waterfalls. Mrs. Dunn made us two large thermoses of vegan hot chocolate spiked with cayenne red pepper. Every time we found another partially frozen waterfall glistening like a strange vertical forest of icicles we'd pour spicy-hot dairy-free cocoa into the red screw-off mugs and toast the glory of mother nature.

On our last night together, we had an early Christmas. I couldn't believe that Mr. and Mrs. Dunn had actually bought me presents and was beyond moved when I opened up a trucker hat and matching sweatshirt, both of which read "Brevard, NC."

"So you remember to come back," Mr. Dunn said.

"Soon!" Mrs. Dunn added.

"Lucas has presents for you too," Jill told her parents, which made me blush because the gifts I brought were stupid. But it was too late to pretend I had nothing to give, so I went to our room and retrieved the two small wrapped boxes.

When I handed the Dunns their gifts, Mrs. Dunn said to her daughter, "Did you wrap these?" because no one believes that a man can wrap a present properly, but I really can and Jill told her mother as much, which seemed to impress her. Once the coffee mugs that I had made with David Fleming in pottery class were out of their boxes, they looked mawkishly amateurish and even deformed to my eye. Without giving ourselves the necessary time to master the craft, David and I had gleefully made mugs for every member of The Survivors, along with Mark and Tony and some of our family members. But this gift exchange with the Dunns was our hasty work's debut. I wanted to call David and tell him not to distribute the rest at the many Survivor-hosted holiday gatherings because the current experience was so humiliating.

But then, as her parents inspected their mugs, Jill rather proudly said, "Lucas made those with his own hands."

"Did he?" Mrs. Dunn said while taking in the bluish-green glaze.

Mr. Dunn stood and left the room, which I thought was a bad sign, but he soon returned with a bottle of what he called "the good stuff," and then we all sat around the wood-burning stove singing along to the old-timey holiday songs playing on the radio and sipping top-shelf scotch from the lumpy mugs David and I had made for Mr. and Mrs. Dunn.

A few hours later, Jill was asleep in her father's recliner and Mr. Dunn had already retired to his bedroom. I was helping Mrs. Dunn dry and put away the dinner dishes when she turned and looked up into my eyes. I looked down into hers and sort of thought they were saying, *I'm sorry*, but then as I looked a little deeper, I somehow knew that Mrs. Dunn's eyes were actually saying *I love you*. Once I recognized that, she put her arms around me and pulled me into her, and then she rested her head on my heart. I wrapped my arms around the old woman and hugged her until I felt myself starting to shake, nearly as bad as I had when I went to Isaiah's church and everyone was touching me and praying. Mrs. Dunn began to rock me back and forth, almost like I was a baby, and she kept saying she was sorry and that I was going to be okay and that she was happy I was with Jill, which was when I started wanting whatever was happening to be over.

When Mrs. Dunn finally let go of me, she turned away and began wiping her eyes with a dishrag and then retreated to her bedroom.

I went back into the living room and looked at the white Christmas lights on the Dunns' fake tree, which was decorated mostly with ornaments that Jill had made when she was a little girl. My favorite was a squirrel composed of a pine cone and pasted-on googly eyes and a tail little Jill had obviously cut off of a stuffed animal. I turned and looked at my friend sleeping under a thick patchwork quilt her mother had made by hand from old clothes. The soft light of the Christmas tree was illuminating her face in a way that made Jill look very young and almost holy. I think I might have watched my friend sleeping in that ethereal glow for hours.

When we left the next morning to make our way to Florida, Mr. and Mrs. Dunn didn't cry, but I could tell they were feeling blue and so I told them that we'd be back soon and often, which is a promise I've managed to keep, as Jill and I now visit them once a season, so four times a year. I have grown to love them both very much—like the parents I never had, but maybe deserved somehow.

Phineas calls this a beautiful compensation and I know you will agree with that.

I could tell Jill was also sad to leave her parents, but she tried to hide it as we made our way down to Florida.

Phineas made me promise not to stay with my mother and her boy-friend, Harvey, saying, "Set yourself up for success. Carve out a space just for you and Jill to regroup, decompress, and heal, in between exposures."

It was strange to think of being "exposed" to my mother, like she was radiation or strong sun on a hazy day—something that could give me cancer. But we took Phineas's advice and, much to the horror of my mother, who was highly insulted by our refusal to stay in one of her and Harvey's three "luxurious" en suite guest rooms, Jill and I checked into a small motel with a life-sized pink neon palm tree out front. Since all of the motel rooms had two beds, we decided to save money and check into one room instead of two.

The next morning we met Mom and Harvey at an open-air breakfast place on the beach overlooking the Gulf of Mexico. It was cooler than I had expected and I regretted not wearing a jacket. Harvey wore a panama hat on his balding head, a thick push-broom mustache under his red nose, and a fishing vest equipped with a ridiculous number of pockets on his body. Mom mostly wore diamonds. They talked about their country club. They talked about Harvey's "state-of-the-art" fishing boat, which he referred to as his "baby." They talked about Harvey's son, Hunter, and his thriving real estate business, letting us know about the many multi-million-dollar sales he had recently closed. They talked about their neighbors, who all were either too loud or had bad taste and, therefore, had decorated their homes the wrong way. The more they talked, the more I felt like I wasn't even there at the table. I tried to tell myself they were only attempting to fill the silences, but whenever Jill tried to speak, Mom and Harvey would talk over her, which started to make me feel like there were sharp knives trying to carve their way out of my belly.

Mom complained about her pancakes being soggy because there was too much syrup and Harvey sent his eggs Benedict back twice, saying the sauce was "off," before he told the waitress he'd lost his appetite. Harvey kind of sulked from that point on, especially whenever our waitress checked up on our table, asking if everything was okay. When Jill smiled and brightly told the young woman that the tomato omelet was excellent, Mom and Harvey actually frowned.

Claiming he had scheduled a day out on his "baby" before he knew we'd be visiting, Harvey left us after breakfast, but not before insisting on paying the bill, which he had managed to have reduced significantly on account of his meal being "inedible." Mom and Harvey didn't notice, but just before we all got up and stepped out onto the beach, I saw Jill slip our waitress two twenties.

After saying goodbye to Harvey, Jill suggested we take a walk on the water's edge, but Mom started interrogating us about what we had bought everyone for Christmas.

Jill said it was a surprise, which is when Mom—with a sober face—said, "Harvey's family takes Christmas gift giving deadly seriously."

She went on to say we needed to give them worthy presents, and suggested shopping immediately. "Especially if you didn't bring anything all that impressive," Mom added.

I thought about David's and my lumpy coffee mugs and I began to feel like all my internal organs were falling out of my body and splatting on the concrete around my feet.

Jill once again suggested a walk along the beach, but Mom said she really wanted to get the Christmas shopping out of the way and that doing so would take a huge load off her mind. She said she'd pay for everything and then joked that it would really be Harvey who would be paying before she put a hand on my arm and said, "And Lucas, my sweet boy, I know exactly what you can get for me!"

It was at this point that Jill said, "You realize that you haven't asked your son a single question, right?"

"I just asked him to go Christmas shopping with me," Mom said.

"Lucas made you a present with his own hands and it's beautiful," Jill said, greatly overestimating the aesthetic quality of my pottery.

"That will never do," Mom said with a worried look on her face.

It was here that Jill started screaming at my mother, calling her names that I don't even feel comfortable repeating—especially in writing—and she didn't stop yelling for at least five minutes. Mom broke down crying and said that Jill was horrible and mean and ugly, which just made Jill yell louder, and at one point, I started to worry that Jill might even hit Mom. Instead, Jill screamed, "Lucas is the best thing in your life and you treat him like he's the worst! He's needed you! He's needed someone to love him for fifty years! And no matter how much the rest of us try to fill in for you, you still have so much power over him and it's like you don't even know how much damage you're constantly doing!"

"At least I'm not sleeping with my dead friend's husband," Mom said through tears, which is when Jill closed her eyes, took a deep breath, and walked away.

When Jill was out of earshot, Mom said, "Lucas, you simply *must* get rid of her."

I looked at my mother's tear-streaked face for a long beat, before I chased after Jill.

My mother called for me but I ignored her.

When I caught up to Jill, I could feel the anger rolling off her in waves, so I simply walked quietly by her side and, somehow, we ended up back in our motel room. Once the door was closed behind us, Jill faced me and said, "Your mother is impossible."

When I didn't say anything back, Jill grabbed my face and pulled my lips to hers and then we were taking off each other's clothes and rolling around on the bed and then—before I had time to think about what was happening—I was inside Jill and we were making love, only it didn't feel transgressive this time, but okay and even amazing and beautiful and like exactly what was supposed to happen on this December morning in Florida.

When it was over, we were on our backs with our arms touching, catching our breath.

"I can't spend any more time with your mother," Jill said. "I just can't. I'm sorry."

"What if we got in the truck and just started driving south until we found another place to spend Christmas?"

We turned and faced each other, which is when I noticed that Jill's hair had gone gray. I knew it couldn't have turned gray all at once, but I simply hadn't noticed before. She was just as beautiful as ever, only she looked more like a queen now—wise, powerful, and self-aware.

"I really hope you made me a coffee mug for Christmas, Lucas."

"David Fleming helped."

She kissed me three times on the lips and then we were in her truck driving south. We found a place on the beach somewhat south of Sarasota and I turned off my phone so I didn't have to deal with Mom's guilt texts and threats and general ugliness.

The day before Christmas, Jill and I made a sandcastle, on which we wrote the names of all eighteen people who had been murdered at the Majestic Theater, including our Darcy. We wrote with the quills of laughing gull feathers. I carved your name into the sand too, right next to Leandra's, of course. And then Jill and I sat there watching. The tide deployed a million gentle waves to tenderly lick the sand back into the Gulf of Mexico, slowly taking all of your names. The long process put me into a meditative trance that really seemed to help, especially since we hadn't done anything official to mark the anniversary of the shooting weeks before, back when we were in Brevard.

I remember video chatting with Phineas on Christmas Day and talking about all of the above, which he said was exactly what I needed to be doing and that I had been listening to psyche. Leaving my mother hadn't been avoidance or a regression, but a conscious choice to protect the most important relationship I had, which was with Jill. And so I spent the rest of the holiday walking hand in hand with Jill on the beach and through town and once in a while I thought I could feel Darcy smiling down on her two favorite people in the world taking care of each other now that she was gone.

When we returned to Majestic, Jill moved into my bedroom and we started sleeping under the same comforter, but everything else continued the way it was before we took our trip. I had three sessions a week with Phineas, who methodically pieced my psyche back together. I spent time with my adult-sitters. Jill worked at the Cup Of Spoons and continued to plan relaxing Saturday adventures for us. And time passed.

Maybe two months ago, before I began writing this last letter, Aliza finally returned to Pennsylvania with her daughter, who shares our town's name. I think little Maj is three now. It seemed like we spent every night of those two weeks either hosting Isaiah's family or being hosted by them. Maj seemed to take a quick liking to her uncle Lucas and aunt Jill and we even babysat one night when Bess and Isaiah took Aliza into Philadelphia to have dinner at 215 on Jill's recommendation. It was easy to fall in love with Maj as her eyes sparkled with delight whenever you merely smiled and said her name.

I remember blowing off a bunch of my adult-sitters and our weekly activities so that I could spend time with Aliza and Maj, while Isaiah and Bess were working. One morning, Aliza and I decided to take a walk in the Kent Woods Preserve. I remember I was pushing Maj in her stroller and Aliza was talking about being a teenager at Majestic High School, back when her father was a young principal and I was a young educator recently tapped to be what they were calling a "natural listener" at the time. In the shade of a gigantic budding oak tree, standing near a babbling brook, Aliza said, "I don't think you realize how much of an impact you had on me."

"I just listened," I said. "It wasn't that big of a deal."

"Then why did you stop?"

"Stop what?"

"Listening."

"I'm listening to you right now."

Aliza raised her eyebrows and lowered her chin. "You know what I mean," she said.

I looked away because I didn't want to talk about what I had done to Jacob and how I had gone on to fail his brother, Eli. I remember my skin burning.

"I think you should start listening again, Mr. Goodgame," Aliza said. When I didn't answer, she said, "I'm pretty sure I know a guy who'd give you a job."

I talked it over with Phineas, saying I understood what Aliza was saying and that I appreciated the kindness. I also had been feeling pretty terrible about draining Jill's house-sale money and relying on the other Survivors to keep me busy. Laxman had long ago begun to overpay me for the filing I did on Wednesdays for his law firm and had many times generously offered to hire me full-time, but the truth was that, while I loved being around Laxman, I didn't much like working at his law firm. Robin Withers had also offered me paid employment at the library, but I refused to take any money from her for the work I'd do on Mondays because, as everyone knows, public libraries are criminally underfunded.

"What does psyche have to say when you think about going back to work at the high school?" Phineas would often ask me.

I'd close my eyes and try to center myself, but psyche seemed to be saying two things at once. Part of me very much wanted my old job back, which had always given me a sense of purpose and even joy. I had once been very good at it. But something in my gut also started to bubble simultaneously, and that part wanted me to stay as far away from troubled teenagers as possible, because of what I had done to Jacob Hansen.

When I got up the courage one night to broach the subject of my return to Majestic High with Isaiah, he squeezed my shoulder and said, "Just say the word and we'll have you working with young people again. I could get that passed by the school board in about three seconds flat," which made me feel simultaneously good and bad. While it was nice to have a vote of confidence, it was hard to know that the decision was in my hands alone and, therefore, I would have to shoulder all of the responsibility.

"When it's time to go back," Phineas would say, "psyche will know. Perhaps there will even be an undeniable sign."

"What kind of sign?" I'd ask.

"The kind you just can't ignore," Phineas would say, and then smile in his usual mysterious yet somehow friendly manner.

Since you were my analyst for less than two years and we only had one two-hour session a week, I've spent a lot more time with Phineas, who sometimes lets our sessions stretch to ninety minutes without charging Jill any extra money. One time I asked why he does that and he said it was simply what psyche was asking of him. I really have grown to love and trust Phineas, but I still miss you, Karl.

The only annoying thing about Phineas was when he started to push for me to see a movie at the Majestic Theater. He had begun referring to our local movie house as another treasure-stealing dragon that was currently sitting on a small mountain of my gold. Every session, he'd ask me to visualize and meditate on returning to the Majestic Theater. "Maybe start by going into the lobby, or even just purchasing a ticket from the box office out front," he'd say, but I would simply close my eyes or try to change the subject, even though I was fully aware of the fact that I was putting off an essential part of my recovery.

I wanted to ask my fellow Survivors what it was like to see a movie at the Majestic Theater now, but every time I tried to bring it up, my heart started pounding and all of the spit in my mouth would instantly evaporate.

My body reacted similarly whenever Phineas tried to get me to finish the letters I had been writing to you, which I also couldn't do until recently.

What changed? I hear you asking now.

Well, I got my sign, of course.

Mark and Tony invited Jill and me over for dinner, saying it had been too long since the four of us had been together in the same room, which was true. Jill asked if she could bring anything and they requested her rhubarb-strawberry summer pie, which she happily whipped up for them, even though it was still technically spring. Then we were seated in their extravagant dining room and being served by the private chef they had hired for the evening. Maybe it sounds a little showy to hire a private chef, but they did it as a gift for Jill, who spent much of the evening in the kitchen talking recipes with Chef Kara, while the rest of us kept our own company.

I remember that we had watermelon gazpacho followed by a salt-roasted squash salad and corn-bread-crusted catfish.

Jill insisted that our cook join us at the table for a slice of Jill's pie, which Chef Kara said was "orgasmic," much to the delight of my favorite housemate.

And then we were on Mark and Tony's screened-in porch, sipping tiny crystal chalices of brandy under what looked like strings of early twentieth-century carnival lights. The talk about how good dinner was seemed to go on a little too long. When everyone started repeating what they had already said, I began to sense that Mark, Tony, and Jill knew something that they weren't telling me.

"What's going on here?" I finally said, which made Jill look down at her lap, while Tony and Mark shared a glance.

Finally, Mark said, "It's Eli."

"Eli?" I echoed. "Is he okay?"

"He's graduating from college in a few weeks," Tony said.

I had sort of lost track of the years, but some quick math confirmed that almost four had indeed passed.

"I'm happy for him," I said, and meant it.

"Well, the thing is," Mark said, and then tipped the last of his brandy down his throat, "Eli had to make what's known as a short for his senior thesis."

"A short film," Tony clarified.

"Okay," I said, because that didn't sound out of the ordinary.

"His won a prize," Mark said.

"Best of his class," Tony added with a hint of pride.

"That's wonderful," I said, still not understanding why everyone was looking at me so strangely.

This was when Mark and Tony looked over at Jill. When I met her eyes, she said, "Eli's film is about you, Lucas."

Mark and Tony both started talking quickly here, saying Eli used a lot of footage he had taken while he was living with Jill and me. They had also supplied him with behind-the-scenes video taken during the filming of our monster movie, which worried me because of how mentally ill I had become during the shoot. I started to feel physically sick, because I suspected that Eli might be trying to get revenge on me for killing his brother. I was worried that he had used his short film to shame me, showing strangers my diseased mind, my fractured psyche. And then I started to get angry because I hadn't agreed to be filmed. How dare Eli share the private moments that happened in my own home when he hadn't even asked my permission, let alone gotten me to sign any sort of contract!

And then, before I really even knew what I was doing, I was walking out of Mark and Tony's screened-in porch and into the night, as they called my name and tried to get me to stay. But I strode on, and when Jill caught up with me, I began to run through the streets of Majestic until I finally shed her, which is when I slowed down to a speed walk.

I didn't know where I was going until the black iron gates of the Majestic Cemetery came into view. Then I was sitting in the grass above Darcy's belly and apologizing for not bringing any flowers. I tried to joke about poor Gary not getting laid, but that gag just didn't seem funny tonight. So I told Darcy about Eli's short film and asked how he could be so cruel after I had taken him into my home and helped him get his monster movie made. But the more I tried to paint Eli as a bad guy, the more I realized that I was trying to project all my darkest feelings about myself onto him, which Phineas later confirmed as accurate. And then I was telling Darcy I was sorry that I wasn't able to make the blood stop coming out of her body and that I hadn't seen Jacob enter with guns blazing in time to step in front of those two bullets; and I apologized for sleeping in the same bed as Jill; and then I apologized for not being able to save winged Darcy from fading back into the unconscious of my imagination, because I would do anything to resurrect her. I talked and talked until I had no words left, and when I finally got up and turned to leave, I was surprised to see Bobby the cop leaning against his cruiser, which was parked a respectful distance away from Darcy and me.

"When did you get here?" I asked.

"A while ago," he admitted.

"You were listening?"

"Just took these out," he said, extending his right hand toward me. There were two white wireless earbuds resting on his open palm. "Phillies are down seven to six against the Mets in the twelfth."

We looked at each other for a moment there in the moonlit cemetery.

Then he said, "Jill thought you might need a ride."

"You must be really tired of driving me home after all these years," I told Bobby.

"It's a lot easier than chasing drunk teenagers out of the woods," he said. "Let's get you back to Jill, okay?"

I nodded, and then I was in the cruiser. When I got out in front of my home, I thanked Bobby for serving and protecting me once again, to which he responded by giving me a salute, before watching to make sure I got inside safely.

"I think you might owe Mark and Tony an apology," Jill said when we sat down on the couch. "They've been worried sick about you."

"I can't believe Eli betrayed me," the dark part of me couldn't resist saying.

Jill looked quizzically at me for a moment and then said, "I've seen Eli's film already."

"How?"

"Mark and Tony have it."

"Why didn't you tell me?"

"I needed to make sure it would heal rather than destroy you."

"Will it destroy me?" I said, sounding too much like a little boy for my own liking.

"Do you really think any of us would let that happen, Lucas? *Really?*"

I called Mark and Tony to apologize, but they quickly brushed aside my attempt, saying Eli was insisting that I watch his short film on the big screen and that they were offering me a private screening in the Majestic Theater's Grand Viewing Room. Apparently, they had long ago been in touch with Phineas, who had already been secretly preparing me for the challenge.

"Eli wants to video chat with you right after you watch it," Mark said.

"And I really think you're going to want to take that call," Tony added.

It was a lot to process, but I couldn't help noticing that this was probably the sign that Phineas had been telling me about. Part of me felt like I was marching straight toward my doom and the other part felt like I was walking toward salvation.

"Can you hold the tension of those two opposites and make the resulting pain meaningful?" Phineas asked me so many times—until I felt like maybe I could.

Finally, Mark and Tony set up a date for me to view Eli's short film alone in the Grand Viewing Room. So many people had volunteered to sit through it with me, but, somehow, I knew I had to face this dragon on my own. "You'd have to share all the gold otherwise," Phineas said many times.

The day before my private viewing, a fully armed Bobby the cop and my Jungian analyst accompanied me on a walk-through of the Majestic Theater. It was the first time I had set foot in a movie house since I had my very public breakdown years before. We walked past the ticket booth and into the lobby—full of historic black-and-white photos dating all the way back to the thirties—where Mark and Tony greeted us and asked if I was ready, to which I nodded. We followed them into the Grand Viewing Room, which was lit up but silent as a tomb. Phineas put his hand on Bobby's chest, meaning hang back, and then I walked forward alone.

I stood on the spot where I had ended Jacob Hansen's life. I sat down in the reupholstered seat where my wife had been murdered. And then I raised my face toward the host of angels frozen eternally above. I sat there gazing up at their strange heaven for what felt like an hour, before I walked back toward Bobby, Phineas, Tony, and Mark, who were all respectfully standing guard by the door that led back to the lobby. I nodded once at them and then we all walked out. No one asked if I was okay, which I took as a good sign.

That night, Jill kept offering to tell me exactly what was in Eli's film and also to sit next to me during the screening, saying she could hold my hand and help me make it through the complicated emotions that were sure to surface. But Jill had already done enough for me over the past four or so years, and I needed to slay this dragon myself. The knight doesn't bring his lady on his quest; he brings the dragon-slaying bounty home to his lady—and my lady had proved more than worthy of the type of gold I was after.

I didn't sleep much that evening.

Phineas and I had an emergency session first thing in the morning, the majority of which he spent staring deep into my eyes and sending his healing energy into me, which may sound very strange to some of you, and I get it, but once you make that sort of connection with your Jungian analyst, there is simply no better fortification. At the end of our analytic hour, Phineas said he was proud of me for finally facing perhaps the biggest of my own personal dragons, which is when I said, "I haven't faced the Majestic Theater dragon just yet."

"But that's exactly the miracle of today, Lucas," Phineas said, "because you really have faced the Majestic Theater dragon already. In a million different ways. And you're still very much alive and getting better every single day."

Before I knew it, I was seated in the Majestic Theater's Grand Viewing Room, right next to the spot where my Darcy was murdered. A quick flutter of panic hit my chest when the lights went down, so I reminded myself that Jill and Bobby and Mark and Tony and Phineas and Isaiah and Bess were standing guard in the lobby along with Robin Withers, Jon Bunting, DeSean Priest, David Fleming, Julia Wilco, Tracy Farrow, Jesus Gomez, Laxman Anand, Betsy Bush, Dan Gentile, Audrey Hartlove, Ernie Baum, Chrissy Williams, Carlton Porter, and even the current governor of Pennsylvania, Sandra Coyle. We were all going to watch our monster movie afterward, which would be the first time I would see it, because of my breakdown the night of the premiere and my subsequent self-imposed ban on movie watching.

Then the screen became illuminated.

The first image I saw was a headshot of the creature Eli and I had created, under which was written: *A Feathered Monster Production.* Then I saw Eli up there on the big screen. He had filled out a little and was sporting a thin goatee that made him look like a neo-beatnik of sorts, but it was still our boy and my heart got a little bigger as soon as I laid eyes on him.

Looking directly into the camera lens, Eli began talking about how his brother, Jacob, had walked into a movie theater and killed seventeen people, one of whom happened to be the wife of a man who was providing Eli with mental health assistance at his high school. Then he said, "Rather than tell you how Mr. Lucas Goodgame responded to his wife's murder, please allow me to show you."

I started to really worry here about Eli's handling of the fact that I had killed his brother.

That's when the swelling emotional music started to play and up on the movie screen Eli's orange tent began to illuminate my backyard. That first image was enough to transport me out of my current reality and send me time-traveling back to my time with Eli, back when he was Jackie Paper and I was Puff, the Magic Dragon. I was no longer in the Majestic Theater but in a fantasy that Eli had crafted for me, mostly using footage he had taken with his phone. *Maybe this was my cherry lane.* Eli narrated over the music, explaining much of what I have already told you in these letters.

And there was footage of thimble-fingered Eli and me sewing feathers onto the wetsuit; and the two of us chucking the Frisbee back and forth in my backyard—which is when I realized that Jill must have sent him footage she had taken with her phone—and me reading Jungian books in the orange tent; and Jill cooking in the kitchen; and the three of us licking massive ice-cream cones at We All Scream For Ice Cream; and Jill and me swinging in Darcy's hammock. And then Eli's in the library closet filming—through the door crack—parts of Other Lucas's speech; and suddenly everyone's goofing around in our costumes in front of Arlene and River's Wardrobe Mobile; and then we're all on set and people are putting on makeup; and I'm rehearsing my lines diligently; and Eli is in his monster costume hugging me; and then I'm playing Frisbee with the monster—which is when I realize that Eli must have had someone else shooting video on set because there are all these shots of me watching Eli directing and acting. And I have such a proud, concerned look on my face. It almost looks like I'm making sure Eli is okay and being treated fairly. And I'm maybe even doing what a good father might. Eli had included footage of all the cast parties Mark and Tony threw. And I'm surprised by how much I'm smiling on-screen. I had sort of come to believe that I had been miserable and selfish the whole time, and yet Eli's video depicts the exact opposite.

At the end of his short film, Eli narrates over a shot of my house. "And to think, I almost didn't set up my tent in this man's backyard," he says, just as the front door opens. I step outside with a big warm smile on my face and wave to Eli. I don't remember doing that in real life and I can't place the footage in any sort of mental time line. I start to worry that this is the part where he'll get around to talking about my killing his brother, but—shockingly—the film ends without Eli mentioning that very ugly fact.

When the lights came back on, I covered my face because I'd been crying for the past fifteen minutes. It took me a bit to get myself together and I was grateful when everyone continued to wait in the lobby, giving me space. After what felt like ten or so minutes, my phone began to ring and when I hit the video-chat button Eli and I were suddenly staring into each other's eyes for the first time in almost four years.

"I can tell from those tears that you absolutely hated it," he said, and then flashed a strong, confident smile, which immediately announced that Eli was no longer a boy.

I couldn't get too many words out, but Eli made it okay by doing all the talking himself, mostly telling me about the prize he had won and all the contacts he had already made, and sharing all of the good things he had created for himself out there in California.

Then he said there were people waiting for me in the lobby so he was going to let me go, but he had just one more question for me.

"Theoretically, if someone had already purchased a plane ticket for you," he said, "and all of your friends were booked on the same flight, including the lovely Ms. Jill, would you please come to my graduation ceremony?"

I nodded and wondered who had purchased a plane ticket for me, but then, before I could even make a guess, everyone was seated around me in the Grand Viewing Room and we were all munching popcorn even though it was only ten thirty in the morning. Our monster movie was lighting up our imagination and each Survivor let out a triumphant cheer every time they saw their gigantic self up there on the silver screen. Our film was campy and kind of even more ridiculous than I had remembered it being, but, as I listened to my friends and neighbors clapping and laughing and even whistling, I knew with deep certainty that what we were watching was our favorite motion picture of all time and that the moment I was currently having was maybe the best movie-house experience I would be given in this lifetime.

Toward the end, when the monster and my character were receiving our medals from the mayor played by Jill, I tilted my head back and tried to see the angels above, but they were hidden by the great beam of light that bridged the projector and the screen.

And I thought, *That's us up there in that beam of light—all of the people in this room and many other Majestic citizens.*

Us.

We are the light.

Right now—as I type the last of this letter into my laptop—I'm sitting mid-flight on an airplane. Like I said before, I won't be writing you anymore. And after Phineas reads this last document, these words will most likely never be read by anyone ever again.

Jill's passed out next to me. Her head is resting against my right upper arm. She's a pretty sound sleeper, but I'm doing my best to type without moving too much. All of The Survivors are on board, except you and Sandra Coyle, who was kept away by "gubernatorial duties." Mark and Tony are in first class, living the high life. Bess and Isaiah are across the aisle from us and are also sound asleep. We're all headed to Los Angeles to see Eli accept his college diploma.

On a whim, in the airport men's room, while we were drying our hands, I asked Isaiah if I could maybe meet with the school board members and interview for my old job. He asked if I was serious and when I said I was, he yelled, "You're hired!" so loudly everyone in the men's room turned and looked at us.

Just this past week, I stole one of Jill's rings so that the jeweler could size it and then quickly make an engagement band, which is in my pocket right now. I called Mr. Dunn yesterday and asked for his blessing, to which he said people really didn't do that anymore because women were not the possessions of their fathers, especially women in their fifties and their seventy-something stepfathers, but he was pleased all the same. Both he and Mrs. Dunn had wondered what had taken me so long. Then he said, "I don't need to officially welcome you to the family, son. You've been with us for some time now."

I have been asking for Darcy's permission too, visiting her gravestone almost daily, but I haven't seen any sort of sign indicating that my deceased wife has given me her blessing, which—for obvious reasons—feels much more important than Mr. and Mrs. Dunn's.

Whenever Darce and I would hear about a tragedy on the news or in conversations with others—back when she was still alive—she would grab my hand and say, "Don't die before me, Lucas, because I don't want to live without you, okay?" It was meant to be half-joke and half-declaration-of-undying-love. So I've been asking her winged grave marker why we never discussed what would happen if she died first. I'm pretty sure that Darce would want Jill and me to continue taking care of each other, but I obviously can't know for certain.

Phineas says that while the unconscious often speaks to us through our dreams, sometimes our awake selves need to make our own dreams.

And so, just as soon as I end this letter, I'm going to open the window shade. Then I'll stare at the clouds until my eyesight softens and my pupils adjust to the light, at which point I'm going to allow myself to imagine winged Darcy just one last time. I'm going to make her powerful wings flap so that she can keep pace with our plane. And—with my eyes—I'm going to ask for her permission to marry Jill. In my mind now, I see winged Darcy looking equal parts sad that her time with me is finally and officially ending and happy for Jill and me, who have been able to comfort each other in her absence. I'm pretty sure Darcy will be able to bear the tension of those two opposites—that she'll be able to make meaning out of that pain.

I'm not sure how long she'll be able to fly alongside the plane while holding eye contact with me, but I'm going to do my best to burn her face and her glorious wings into my memory. I imagine at some point she'll wave goodbye and then she'll shoot up fast as light toward the great unknown above.

I'm looking forward to throwing my arms around Eli and telling him I'm proud of him. It will be good to thank him in person for all he did for me. And I'm pretty sure I'll be able to convince my fellow Survivors and friends to help me throw an engagement party for Jill. It will be nice to see Aliza and young Majestic too, in their home state. I'm even set to meet Aliza's husband, Robert, for the first time, whom I'm sure will be worth meeting.

I want to thank you, Karl, for being here with me just when I needed you most. I don't think I could have done any of this without you.

I remember this one session early on in my analysis when you looked in my eyes and told me you loved me. I didn't believe you. I had too many broken places inside to accept that gift.

I'm able to accept it today.

So thank you.

And I love you too.

Jill's beginning to stir. I've just kissed the part at the top of her head. It still smells like honeysuckle.

Okay, now I have to go say goodbye—once and for all—to winged Darcy.

I didn't expect this to hurt so much, but Darcy was irreplaceable.

So were you.

Your most loyal analysand,

Lucas

Acknowledgments

This book was written at the tail end of a tremendously dark period of my life, one that at times, quite frankly, felt like the end of Matthew Quick. Writing fiction has always helped me manage my depression and anxiety. For this reason, the addition of severe writer's block—which humbled and humiliated me for the better part of three years—was a particularly difficult cross to bear.

A precious few men lightened my load: my optimistic lunch partner and trusted confidant, Matt Huband; my movie club cofounder, Kent Green; my swimming and kubb buddy, Adam Morgan; my loyal brother, Micah Quick—long live the Saturday-morning phone call; and fellow writer Nickolas Butler, who encouraged me to write another epistolary novel.

RIP to my email pen pal of two decades, Scott Humfeld. I miss you, old friend.

For three excruciatingly long years, my two ace agents, Doug Stewart and Rich Green, astounded me with a relentless patience and what often felt more like friendship than business. You are both appreciated.

Additional thanks to Kat Morgan, for making me laugh and answering my questions; the aforementioned Kent Green, for the monster movie recommendations and talks; my nieces and nephews—Isla, Oliver, Brexley, and Archer—for making it easy to love; OBX Realty Group, for "Representing Buyers & Sellers Since 2003 From Corolla to Hatteras"—"you can check [them] out on the web"; Mom and Dad, for giving me life; Barb and Peague, for making Alicia; Megan Shirk, for her fight; Dr. Dixie Keyes, for her light; Roland Merullo, for his grace; Evan Roskos, for his endurance; David Thwaites, for his tenacity; Henning Fog, for his kind support over many years; Liz Jensen, for her forgiveness; Cecelia Florence, for Sundays at Celie's; Scott Snow, for introducing me to Brevard and Pisgah National Forest; Woo Casa Kitchen in Nags Head—especially Katie and Brooke—for excellent food and steady kindness; Erik Smith; Wally Wilhoit; Scott "Mr. Canada" Caldwell; Bill Rhoda; Justin Cronin; and Paul King.

Special thanks to *This Jungian Life*, featuring the generous, psyche-nurturing wisdom and compassion of three Jungian analysts: Deborah C. Stewart, Lisa Marchiano, and Joseph R. Lee. During my dark night of the soul, this podcast was a trusted weekly balm and greatly informed/influenced the writing of this book.

Immense thanks to every single bookseller, librarian, internet book person, teacher, student, fan-mail writer, reviewer, and/or Matthew Quick enthusiast who has ever said or written a kind word about my work.

Magical thanks to HeroKing (aka Zac Little) of Etsy for handcrafting me a powerful writing talisman in exchange for a relatively trifling sum of money.

When I was creatively blocked, magical thinking convinced me that to get unblocked I had to work Gordon Lightfoot's beautiful song "If You Could Read My Mind" into the opening chapter of this novel. Magical thinking was dead wrong about that. As you know by now, the song doesn't make a single appearance. But as I slowly worked up the courage to take another serious fiction-writing leap of faith, I listened to "If You Could Read My Mind" over and over again for many months—maybe thousands of times on repeat. I started writing the opening lines of this book when I finally turned Mr. Lightfoot off, but I wanted to acknowledge the spirit of the song and its influence on my subconscious.

Gigantic thanks to my editor Jofie Ferrari-Adler, whose insightful, no-nonsense approach elevated the text in many ways. His infectious enthusiasm also pushed me to really polish and tell the best story I possibly could. Thanks, Jofie, for getting and championing *WATL*.

A single person can write a novel, but it takes an entire team to publish one. Thanks to everyone at Avid Reader Press. You are all very much appreciated.

Thanks also to the hardworking professionals at Sterling Lord Literistic.

No Matthew Quick book would exist without the writer Alicia Bessette, my wife of more than a quarter century. Alicia's empathy, patience, listening skills, professional sentence-level editing, life-affirming morning hugs, and quiet—yet powerful—wisdom made this book (and me) better in every way imaginable. She also introduced me to *This Jungian Life* and was the first to suggest that I write another epistolary novel.

I've done a colossal amount of Jungian-related reading, all of which greatly informed what you just finished. I'd like to acknowledge a few Jungian and Jungian-adjacent authors I found particularly influential: Robert Bly; Paul Foster Case; Tom Hirons, who wrote the poem "Sometimes a Wild God"; Robert A. Johnson; Donald Kalsched; Eugene Monick; Sylvia Brinton Perera; and, of course, Carl Jung himself. The Jungian acknowledged earlier on this novel's dedication page recommended almost all of the aforementioned writers—and many more—to me. That same Jungian massively informed/influenced the writing of this novel.

While I fully submerged myself in all things Jungian for years, I'd like to clearly state that I am absolutely not an expert on Jung. I'm just a fiction writer who got very curious. I'm also a human being whose mental health was vastly improved by many of the Jungian ideas I encountered throughout this journey.

Finally, thank *you*—the person reading these words right now. Without your hands turning the pages, without your eyes scanning the lines, these ideas would remain dead on the page and the book jacket would effectively become a coffin. The hope of once again connecting with readers kept me putting one metaphorical foot in front of the other during my darkest hours. With gratitude and love, I'm wishing you all the best.

About the Author

MATTHEW QUICK is the *New York Times* bestselling author of *The Silver Linings Playbook*, which was made into an Oscar-winning film; *The Good Luck of Right Now*; *Love May Fail*; *The Reason You're Alive*; and four young adult novels. His work has been translated into more than thirty languages, received a PEN/Hemingway Award Honorable Mention, was a Los Angeles Times Book Prize finalist, a *New York Times Book Review* Editors' Choice, and more. *The Hollywood Reporter* has named him one of Hollywood's 25 Most Powerful Authors. Matthew lives with his wife, the novelist Alicia Bessette, on North Carolina's Outer Banks.

WE ARE
THE
LIGHT

MATTHEW
QUICK

This reading group guide for We Are the Light *includes an introduction, discussion questions, ideas for enhancing your book club, and a Q&A with author Matthew Quick. The suggested questions are intended to help your reading group find new and interesting angles and topics for your discussion. We hope that these ideas will enrich your conversation and increase your enjoyment of the book.*

Introduction

From Matthew Quick, the *New York Times* bestselling author of *The Silver Linings Playbook*, comes a poignant and hopeful novel about a widower who takes in a grieving teenager and inspires a magical revival in their small town.

Lucas Goodgame lives in Majestic, Pennsylvania, a quaint suburb that has been torn apart by a recent tragedy. Everyone in Majestic sees Lucas as a hero—everyone, that is, except Lucas himself. Insisting that his deceased wife, Darcy, visits him every night in the form of an angel, Lucas spends his time writing letters to his former Jungian analyst, Karl. It is only when Eli, an eighteen-year-old young man whom the community has ostracized, begins camping out in Lucas's backyard that an unlikely alliance takes shape and the two embark on a journey to heal their neighbors and, most important, themselves.

Topics & Questions for Discussion

1. Lucas writes that Karl, his analyst, was the first person besides his wife to ever say to him "I love you" and mean it. Karl loved him in the way that "the best part of my soul loves the best part of your soul," a phrase which becomes a refrain throughout the book. What is the power of this type of love as seen in the book, and how is it distinct from romantic or familial love? How is it different from the love that is earned through one's actions?

2. In the aftermath of the movie theater tragedy, Lucas is consoled by his vision of the victims turning into angels, and takes comfort from the following visitations of his wife in the form of an angel. He believes that it would "be cathartic for everyone to understand that their loved ones did not suffer and were not afraid, but were instantly transformed into higher beings who were far more beautiful and enlightened than humans could ever be." In which ways is this angelic secret constructive to Lucas, and in which ways is it detrimental?

3. "I wish there was something we could do, other than be angry," the survivors say to Lucas in the months after the tragedy. How is anger treated in the book? Can it ever be a force for good?

4. Lucas can't bring himself to return to his work at the high school, so Eli seeks him out at home. Lucas writes that Eli's anguish "made me feel guilty about abandoning him and all of the students who relied on me the way I relied on you, Karl. The irony is not lost on me." How does the help that Eli needs from Lucas compare to the help that Lucas needs from the absent Karl? How did you feel about Karl as you read the book, and how did your feelings change by the end?

5. Sandra Coyle urges Lucas to give up helping Eli make his amateur film project and come work for her anti-gun political crusade instead. She tells Lucas, "If you want to be part of a *real* solution, if you want to *really* honor Darcy, you've got to put childish things aside and be a man." How does her idea of "being a man" differ from the ideas expressed by Lucas, Karl, Isaiah, and others?

6. Lucas goes to great lengths to help Eli carry out his monster movie project, guiding and partnering with him to make the whole thing possible. But before they hatch a plan of action, Lucas helps lift Eli's pain by simply keeping him company without saying a word: "We sat in silence for a long time, quietly looking at each other. . . . As I sat in the tent with young Eli, I could feel his pain and frustration and loneliness leaving his body." What does this book teach us about the different ways of helping someone to heal? How does the rest of the town later pitch in to help Lucas?

7. Lucas insists that "No one in our movie is good or bad. . . . Just true depictions of whole people, each with both a shadow and a light side." The fictional scripted movie doesn't match the messiness of reality, or does it? In real life, Lucas still refuses to vilify Jacob Hansen,

because he doesn't believe that anyone, even Jacob, is entirely bad. Do the other characters in the novel agree with him? Why do you agree or disagree?

8. In the eyes of many of the townspeople, Lucas is Jacob's opposite, Majestic's savior and white knight. How does this hero worship affect Lucas, who is struggling with his complicated feelings about what he did to stop the massacre? Lucas himself holds a worshipful view of Karl, believing that he holds all the answers that Lucas needs in his wounded state. What do you think are the downsides of idolizing people who are all too human?

9. Other characters draw a hard distinction between Jacob and his seventeen victims, but Lucas is firmly attached to the number eighteen—he compulsively walks eighteen miles in a day, he circles around Karl's house eighteen times, and he writes eighteen letters total. He even convinces the survivors to agree to "an in-memoriam section listing the names of all eighteen people who were killed at the Majestic Theater, including Jacob Hansen." How do you think this reflects Lucas's search for closure? Does the book suggest that all healing requires forgiveness, and do you agree?

10. Lucas is profoundly shaped by his trusting, tender relationships with the other men in his life, and the vital importance of healthy masculinity is a major theme in the book. Yet not to be overlooked are the female characters in the book, who play an equally important role in helping Lucas and the town on the journey to wholeness and healing. Consider all the big and small ways in which the women step up: what is their part, and how is it complementary to the man-on-man healing approach?

11. In the novel, many people who are not related by blood extend unconditional love and support toward one another. Many biological relationships, such as between Lucas and his parents, Jill and her father, and Eli and his mother, are twisted and toxic rather than truly caring and nurturing. What does it mean to treat someone like family? What is special about a chosen family, and what does the book say about belonging to and taking care of a community?

12. In addition to Eli's monster movie, the other film that holds great meaning in the book is the cinematic classic *It's a Wonderful Life*, which was beloved by the town until tragedy struck. How does the story of *It's a Wonderful Life* connect to the story of the monster movie and the overarching story of the novel?

Enhance Your Book Club

1. Vote on a favorite classic movie to watch together. Keeping in mind what you learned from the book about how movies are created, what did you notice this time? Reflect on the art of filmmaking and the experience of watching.

2. Set aside some time for individual journaling and invite each member to write a private letter of their choice, in the spirit of Lucas's letters to Karl. Members can choose to share their letters. How does it feel to put thoughts into words?

3. The close-knit townspeople of Majestic, PA, come together to take care of their own. Is there a way that your club can give back to the community? Sign up for a group volunteer opportunity and enjoy a meal afterward at a local diner like the Cup Of Spoons.

A Conversation with Matthew Quick

How did you decide to write *We Are the Light* as an epistolary novel?
I got 100% sober in June of 2018 and was immediately rewarded with crippling writer's block. I'd sit at the computer all day and struggle to complete a paragraph. And the paragraph would not be good. This went on for years. My wife, Alicia, began encouraging me to write another epistolary novel. She pointed out that I was still able to write letters. I've always had pen pals. I enjoy writing long letters and emails to friends. I resisted Alicia's suggestion. But when the writer, Nickolas Butler, echoed my wife's opinion without my having shared it with him, I finally went up to my office, typed the words "Dear Karl," and was off. After years of not being able to write, I was suddenly writing happily for eight to twelve hours a day. A lot happened during those years of writer's block, including my entering into Jungian analysis. I'm not suggesting that writing epistolary novels is some sort of magic cure for writer's block. But the intimacy of letter writing helped me find my way into the heart of this story, which is perhaps my most intimate to date.

The loving bonds between Lucas, Eli, and the other male characters in the book are expressed loud and clear. Why do you think this is important to show?
The loving relationship I had with my grandfather probably saved my life when I was young. I grew up at a time when—and in a community

where—men were not really encouraged to be openly intimate with each other. There wasn't a lot of male hugging going on back then. Nor were there too many male-only heartfelt discussions. My grandfather was a WWII veteran and he wasn't exactly warm and fuzzy either, but he held my hand every morning at the breakfast table and prayed for me with an earnestness that felt sincere. I also remember being saved by sweaty male hugs on the basketball court. These were, of course, justified by difficult baskets made and victories over our enemies, but as a boy starved for male affection, I made do with them. And during my recent depressions and anxiety battles, a few of my best male friends really showed up for me. I regularly have conversations with male confidants about my feelings and aspirations and dreams and fears and hurts. I have found that many men are hungry for such talks and light up when you give them the chance to participate in such experiences. I think there are a lot of lonely, hurting men out there. Lonely hurting men pushed to extremes sometimes do horrific unthinkable things—like Jacob Hansen does in the movie house. But when lonely hurting men are loved by their communities and given the chance to bond in healthy ways with other men, sometimes they contribute beauty and unity to their communities—like Eli Hansen does. I would like there to be more Elis in the world than Jacobs. That's why it's important to let men know that we love them and that they are allowed to love us back.

How did Jungian analysis come to play a starring role in *We Are the Light*?

I had been Jung-curious for a long time. And during my most recent dark night of the soul, when my worldview was perhaps at its bleakest, my wife encouraged me to give the *This Jungian Life* podcast a listen. When I did, I heard Jungian analysts Deborah C. Stewart, Lisa Marchiano, and Joseph R. Lee discuss many topics through a Jungian lens, as well as analyze the dreams of listeners. I binged the T.J.L. archive and became more and more interested in Jung's ideas. Finally, I found an analyst and entered into Jungian analysis myself. To say that my analysis has radically reshaped who I am, would be a gross understatement. Since 2014, I had also been trying to write a novel about a tragedy at a historic, cathedral-like movie house, but could never figure out how to tell the tale. It was only when I started applying a Jungian lens that the story began to flow out of me in a way that felt meaningful.

Lucas finds his calling as a school counselor for teenagers. Have you ever worked with young people? What do you think teens like Eli need from the adults around them?
From the fall of 1996 to the summer of 2004, I worked with teenagers. I taught, coached, counseled, chaperoned, and spent the majority of my time around young adults. One of my undergraduate professors once told me that what children need most from adults is proof that one can make it to adulthood and be okay. At the time, I took "okay" to mean adult life could be enjoyable and honorable and purposeful—that you didn't have to be miserable or abusive or settle for something you never really wanted. The deeper I go into my Jungian work, the more I believe that "okay" means remaining whole in adulthood without splitting off essential parts of one's identity. Or if those parts have gotten temporarily split off by life's hard knocks, we can show young people that it's possible to reclaim those split-off parts and become whole again, albeit through difficult inner work. And when you talk honestly and sincerely to teens about this possibility—becoming who they were always meant to be—their eyes almost always light up.

How long did it take to write *We Are the Light*?
Like I wrote above, I had the basic idea in 2014 and—for seven years—had been trying to write my way into a voice and an opening. But—again,

after years of my subconscious working on it—the first draft of what became this novel was written in under a month. I got pretty obsessed and was working seven days a week and writing for eight to twelve hours a day. My wife and I edited additional drafts together for a few more weeks. And then my editor, Jofie Ferrari-Adler, provided many valuable insights and really helped me polish.

The monster movie screenplay that Eli and Lucas write is an extremely personal piece of art. Was writing *We Are the Light* a similarly personal experience for you?

Yes. Although, the novel is in no way meant to be autobiographical. I never experienced a tragedy in a movie house. Lucas Goodgame doesn't struggle with alcohol abuse. But we both have bonded pretty intensely with our Jungian analysts. We both have relied on the therapeutic value of art and story. We both have had places deep inside of ourselves shatter. And we've both benefited from the healing properties of friendships. I've also written screenplays, although never a monster movie.

What is the most interesting research you did for the book?

My parents have a home in Ambler, PA. Whenever I'd visit, I'd go to the historic Ambler Theater with my dad and try to dream up the plot for my movie theater novel. Even though the theater in *We Are the Light*—the Majestic Theater—is fiction, I had the general look of the Ambler Theater in mind when I wrote the book. I'm in a two-man movie club. The other man is my buddy, Kent, who has made horror films in and around south Jersey and loves monster movies. Kent gave me a list of old monster films to watch, all of which I found interesting and great fun. I particularly dug Jacques Tourneur's *Cat People* and *The Leopard Man*. Again, my deep dive into all things Carl Jung would take the prize for most interesting.

Was there a scene in the book that surprised you as you were writing it?
In chapter 17, during an evening rainstorm, a soaked-to-the-bone Tony shows up at Lucas's home and then begins to emotionally unburden himself on the couch. We learn that the Majestic Theater tragedy created a rift between Tony and Mark, but the film project and working with Eli allows Tony to believe in his community again, which in turn helps him reconnect with his partner too. It's a tender and vulnerable moment. When I had the impulse for a rain-soaked Tony knocking on Lucas's door, I didn't know what Tony was going to say once Lucas let him in. So that surprised me.

We Are the Light **plays homage to cinematic magic as well as the real behind-the-scenes work of moviemaking. What did you want to capture about the moviegoing experience? Have you ever been behind the camera in real life?**
I've never been behind a movie camera. I spent a day on the *Silver Linings Playbook* movie set. And I've worked with directors and actors and producers on several screenplays. But the book was more informed by the many hours I've spent in dark movie houses gazing up at the great beam of light dancing on the screen. In the first half of my life, whenever I was feeling depressed or anxious, I almost always did one of two things (when I wasn't writing): drink alcohol or go to the movies. While drinking almost always led to a worse state of mind, the cinema often buoyed me through rough spells in a way that was positive and constructive. It's where I went to dream, to cheer, to cry and laugh, to study the human condition, and to learn about storytelling—how you do it and why. The best movies activate something deep within us and help us get in touch with our feelings. We often call it being moved, but I think it's so much more than that. Maybe it's being reconnected with what makes us feel most alive—the transcendent spark within all of us. The movie-going

experience—when the film is good—lifts us above the everyday grind. It can remind us of what's possible. It can encourage us to be our best selves.

Do you have any unwritten ideas about how Lucas, Jill, Eli, and the other townspeople of Majestic lead their lives after the story ends?
I think the Majestic Theater has been sanctified once again by the end of the novel and that everyone will continue to have cinematic experiences, despite the tragedy. And that's the metaphor, right? There is real evil in the world and it wants to rob us of the good. But if we look with the right eyes, we will see that there is always more good than evil, which is primarily the reason why such things as love and friendship and community are even possible at all. I think Lucas and Jill will take care of each other, just as Darcy would have wanted it. And I think Eli will continue to untether himself from the post-tragedy womb that Lucas and the town of Majestic create for him. Eli will go out into the world and have his life's adventure, leaving boyhood behind and becoming a man. And when he's far enough along on his journey—when his adult identity is established—he will return in some way to Lucas and Jill and Tony and Mark and the town of Majestic. They'll be waiting with open arms, ready and willing to celebrate the first-half-of-life completion of his wondrous maturation process.